"Nancy Haddock had me hooked from page one with *La Vida Vampire*. The wonderfully charming heroine, sexy-as-sin hero, and fabulously engaging mystery kept me turning pages into the wee hours of the morning!"
—Julie Kenner

"A sultry setting, a clever mystery, and strong, sparkling characters...Nancy Haddock delivers everything it takes to make a fan out of me!"
—Jane Graves

"*La Vida Vampire* is fun, fun, fun! Nancy Haddock's fresh and sassy new voice enlivens a well-known genre, and her heroine is one of the most entertaining in years. Readers will enjoy the snappy dialogue, irreverent tone, fabulous setting, and the fascinating world. Wonderful!"
—Kathleen Givens

"Vampires, shape-shifters, and wizards...oh my! *La Vida Vampire* has it all. A clever mystery, an engaging, undead heroine, and a make-your-fangs-drool vampire hunter."
—Lynn Michaels, author of *Nightwing*

"Get a new lease on afterlife with *La Vida Vampire*, a fresh and original paranormal mystery, steamed up with a touch of romance. Nancy Haddock's debut is devilishly delightful!"
—Catherine Spangler,
national bestselling author of *Touched by Fire*

continued...

LA VIDA VAMPIRE

NANCY HADDOCK

BERKLEY BOOKS, NEW YORK

THE BERKLEY PUBLISHING GROUP
Published by the Penguin Group
Penguin Group (USA) Inc.
375 Hudson Street, New York, New York 10014, USA
Penguin Group (Canada), 90 Eglinton Avenue East, Suite 700, Toronto, Ontario M4P 2Y3, Canada
(a division of Pearson Penguin Canada Inc.)
Penguin Books Ltd., 80 Strand, London WC2R 0RL, England
Penguin Group Ireland, 25 St. Stephen's Green, Dublin 2, Ireland (a division of Penguin Books Ltd.)
Penguin Group (Australia), 250 Camberwell Road, Camberwell, Victoria 3124, Australia
(a division of Pearson Australia Group Pty. Ltd.)
Penguin Books India Pvt. Ltd., 11 Community Centre, Panchsheel Park, New Delhi—110 017, India
Penguin Group (NZ), 67 Apollo Drive, Rosedale, North Shore 0632, New Zealand
(a division of Pearson New Zealand Ltd.)
Penguin Books (South Africa) (Pty.) Ltd., 24 Sturdee Avenue, Rosebank, Johannesburg 2196,
South Africa

Penguin Books Ltd., Registered Offices: 80 Strand, London WC2R 0RL, England

This book is an original publication of The Berkley Publishing Group.

This is a work of fiction. Names, characters, places, and incidents either are the product of the author's imagination or are used fictitiously, and any resemblance to actual persons, living or dead, business establishments, events, or locales is entirely coincidental. The publisher does not have any control over and does not assume responsibility for author or third-party websites or their content.

PRINTING HISTORY
Berkley trade paperback edition / April 2008

Library of Congress Cataloging-in-Publication Data

Haddock, Nancy.
    La vida vampire / Nancy Haddock. — Berkley trade paperback ed.
        p. cm.
    ISBN 978-0-425-21995-9
    1. Vampires—Fiction. 2. Tour guides (Persons)—Fiction. 3. Saint Augustine (Fla.)—Fiction.
I. Title.
PS3608.A275V53 2008
813'.6—dc22   2007036807

PRINTED IN THE UNITED STATES OF AMERICA

10 9 8 7 6 5 4 3 2 1

This book is dedicated to my parents,
Gene and Virginia Hendrix,
who encouraged my passion for reading

And to my husband and children,
Jerry, Rob, Rick, Adam, and Leighanne Haddock,
who supported my passion for writing

ACKNOWLEDGMENTS

Thanks are due to so many, I may not get them all in this go-round. They start with my editor, Leis Pederson, and the entire Berkley Publishing Group for making my first sale a blast, and to Roberta Brown, agent extraordinaire, for being her fabulous self.

The outstanding men and women of the St. Johns County Sheriff's Department answered my questions with their usual professionalism and humor. Any errors and/or embellishments are mine. Justice must be served, but so must fiction.

I deeply appreciate my friends at Starbucks (Store 8484) for the triple shots of caffeine and limitless caring, and my chapter-mates and online group friends for their encouragement and support.

Last, big dancin'-on-the-beach thanks to my critique coaches— Lynne, Jan, Cathy, Julie, Valerie, and Kathie. You made my work better, and you make my life brighter. I appreciate the Light in you all!

ONE

I hurried up St. George Street, wrapping a finely woven shawl and the soft Florida night around me. Fog would shroud the city in a few hours. I felt it creeping in the early March air as surely as the bay waters lapped gently against the seawall.

Nostalgia hit me in waves. More than two hundred years ago, I'd happily skipped through these carriage-narrow streets as a rebellious child, then sedately strolled them as a young woman. Faces and voices, laughter and tears of long ago danced through my memory.

Then a man on a silver Vespa zipped by on a cross street, and I snapped out of it.

Sheesh, why was I brooding over my lost past when the present was such a kick? Note to self: Knock it off.

Being a vampire had *some* advantages, I admitted as I wove my way past window-shoppers on the pedestrian-only main drag. Near-immortality counted, right? And enhanced senses.

Then there was vampire strength and speed—if I bothered to use either one. Since I'd never really taken to being vampy, I'd refused to practice the tricks of the fang brigade. Plus, life was pretty laid back in my hometown of St. Augustine. Why rush?

As for drawbacks to the vampire life, extended daylight savings time could be a bummer if I was in the sun too long. Still, sunlight was a minor issue for me and always had been. Why? Who knows?

I for sure had it better than I did back in the 1800s. Captured because I had The Gift of psychic visions and telepathy, then turned so the big jerk vampire king Normand could control my so-called power, I'd had no choice but to live with vampires and drink from whoever was served. Yuck.

But, hey, I'm a free woman now. I have artificial blood in a bottle, super sunblock, and all-night shopping at Wal-Mart. I'm part day-walker and all night-stalker, especially when my prey is a bargain in a near-empty discount store.

If that sounds silly, *you* try being trapped underground for over two hundred years. Once the stark terror had passed, boredom reigned. Now that I'm out, I want to learn things, do things, see things—in short, make my new lease on afterlife perfectly normal.

I'll fight to keep it normal, too. I even have a job. Yep, meet the newest certified guide working for Old Coast Ghost Tours. Me, Cesca Marinelli. A vampire telling ghost stories. Is that a kick or what?

My first shift was due to start in fifteen minutes, so I had time for a spot of eavesdropping on my favorite couple. Enhanced senses *can* be useful, especially since they don't overwhelm and overload me anymore. I'd honed the skill to filter sounds, smells, heartbeats—all kinds of sensations—and focus in on what I wanted to. Besides, I couldn't help myself. Watching the Maggie and Neil show was better than watching TV Land on cable.

Too bad I didn't remember that eavesdroppers never hear good of themselves—even from a block away. The shock and awe of finding me had worn off, but my petite blonde dynamo roommate, Maggie O'Halloran, and Neil Benson, her black-haired, green-eyed sweetie, still forgot I hear like, well, a vampire. Never mind seeing them plain as day at the spot where my tour group was already gathering.

Neil, in blue jeans, deck shoes, and a sweater-shirt the same gray color that salted the hair at his temples, also wore a sour expression.

"She's Gidget with fangs and an accent," I overheard him say as I continued strolling up the block.

Maggie laughed, facing me but not yet seeing me. Neil may be a little younger than Maggie, but she looked gorgeous in teal cotton pants, a boatneck top, and navy blue tennis shoes. She exuded confidence and the scent of magnolias that I easily picked up amid the myriad scents on the night.

"The accent is barely noticeable, honey," she said, "and Gidgets are, by definition, short. Cesca's five eight."

"Mags, she surfs. You have to admit that's odd."

"No odder than you surfing with her. Besides, you only have yourself to blame for getting her hooked. Renting those Gidget movies was your idea of a joke, not mine."

"Well, she got me back in spades when she held that seven-foot board over her head and ran to the ocean yelling, 'Cowabunga.'" He heaved an exasperated breath. "Cowabunga, for pity's sake."

Maggie snorted and covered it with a cough. Me, I chuckled out loud. Hey, from a half block away, he couldn't hear me.

Neil crossed his arms over his chest. "It's not funny, Mags. Do you have any idea how weird it is to be on the beach at five in the screamin' afternoon with a vampire? She should be toast in the sun. Instead, she's got that long hair in a bushy ponytail, and she's wearing a gouge-your-eyes pink bathing suit."

"It's coral, not pink, and look on the bright side. Her olive complexion makes her look tanned instead of dead white."

Neil turned enough for me to see him glower. *Guess he's not impressed with my perpetual tan.* A few shop doors away from them, I paused.

"Okay, honey, I won't ask you to take Cesca surfing again. Her truck should be out of the shop tomorrow anyway." Maggie spotted me, then gazed back at Neil. She sighed dramatically. "It's too bad, though."

"What's too bad?" he asked, his back to me again.

"It's just that Cesca was so excited when she got back from the beach. She said she learned more from you in two hours than she did in two months of surf school."

"She did?"

"Mmm-hmm." Maggie stepped closer to him. The aroma of pheromones spiked.

"She *is* a quick study." His voice went just a little hoarse. "And a natural shark repellent."

"Uh-huh. Plus she's got a job now. A night job. She'll be busy for at least two hours, and we could be, too." Maggie let her fingers do the walking up Neil's shirtfront. "Moondoggie."

He gulped so hard, it practically echoed in my ears.

"Cowabunga," he choked out.

Maggie smiled. "Exactly."

She kissed Neil, long and slow. Then she winked at me over his shoulder.

I rolled my eyes hard enough to give myself a headache, but believe me, I was taking notes as I watched them walk toward the bay front, arm in arm. Not that men were falling at my feet or ever had—which made me doubt the whole vampires-are-sex-magnets thing. But, hey, if I ever find a guy who doesn't break Olympic speed records running away, I'll be ready to wind him around my little finger.

Granted, that bushy ponytail crack *did* sting. I mean, I can't control what genetics and humidity do to my hair, unless—

I patted my French twist plastered with hair spray and put chemical straighteners on my next Wal-Mart shopping list.

All in all, Neil wasn't so bad. He *had* stopped calling me Cesspool, and deep down, hidden in the depths of his soul, I bet he'd even miss me if I were gone. Besides, the guy could surf, and with Maggie busy seducing him, she wouldn't be trailing after my tour.

Don't get me wrong. It was sweet of Maggie to see me off on my first job. She'd discovered me seven months ago under the once-grand Victorian house she bought to restore. I appreciated her mentorship and unwavering support in getting me up to speed with the twenty-first century. Sure, I'd been able to astral travel, to "see" and "hear" from the coffin in that long-forgotten basement. But walking in the world after two hundred years plus of entombment was a whole new trip.

Maggie taught me to power shop and hired a tutor for academics. We rented almost every movie Blockbuster stocked in-store, and I'd joined the online service as soon as I qualified for my own credit card. We also checked out scads of library books to round out my crash course in modern culture. In short, Maggie was my fairy godmother, and without her, I'd be dead.

Or rather, still buried.

But I climbed out of that coffin last August thirteenth (a lucky day for me!) ready and raring to embrace every modern marvel. Now I'm living *la vida* vampire—my version on my terms. Except for the rules of the Vampire Protection Agency, of course. My VPA handler in Jacksonville, Dave Corey, is a pretty cool guy though, and I only have to report to him every quarter.

Maggie didn't *need* to hover anymore, especially when Neil was so grumpy about sharing her.

I'd get Neil for the bushy hair crack sooner or later. Meanwhile, it was almost time to take my next step toward a normal, independent afterlife. Work. I was on in five minutes.

I reached the tour substation near the two-story waterwheel where a real mill operated in the late 1880s. Now the Mill Top Tavern was a hot spot for live music.

I twitched the skirt of the deep gold Empire gown I'd designed and sewn with Maggie's help and her Singer sewing machine, and eyed the mortals ambling in the cobblestone courtyard. Their blood pumped so loudly it seemed as though a thousand hearts beat in my ears instead of those of the thirty who'd signed up for my tour.

In small and large groups they approached, handing their tickets to Janie and Mick, fellow guides assigned to help me corral the crowd tonight. Janie Freeman is thirty-two and as upbeat as her short, breezy hairdo and sweet Oklahoma drawl. Mick Burney is forty-four, says he's from Daytona Beach, and has hard edges that soften a bit around Janie. I'm pretty sure these two are dating, but they're very secretive, and I don't pry.

I gave up trying to catch a lingering glance between them. Instead, I blocked the ambient sights, sounds, and smells around me to size up the tour-takers as they drew closer.

On my left, a couple smooched and whispered endearments in French, stuck tongues down each other's throats, and whispered more. They positively reeked of pheromones and wore shiny wedding bands, so they had to be newlyweds. Question was why they bothered to leave their room.

On my right, a handful of broad-shouldered men who spoke like *The Sopranos* characters bragged about haggling over the prices of antiques. One with a camera was especially loud and animated. Did real wiseguys haggle over prices?

A lanky guy dressed in a flannel shirt, polyester slacks, and an unzipped windbreaker—the sleeves, pant legs, and shirttails all a smidge too short—trailed the wiseguys. Next to them, he looked so shabby, I had a pang that he couldn't afford better-fitting clothes. With a cowlick in his muddy brown hair and a happy puppy expression as he looked around, he reminded me of Gomer Pyle. Except when his glance landed on the French couple. Then something brooding moved behind his gray eyes.

I shrugged and peered behind me where twelve middle-aged ladies each wore teal Jacksonville Jaguars outfits and matching visors embroidered with the words JAG QUEEN. I could deal with women who liked the Jacksonville football team. *I* liked football, and the Jag Queen visors were darling. But, whew! The mix of perfume was an olfactory assault, especially the Shalimar. Too bad sticking cotton up my nostrils would look tacky.

Ahead, a smattering of parents towed children past the sick-eningly sweet lure of the fudge and candy store. Five teenagers brought up the rear. The two boys and three girls were decked out in goth-look black right down to their fingernails.

The tallest of the Jag Queens, the one my nose pegged as being drenched in Shalimar, gave the goth gang a disapproving sniff, then glared at the French bride. For the public display of affection going on? I didn't think so. Not from her stiff posture or the way her narrowed eyes shot venom. But only for a split second. When another Jag Queen spoke to Shalimar, she was all grandmotherly smiles again.

An odd byplay, but I didn't have time to dwell on it as the members of the tour group stopped a full seven feet away. They eyed me with mixed eagerness and fascinated dread, half expect-ing me to pounce.

As if.

I'm a vampire. The only one in town, but big deal. I do have self-control, never mind self-respect.

Last fall, the *St. Augustine Record* ran a story on how Mag-gie found me in King Normand's own coffin, the almost petri-fied wood still bound by silver chains. We didn't tell the reporter the coffin had a false bottom filled with real treasure—King Normand's version of stuffing money under a mattress—or that I'd shared the bounty with Maggie and Neil. The writer made a sensation enough of Normand being a then-hated Frenchman that local history had omitted from the records. The article went on to paint me as the spunky hometown girl who defied the vampire king, was punished by burial, and was then for-gotten when Normand and all his vampires were killed by the villagers. Suddenly, *wham!*, I was the oldest citizen, a heroine who'd given *time-out* a whole new meaning and an added tourist attraction in the Oldest City.

Big whoop. I shrugged off my fifteen minutes of fame, studied my tail off in tour guide training, and was ready to be all I could be on every shift. Monday, Tuesday, Thursday, and Saturday this week. Tuesday, Thursday, and Sunday next week.

Wednesday is bridge night. Forget being a fiend for blood. I'm a fiend for bridge.

But the tourists didn't know that. I smelled real fear from some of them. I wasn't quite sure how to put everyone at ease but I hoped inspiration would strike.

The night-glow Timex Maggie gave me read eight o'clock straight up. It was showtime. I pulled my fragile psychic shields up, squared my shoulders, and—

The humans clustered near me jumped.

Except for a cute towheaded boy of perhaps five years and a fiftyish stone-faced man with a scar trailing down his right jaw, who drifted up to stand near the newlyweds.

The boy gave a single nod, wiggled his shoulder from his mother's grasp, and dashed up to tug on my skirt.

"Hey, lady ma'am," he yelled, "are you a real vampire?"

His mother surged forward and croaked a frightened, "Robbie, get back here."

I held up a hand to reassure her he was safe and looked down. The child didn't blink, didn't budge. Streetlights made a halo over his blond mop of hair.

I smiled, sank into a crouch, and answered as loudly as he had asked, "Indeed, Master Robbie, I am a vampire."

"Huh." He cocked his head at me, obviously thinking. "My babysitter says vampires are monsters that 'thrall you with their eyes and then they—" He chomped his teeth twice. "—bite you. Are you gonna bite me?"

This kid needed a volume knob, but he was a cute corker. "Well, sir, I'm not good at enthralling because my eyes always cross. Like this." I crossed my eyes hard. Robbie laughed the way the children of the old Spanish Quarter used to. A sound I'd missed.

"And you're not gonna bite me either?" he asked, not quite as loudly.

"Ewww, no way." I pulled a face that made him laugh again. "I don't like biting people. It's icky."

The mother released the breath she'd been holding, a few in the crowd chuckled, and Robbie grinned.

"You're not much of a monster, are ya?"

"Nope, but you're a fine young gentleman." I ruffled his hair, and stood. "Now, if you'll scoot back to your mother, we'll start the tour."

He did, and I faced a marginally less wary, more attentive crowd. Problem was, between the group's high emotions and intense curiosity, they shattered my psychic shields. Thought-questions flew at me left and right. What was my heritage? Where did I live? Where was I buried? Do I like this century, what do I do with my spare time? Do I show up on film? Does the tracker hurt? How do I eat? Do I shave my legs?

Shave my legs?

I couldn't pinpoint exactly who thought each question, not this close to the new moon. Heck, with the dark moon so close to shutting The Gift down entirely, I was surprised the impressions were this clear. Then again, they'd handed me inspiration.

If knowing more about me would calm fears, I'd handle their avalanche of questions as part of my spiel.

Only Stony—who looked like he'd have more fun getting his teeth extracted with a crowbar—and the newlyweds didn't seem to mentally bombard me. The petite brunette bride tossed her long hair back so often, I wondered if she had a kink in her neck. She wore skintight black slacks and a semi–see-through black camisole. If that was the fashion in Paris, I'd pass. Her hubby wore gray trousers and an Oxford striped shirt. Their long, speculative glances at me didn't hold fear. In fact, I could've sworn they leered. And the bride's head tossing? It almost looked flirtatious. Sure had Gomer gawking at her.

Too creeped to try taking a psychic peek at them, I focused on being tour guide extraordinaire.

"Welcome to the Old Coast Ghost Walk. I am Francesca Melisenda Alejandra Marinelli, your guide, born here in St. Augustine in 1780. I know you have questions about me, and I'll get to those in a second. First, let me introduce my friends and assistants, Janie and Mick. Janie's dressed in a Minorcan ensemble of the late seventeen hundreds, and Mick's wearing a Spanish soldier's costume."

"Why are you wearing an Empire gown?" the Shalimar Jag Queen asked. "Isn't that from the Regency period?"

"Yes, ma'am. Mine is circa 1802, and I chose it because I love the style." The two oldest Jag Queens tittered, and I continued.

"We're standing at the north end of what used to be the Minorcan Quarter, or the Spanish Quarter, or simply the Quarter. We'll go through the city gates to the Huguenot Cemetery, then loop through the historic district to end our tour on the bay front. You're welcome to ask questions as we visit the sites, but let's see if I can address some of your personal questions before we start.

"First, please call me Cesca. You *can* take pictures, I *do* show up on film, and I *hope* you'll get my best side." The loud wise-guy waved his camera and laughed. "Seriously, if you get any ghostly photos of the haunted sites, the tour company would love to have copies."

"Ghost pictures?" Gomer breathed, goggle-eyed. "Honest to goodness ghost pictures?"

I nodded.

"Goll-lee."

Biting the inside of my lip to keep from laughing at the Gomer-ism, I turned toward the Jag Queens and regrouped.

"Now, I mentioned this was called the Quarter. My parents were among those immigrants from Minorca, Italy, and Greece who came here as indentured servants to work the New Smyrna Colony. When the immigrants didn't get what they were promised, they fled to St. Augustine for asylum. My mother was Minorcan Spanish, my father an Italian mariner, and my family home was on the bay front. The house we lived in is long gone, but I'll show you where it was when we get there.

"I was buried for two hundred and four years," I continued as twelve pairs of eyes got rounder, "in a tiny basement of coquina that had a small trapdoor flush with the ground. The original house over the basement was coquina stone and wood. It's also long gone, and a late eighteen hundreds Victorian house is on the site now. My friend, Maggie, is restoring the house, so it's a construction zone and not safe to visit.

"I love living in this time," I said to the goth gang, "and the

GPS tracker I wear is in my arm. I don't get headaches like Spike got in *Buffy*. I do watch a lot of TV and movies, and I read a lot. Classic TV, old movies, and mystery novels are some of my favorites. Oh, and I truly don't bite people. I get artificial blood from the health food store, and it's bottled just like cola, except they come in six and eight ounces instead of larger sizes."

I paused for a breath, and Shalimar jumped in.

"Ms. Marinelli, Francesca, you just answered half the questions my group planned to ask. I've heard vampire senses are sharper than human ones, but this is ridiculous. Do you read minds?"

"Not exactly," I fudged, "but I am a bit psychic when certain moon phases don't fritz me out."

"A *bit* psychic, my best pearls! Invite us along next time you play the lottery."

The group laughed, and Skinny Goth Boy spoke up.

"Hey, the newspaper said you were a princess before you were, you know, in the basement. Were you really some kind of royalty, like from Spain?"

"No. The head vampire here called himself a king because he could get away with it. He declared me the princess because he sort of adopted me."

"So you were heir to the bloodsucker's throne?"

Stony asked the question, his voice grating like coquina on a chalkboard. Dressed in a black turtleneck, black Wranglers, and black sneakers, his hard eyes were a startling pale blue. I didn't mind the other questions, but his annoyed me.

"I'd appreciate it, sir, if you'd use more tactful language in front of the young children," I said polite as could be. The tour company and my mother would've been proud. "To answer you, in a sense I suppose I was being trained, but I was a most unwilling and uncooperative heir."

"So, eh, Princess Vampire," the loud wiseguy said, "you see dead people?"

Corny, but I could've kissed the man for asking the perfect question to get us on tour-track.

"I do see our ghosts when they want to be seen," I said as I retrieved the battery-operated lantern from the substation's small storage shelf. "Let's get along with our tour and find out if they're active tonight. Now, please watch your step, watch the children, and stay together as I tell you of the ghosts of St. Augustine."

An hour and thirty minutes later, the fog began to thicken, and the air was cooler, but the tour had been successful. Wildly successful, judging by the unusual number of sightings. I mean, the disturbed energy of storms can bring our ghosts out of the woodwork, but plain old fog?

Nevertheless, Wiseguy saw Judge John B. Stickney's ghost in the Huguenot Cemetery, my little friend Robbie saw both a cat and dog ghost, and two teens swore they saw an angry woman in the window of Fay's House on Cuna. Gomer must've seen her, too. I almost lost it when he uttered a shocked, drawling, "Shazam." He sounded too Gomer-ish to be for real, but he did look shaken. The French couple actually took their eyes off each other long enough to exclaim over orbs of light zipping around the Catholic Tolomato Cemetery.

I saw my favorite spirit, the Bridal Ghost, in the Tolomato and told her story, the one I'd "seen" from my basement grave. It wasn't a tour-sanctioned story, but the ghost nodded as if satisfied I had gotten the basics right. I hoped neither Janie nor Mick would turn me in for telling a tale not backed by specific historical data.

Then again, I could argue I *was* the historical data.

I wrapped up my last ghost story at the final stop and scanned the crowd. We'd covered less than a square mile on the tour, but the children were drooping or sleeping in their parents' arms. Wiseguy and his friends were quiet, and even the teens were subdued.

The newlyweds and Stony hung to the left side of the group. In fact, Stony seemed to be shadowing the couple during the tour. I didn't lower my reinforced shields to read the dynamics there. Nope, no idle snooping for me. I curbed my curiosity and conducted myself professionally.

"Ladies and gentlemen, this concludes our tour, except that I wanted to answer the lady's earlier question about where I lived."

I pointed at the newest bayfront hotel, pleased that seeing the site where my family had lived no longer gut-punched me.

"My home was about in the middle of this stretch of property. This hotel is new, but it replaced a motor inn where Martin Luther King, Jr., once jumped or was thrown into the motel pool.

"Thank you for joining us on the Old Coast Ghost Walk this evening. If you'd like to leave from here, you may, but I'll escort those who wish it back to our meeting place. Also, if you want to turn in an evaluation form, you can get a discount on a future tour."

The parents and children headed north toward the new tourist center parking garage. Wiseguy's group started south. That left the goth gang and Gomer, the Jag Queens, the newlyweds...and Stony, who stalked toward me.

"Hold it," Stony's gravel voice rumbled. "I want to know what happened to your family home. Why didn't it survive like these others did?"

I gave him my polite demeanor, just as I had before. "Many homes here were destroyed by fire over the years and have since been rebuilt. My home burned in 1802."

He took another step. "And you became a vampire in...?"

I gave him *very* polite. "Eighteen hundred."

One more step put him and his bad breath nearly in my face. "Did your family die in the fire?"

The Jag Queens gasped en masse, and Mick moved away from Janie to help me, but I held up a hand to show I'd handle the problem myself.

I gave Stony a polite smile so tight my teeth ached. "My parents were out visiting at the time of the fire and weren't harmed."

"Bull. I bet you slaughtered them. That's the truth, isn't it? You tore out their throats like the undead monster you are and set fire to them, didn't you? Didn't you, *brusha*!"

He grabbed my shoulders and shook me so hard I dropped the battery-operated lantern.

That's when I ran out of polite.

TWO

I may not use my vampire strength or speed, but in that moment I could've cheerfully snatched Stony's head clean off and handed it to him before he fell.

My good manners, good sense—and his breath—stopped me.

Mick moved behind Stony, but I waved off his help again and glared into the man's pale blue eyes.

"You're invading my personal space here, and you need a mint, jalapeño breath."

He smirked. "It's garlic, bloodsucker."

"It's both," I shot back, "with the underlying scent of cheap cigar. And for the record, I'm a blood sipper not a sucker. Starbloods caramel macchiato, if you want to apologize for this outrage with a case or two. Plus," I added, ducking easily out of his grasp when he didn't have the courtesy to let go, "I don't consider myself undead, just *underalive*. I mean, zombies, now those things are undead. And they stink almost as much as you do."

"We're locked and loaded and have him covered, dear," Shalimar Lady said. "Shall we phone the police, too?"

I leaned sideways around Stony and blinked. Six of the Jag Queens pointed guns at the man, though Shalimar's seemed to veer toward the bride, who stood just to the right behind me. Three other ladies held cell phones at the ready. What, did they each have different calling plans? The goth gang wore bug-eyed expressions, and Gomer and Mick stood tensed for action, but the ladies looked calm. Maybe because they'd raised children. Takes a lot to freak out mothers.

"No need for the police, ma'am." I smiled and straightened my shawl. "I'm sure Stony, um, this…gentleman…is leaving now."

"My name is not Stony," he ground out, his face turning apoplectic purple.

My genteel upbringing aside, I wouldn't have been crushed had he stroked out on the sidewalk then and there. He'd dug his fingers into my right arm where the GPS chip was implanted, and that puppy hurt. Alas, he didn't drop dead, and I didn't give him the satisfaction of rubbing my sore arm.

"Another time, vampire. You'll be alone, and you *will* die. One way or another, we'll make sure you all die."

He shouldered past me and stomped off, nearly barreling into the newlyweds, who watched him with raised brows.

As the ladies stowed their weapons and cell phones, Shalimar said, "What did he call you? *Brusha?* What is that?"

"It's a Minorcan word." I nonchalantly smoothed my skirt and hoped no one saw my hand shaking. "He either called me a witch or insulted my hair."

Which would make the second time today my hair took a hit.

I bent to pick up my lantern. Gomer lurched in at the same time, and we bumped heads.

"Oh, sorry, Miss Cesca," he said. "Let me get that so's you don't get cut."

"Thank you, but it's plastic." Dang, his head was hard, but his heart was in the right place.

"Here you go, ma'am. Sure sorry that man was rude to you."

I took the lantern by its twisted handle. The metal base and cage were dented, and the plastic hurricane lamp cracked, but at least we didn't have glass all over the sidewalk.

"That Stony guy's a real jerk," Skinny Goth Boy said. "Why'd he go off on you?"

Though I had a good idea, it was best to get over rough ground lightly. I shrugged. "Probably needs more fiber in his diet. Now, if you're all ready to walk back, let's head up Treasury Street."

"Just a moment, dear," Shalimar said. "Don't you need to file an incident report? Let us give you our names as witnesses."

"*Oui*. That man, he must be considered *dangereux*," the bride said, her sultry voice sounding more peeved than concerned. "He attacks you, and he follows my Etienne and me everywhere." She did the hair-tossing-over-the-shoulder thing again. "He is spoiling our honeymoon."

It shouldn't have been funny, but I felt a grin coming on because I wanted to send the bride to a chiropractor. The comic relief helped calm me, and I held up a steadier hand.

"You're right, of course. We'll report this to the tour company and possibly to the police, but," I said to the bride, "you need to make your own report if you feel threatened."

I clapped my hands like a teacher getting attention. "Right, now we really do need to head back to our starting place."

Janie whispered that she and Mick would take a shortcut back to the tour substation. They'd alert a tour supervisor by phone, and get started on the report paperwork.

To end the evening on a higher note than the scene with Stony, I joked and answered more questions as I led my reduced group back to St. George Street.

Did I breathe and have a heartbeat?

Yes to both. It takes breath—air moving over the vocal cords—to speak and laugh. My heart beats at a comatose snail's pace, but it does thump ten or so times a minute, more when I'm exercising. Unless I'm sleeping or being very still, in which case I may not breathe but once in a while or have a pulse over five beats a minute, but I didn't tell them that.

Could I eat and drink, like, regular food?

Yes again. I'm full after a few bites because a shrunken stomach doesn't tolerate food well, but I buy gelato at the shop on St. George Street every chance I get. It looks like colored whipped cream, and talk about smooth!

What do I do in my spare time besides watch TV and read?

Surf, rollerblade, listen to music, and play bridge.

The surfing and blading intrigued the teens, as did my music interests from jazz to Jimi Hendrix. The ladies played more Texas hold 'em than bridge, they said, but they oohed over some of my favorite actors. Cary Grant and Sean Connery are two. Then I mentioned Adrian Paul in the *Highlander* TV series, and Etienne struck a pose.

"Ah, yes. My Yolette, she collects the *Highlander* DVDs and jewelry. Even the swords. Very expensive, *non*? But my little wife loves these things, and she can buy what makes her happy."

Little wife? Was that condescending or what?

To turn the conversation and satisfy my curiosity, I asked the newlyweds, "What made you choose St. Augustine for your wedding trip?"

Yolette tossed her head again. "Oh, I learned of the city from a friend. Then we heard of you, and I decided we must come."

I blinked. "You heard of me? In France?"

Her jerky husband laughed. "My Yolette, she is fascinated with *vampires*, so *naturellement*, we came to—" He paused a nanosecond. "—investigate you."

I'm not often speechless, but I stopped and gaped. Shalimar, bless her, stepped forward. Literally stepped in front of me, almost confronting the couple, though her voice was mild.

"Are you staying at one of our beautiful bed-and-breakfast inns downtown?"

"*Non,*" Etienne said. "We rent a house on the beach. *C'est très moderne* where we may watch the sunrise. We spare no expense."

Yolette wrinkled her pert nose at the older woman. "*Madame,* your perfume is very strong. Shalimar, *n'est-ce pas?*"

"Yes."

"My late husband spoke of an aunt who wore too much Shalimar. I never met her, you understand, but he says to me it made him sick and I—I am allergic."

Shalimar stiffened, her expression stricken. Probably as insulted as I was for her, but she stood her ground. "What happened to your first husband?"

"He tragically died by—"

"Accident," Etienne said.

Murder, I heard in my head.

I glanced at Shalimar's set face. Had the thought come from her? If so, she sounded a lot different in my head—almost masculine. I glanced at Gomer, who watched intently. When he caught me looking at him, the edge drained from his eyes and he shrugged slightly.

Ready to see the last of this crew, I led them the final half block to our starting place, where Janie and Mick waited with the forms. As promised, each group member gave me contact information, even the goth gang and Gomer. Music from the live band at the Mill Top Tavern made conversation difficult, so the group drifted off quickly.

"You did great, Cesca," Janie said as the newlyweds left and Gomer trailed along behind, pelting them with drawled questions about France. "Grace under fire, for sure."

I sighed. "That guy was one of the famous Covenant freaks, right? The group that stalks vampires to kill them?"

"The one you called Stony? From the way he acted, I'd say so, yeah. In the nasty flesh." Mick tapped the sheaf of papers against his palm.

"Charming. Of all the tours in all the cities in all the world, a nutso vampire watchdog shows up at mine."

I'd read that a cell had provoked a lone vampire a few years ago, then cried foul when the vamp defended herself. Perhaps too forcefully, but she hadn't killed any of them. Still, the bullies had run to the law, demanding an execution. And got it.

Wait, a cell. Teams.

"Don't these guys work in teams?" I asked.

"Yeah, they do," Mick said slowly. "They also catch vamps alone, not with an audience around." He paused. "We could report him if we knew his real name."

Janie frowned. "The French couple said he was tailing them, but they aren't vampires, right?"

I had to smile. Me, Janie could take. More vampires, probably not. "No, they're just folks."

I glanced at Mick, who seemed to know about cults of all kinds. Someday I'd ask him why. "Mick, was tonight just a chance opportunity to harass me, or is there more to it?"

He scratched his jaw. "I don't know. Could be chance, if he's really following the Frenchies. Could be a change in tactics. Even a shot at getting publicity for his cause. Tell you one thing. I'd watch my back, if I were you."

Janie patted my arm. "At least you're forewarned now. I wouldn't lose sleep over him."

Janie is ever the optimist, and I grinned. "You're right. Hey, those sweet ladies tipped me forty dollars to share with you. How about a drink at Harry's? We can work on the report while we unwind."

Mick grimaced. "No offense, Cesca, but if you're drinking blood—"

"No, no," I interrupted, "I don't drink in public unless it's sweet tea. But I do like crunching ice. Will that bother you?"

"Ice?" Mick blinked. "You're kidding."

Janie, who'd caught a snack with me a few times, gurgled a laugh. "Why would she kid, Mick? Geez. I can go out for a while, but not to Harry's. The ghost in the bathroom creeps me big time. How about Scarlett's?"

The musty smell upstairs at Scarlett's where the bathrooms are creeps me, but I don't have to use the facilities often, so I agreed.

We strolled south on St. George, then took a right on the side street Hypolita, chatting about the cute little boy, the Jag Queens, and Gomer. Mick and Janie both thought Gomer was too much a caricature, but none of us had a clue what the man might have been up to. Then I asked if the wiseguys were really mobsters, and Mick told me I watched too much TV.

He may have a point, but I won't give up my mystery shows. Or HGTV.

Scarlett O'Hara's is plain fun. Good food and drink (when I nibble or sip any of it) and live entertainment nightly, so the place was usually packed with tourists and students from Flagler College right down Cordova Street. The exterior is cypress and cedar, and the two now-joined buildings dated roughly from 1865. The coolest thing? Three palm trees grow right through the floorboards where you walk up the steps.

Seats in the rustic outdoor oyster bar were taken. We peeked inside at the *Gone with the Wind* movie posters and portraits of Scarlett and Rhett, but Mick wanted to smoke, so we snagged a table on the porch when four men in business suits left.

Our waitress, Cami, appeared almost immediately to scoop up her tips, wipe down the tabletop, and hand us menus. A pert twenty-something and very slender in her black slacks, black rubber-soled shoes, and a wine-colored T-shirt with a white Scarlett's emblem, she'd waited on me a lot when I came in with Maggie and Neil. She always put a little sweet tea in with my ice but never offered to serve blood. She knew I didn't drink in public, because I'd told her so.

"Hey, Cesca, where's Maggie? Off with that hunk of hers?"

"You got it. These are friends from the ghost tour company."

Cami acknowledged them with a smile and took Mick's order, a pint, Black & Tan. Janie considered a decadent chocolate dessert but went with a drink, a mudslide. I nursed my glass of sweet tea and ice as we worked on the incident report and leafed through the tourists' names and addresses, trying to match them with faces. Laughter and music swelled and ebbed, but it was quiet enough to converse on our corner of the porch, and I was enjoying myself.

Until Cami approached us with a bottle, a glass, and a nervous frown. I recognized the label, my favorite brand of artificial blood. What the heck?

She shrugged her apology. "Sorry, Cesca, but a couple inside sent this to you."

Starbloods bottles are tinted tan so the contents aren't in-your-face obvious. Still, I whipped my shawl off and around the bottle as she handed it to me before Mick or Janie could be grossed out. It was cold and still capped. Good for Cami.

"That couple, they wouldn't happen to be speaking French, would they?" I asked, knowing I wouldn't like the answer.

She nodded. "They're sitting at the fireplace table."

Janie tensed next to me. "Is a guy with a scar on his jaw in there, too?"

"Yeah, and he's driving the waitstaff crazy. Won't sit down. Keeps pacing and getting in our way. Why?"

"The lone guy is a troublemaker," Mick told her, then turned to me. "Want to get out of here, Cesca?"

I was tempted, but he still had half a pint left, and Janie had her drink.

"Naw, I'll go talk to the newlyweds for a minute." I used my best shucky-darn tone, made like it was no big deal, and felt Janie relax.

I didn't, and I tensed even more as I approached the front

porch entry door. Through the glass I saw Stony standing at the foot of the stairs, arms crossed, his back to me.

I clenched the Starbloods bottle with both hands, my shawl trailing around it, and bit my lip. I could blow by this jerk with just a touch of vampire speed if I knew how to turn on the power. Open the door, slip past him, nothing to it. Maybe it would work.

I took a breath, thought *speed* and zip, I did it. True, I stumbled when I put on the brakes to avoid knocking over a waitress, but I reached the table by the fireplace where the newlyweds sat without flattening anyone.

I gave the couple a bright false smile. "Hi, are you enjoying your meal?"

As inane as asking about the weather, I know, but my manners are ingrained.

"*Oui,* very much," Yolette answered. "But I see you do not drink your blood. Why?"

"Much as I appreciate the gesture, I don't drink in public." I smiled again to remove any insult. "Thank you anyway. I'll be sure your waitress takes it off your bill."

"Wait!" Yolette sprang from her chair and slid an arm around my waist.

She smelled faintly of fresh blood, and my stomach turned queasy. Did she have a cut? If so, I didn't want to be blamed for it, especially when someone bellowed behind me. It sounded a lot like Stony's voice, but Yolette's caressing hand was scarier.

"*Mon amie,*" she said, even as footsteps shook the floorboards. "Why do you not drink with your good friends? Surely they cannot be offended if they are intimate with you."

"Uh, intimate?" Language barrier alert. She couldn't mean—

"But of course. Vampires bring such spice to lovemaking. Etienne and me, we often have vampire lovers."

Yikes. She *did* mean.

I stood mute. Stony hovered two feet at my back, making froth-at-the-mouth sounds. Yolette's hand kneaded my waist. I felt faint and wanted to disappear, but flinched when Etienne laughed, harsh and startling.

"Ah, Yolette, I think this little vampire is an innocent. See? She blushes."

"*C'est vrai?* Truly you do not share a bed with your friends?"

"No," I blurted, and meant *hell* no.

"We would welcome you then." She moved her hand from my waist—finally!—but lifted it to caress my cheek. "We could teach you so much, *d'accord*, Etienne?"

"*Oui,*" Etienne said, his voice rich with speculation as he eyed me like I was the rarest dish on the menu.

Stony moved then, jerking me sideways by the arm so fast a mortal would've had whiplash. Though his fingers dug smack into the same spot on my right arm where he'd grabbed me earlier, I kept both hands on the Starbloods bottle. Points for me.

Stony stuck his face close to Yolette's. "I'm warning you, I'll see you dead before you screw a vampire in my town."

"Is there a problem, folks?"

I turned to see Larry Hardy, the night manager, a smile in place along with his business suit and name badge, but his narrow gaze measured the scene.

Etienne rose from his seat and waved a languid hand. "*Non, non. C'est* a mere misunderstanding."

Yolette tossed her hair and stamped a foot. "*Quel problème!*

This man," she pointed dramatically, "he follows us and he threatens me just now. I demand he be removed at once."

"Sir?" Larry's tone made Stony let me go and back up.

"All right, I'm leaving." Stony glanced from Yolette to Etienne to me. "But you remember what I said. I *will* be watching."

Larry followed Stony out to the oyster bar, I guess to be sure he left. I turned to Yolette and Etienne. I didn't like their game, but maybe they were in true danger.

"I need to rejoin my friends and finish our paperwork, but you ought to file a report with the St. Augustine police."

"*Oui*, perhaps we will." She paused. "But tell me, have I offended you, *ma petite*?"

"You surprised me." An honest understatement.

"I suppose you do not wish to be our lover while we are here?"

That'd be a big ten-four. I put it nicer. "No, but have a nice honeymoon."

I didn't need vampire speed to flag down Cami, return the bottle, and have it deducted from the newlyweds' bill. I paid our tab, too, while I had Cami's attention, because I wanted to call it a night.

"What the hell happened in there?" Mick demanded when I stepped back out on the porch. "Stony damn near knocked over three people on his way down the stairs."

"He threatened the French couple," I answered, dropping into my chair.

"Not you this time?" Janie asked.

"Not directly."

"You're rubbing your arm again," Janie said with concern. "We need to add your injury to the form."

"Cesca." Mick's hard edges showed in his face and clenched fists. "What aren't you telling us?"

Embarrassing as it was, I spilled it. "The bride, the newly-wed bride who was wrapped around her groom all night? She propositioned me."

"Huh?" they said in unison.

"My reaction exactly." I rubbed my temples. "Seems the happy couple is into sex with vampires. I never quite got whether she meant solo or ménage à trois or both, but Stony heard every word and went ballistic."

Janie's eyes nearly popped out of her head. "Damn, Cesca, what did you do?"

"Other than mumbling incoherently? Not much. After Stony threatened death to vampire lovers, the manager escorted him out. I told the couple no thanks and split."

Mick's lips twitched. Was that a grimace or a grin fighting to break out?

"Let me get this straight," he said, his voice slightly choked. "The Frenchwoman put the make on you for some vampire nooky? Seriously, you?"

I nodded.

He burst full-out laughing.

Janie punched his arm. Hard. I swear my own arm throbbed in response. "What's the matter with Cesca?" she demanded. "She isn't attractive enough to be propositioned? Is that what you find so funny?"

"No, no, not at all."

"Then what are you implying?"

"That she's not the type to roll in the hay with...just anyone."

"You mean I don't roll in the hay at all," I said and waited as

Janie turned wide eyes on me. I shrugged. "It's true. I haven't, uh, had much experience."

"You have nada experience," Mick corrected. "Most vampires bed hop as fast as they can move. They're sensual, they're—"

"Too sexy for their fangs?"

Mick grinned. "Pretty much. Your sexuality meter is on dead stop. Pardon the pun."

"Thanks for the brutal honesty, Mick. I'll remember that on your birthday."

"It's almost a year away."

"I have a long memory."

"So do I." Janie gave him laser eyes. "How come you know so much about vampire sex antics?"

His gaze darted away then back. "I worked as a bouncer in a bar in Daytona. About fifteen years ago before vampires became a protected species. The vamps who hung out there were a wild bunch."

"Wild with you?"

Mick laid a hand over Janie's. "Never."

"Hunh, like I care." She slipped her hand from under his and homed in on me again. "Ignore him, Cesca. You're plenty sensual and sexy. You don't have a hot honey because you're discerning. But I can fix that. The hottie part, I mean." She grinned and rubbed her hands together. "I know these guys who'd love to take you out. There's Max Malone—"

"No, Janie, stop," I interrupted, gripped by a full-on fix-up terror alert. "Look, it's nice of you to offer, but I'd rather be staked than go on a blind date."

"My friends aren't *that* bad," Janie huffed.

"Of course, they aren't," I soothed. "I'm sure they're great, but where can these guys take me? As little as I eat, going for drinks or dinner is a waste."

"That's for sure," Mick said. "You'd give new meaning to the term *cheap date*."

"Mick, you're not amusing," Janie snarked and turned back to me. "Cesca, I see how it could be awkward, but a movie isn't out of the question. Or dancing." She frowned. "Then again, people tend to work up a thirst when they dance."

"Right, and how many movies can I see without dying of popcorn envy?" I do love the aroma of fresh popcorn.

"Hmmm. You need a guy who's creative about dates."

"I don't *need* a guy at all. Really. I'm busy every night."

"But I'd like to help you find someone special."

Janie looked so crestfallen, I took pity. "Tell you what. If I decide I have the time and interest in dating, I promise you'll be the first to know."

"Can't ask for more than that, Janie," Mick said jovially. "And, Cesca, since you'll need to sleep in, I'll hand deliver the incident report and the tourist list when the company office opens in the morning."

"Sure, Mick, thanks," I said, suppressing a chuckle at his eagerness to repay me for getting him out of a double date.

He went so far as to pat my shoulder as we left Scarlett's, and since Mick never touches me, the gesture was huge—like kissing my feet in public.

We split up on Cordova, Mick and Janie heading north to Mick's car, me heading south for Maggie's condo on Cathedral Place. I took all of five steps before the impact of what just happened hit me.

No, not my near escape with a fixup.

Mind reading. Telepathy.

Holy guacamole, I'd read minds tonight. Not just those of the overexcited tourists. I'd seen men's names form in Janie's thoughts and read Mick's gratitude to be off the double dating hook. Not just his face, his mind. Heard the thoughts in his own voice tone and pattern.

My psychic abilities were like water in a sieve this close to the dark of the moon. For over two hundred years it had been that way. Could they return to normal after all this time?

Nah, probably not. Not for good, anyway. Best not to wish for more out of my afterlife when I already had so much.

THREE

Among other provisions, the Vampire Protection Act required me to live within five miles of my sponsor. I could've rented an apartment, but they aren't as easy to find as one might think. Then there's the whole vampire-daytime-resting-place protection issue, and, well, the quickest fix to my unique housing need was to move into Maggie's penthouse guest room.

Maggie lives in the old First National Bank of St. Augustine building, circa 1928, right in the heart of the colonial part of the city. The building, now housing another bank and various professional offices on the lower floors, is across the street from the Plaza de la Constitución. The plaza is a public park opposite the Bridge of Lions, and it's been a gathering place virtually since the city was founded in 1565.

The city fathers never held with skyscrapers, so the whole bank building is only six floors high and just the top two were converted to condos—three of them on the fifth floor.

Maggie has the entire sixth floor, a modernized loft-esque space with amazing views of the bay, the lighthouse, the old fort, and even snatches of St. George Street and the city gates.

Maybe it was the result of my confrontations with Stony and the newlyweds—and the blind date scare with Janie—but I was drained. My nice, normal afterlife had taken hits of excitement I didn't like. I would've loved to crawl into bed and watch a movie marathon, but I couldn't. Not if I wanted to keep up with my online classes. Then again, studying would put me squarely back in my routine, and that was a good thing.

Design was my class *del día*, or *del giorno* as my papa would've said. Interior design tonight, exterior design tomorrow. Specifically, matching landscape plans with architectural styles. Neither was a college-level course. I couldn't enroll in college until I finished my GED. I was on track to do that, but in the meantime I indulged my HGTV-discovered love of architecture and design by taking the lecture and project classes offered through continuing ed.

In addition to the old Victorian, Maggie was also restoring the carriage house cum cottage on the back-of-the-house grounds for me. She wanted me to decorate my own space, and I would, but Victorian and other ornate styles weren't my thing—not like they were Maggie's. Now, give me Frank Lloyd Wright, Art Deco, Art Moderne, or midcentury modern, and I'm drooling. Lost in lines and curves and colors.

I was two blocks from the condo, thinking about the Craftsman-style cabinet I was designing for class, when I heard muffled footsteps behind me. Stony? Didn't smell like him, no menace in the air. The hinky honeymooners? No pheromones or fresh blood stench.

I stood still, and an essence wafted around me. Faint in the fingers of the fog, but there. It wasn't a fragrance. It was almost a touch. A ghostly touch, yet not a ghost. It could be only an overpowering memory. Or it might be what—or rather who— sprang to mind.

Shape-shifter. Specifically, Triton. My friend from the time of our childhoods until the day I insisted he leave town to escape the vampires.

Shifters had been hunted to extinction, logic argued.

No, the werecreatures—the true lycanthropes—were dead. Those not slaughtered outright had died from contracting a virus engineered to kill them. The virus hadn't harmed humans, and it hadn't harmed other shifters.

Magical shifters lived on.

Two things were sure. I hadn't felt that kind of magical energy scrape my skin in centuries, and I didn't know what I'd do if it were real. Correction, if Triton were real and right there behind me.

I walked faster. Not at vampire speed, just faster. The soft plopping sound of steps got closer. Probably a runner. A guy on the Flagler College track or tennis team. So why didn't he pass me? The footfalls seemed to keep pace with mine. Now that I listened harder, they sounded odd for a human. Sounded more like an animal, and smelled like—

I spun around, and a cat the size of an end table pounced on the hem of my gown.

"Rrryyyow!"

The sound was high-pitched, part scream, part supersized meow that vibrated in my skull. If I were mortal, I'd be in cardiac arrest. As it was, I clutched my shawl and blinked at the feline who was definitely not Triton. It batted at my hem once more, then sat on its considerable haunches and stared up at me. I stared back.

The collarless cat wasn't fat and wasn't really quite the size of an end table, just a giant domestic cat with a tail that looked longer than my arm. Short-haired, tawny reddish gold, with lighter fur on its belly and the insides of its legs, it reminded me of a Florida panther I'd seen back in my old life.

I swallowed. Kitty didn't seem right, so I said, "Hi, Cat."

Cat stood, stretched, and pranced around to walk in front of me. When I didn't immediately follow, it shot an impatient glance over its shoulder and curled its tail as if crooking a finger.

First the mind reading, now a magical cat wanted to walk me home? My night couldn't get much weirder.

Cat padded down the street, past the cathedral and shadowed shops. Smack at the entrance to Maggie's building—not the main bank entrance, but the all-but-hidden one for tenants—Cat stopped, sat, and gave me an expectant glare.

"Oh, nonono," I told it. "Magical or not, I can't bring a stray cat to Maggie. In the first place, I don't know if she likes cats. Plus, we don't have food. Or a litter box."

Cat's response sounded suspiciously like a snort. As if I'd offended it by suggesting it would deign to use a box when it ruled the great outdoors.

I drew my key from the hidden pocket of my skirt, ready to block the door with my foot to keep the cat out. As soon as I began wedging through the entrance, the cat rose and trotted across the street to the plaza. The deeper into the fog it went, the bigger it seemed to grow. A high-pitched, teeth-jarring *rrryyyow* rolled back through the mist just before its tail flicked out of sight.

The essence of magical energy lightened on my skin as the cat disappeared, but I *had* to be seeing things. Right? The cat hadn't grown to panther size. My imagination was in overdrive. Stress. That's all it was.

When you've been buried 204 years, the smallest space you want to be in is a car. That's why I usually don't take the elevator unless I'm hauling something awkward like my bicycle or surfboard.

Tonight, though, I punched in the elevator code and spent the ride up thinking that a hot shower in Maggie's fabulous guest bath would soon calm me. Heck, just being in her condo was a tranquilizer. With fifteen-foot ceilings, exposed ductwork, huge old windows, and an open floor plan, I never feel claustrophobic at Maggie's. The living, dining, and kitchen areas flowed into each other with only an area rug here, a sofa there to define the rooms.

Neil was still with Maggie when I let myself in. They were cuddled on the marine blue sectional sofa (one of the few non-antiques in the place) watching an old *M*A*S*H* episode on the Hallmark Channel. Maggie muted the sound.

"Hey, Cesca, before I forget, Tom called from the auto paint shop. Your truck is ready, and he'll be in by seven thirty tomorrow morning. I don't have to be at the office until nine, if you want a ride over there."

"Great, Maggie, thanks."

I sank into a wing chair she'd found at an estate sale and recovered in blue and tan plaid.

"You look funny," she said, cocking her head at me. "What's up?"

I wasn't sure I wanted to go into my misadventures with Neil there, so I sidestepped her. "Nothing. Just tired, I guess."

"Bull. I just told you your truck, the previously owned baby you paid a small fortune for, is ready to come home tomorrow with a new paint job, and you didn't so much as smile. What happened on the tour to upset you?"

That Maggie, she knows me too well. And she'd find out what happened through the friends of her friends who ran the tour company if I didn't tell her. Might as well spill it.

I launched into the recap of Stony and the newlyweds, making light of it. As I spoke, Maggie sat ramrod straight on the edge of the cushions. More surprising, Neil's expression grew grim.

"Damn it, Cesca," he said when I finished. "Those Covenant guys are no joke. They're the KKK without the robes and hoods."

Maggie raised a brow. "How do you know about the Covenant?"

Neil pushed off the sofa and paced. "I didn't tell you this because I didn't want to make you mad, but I went to one of their meetings. It was last August, a week after you found Cesca."

Maggie shot to her bare feet. "You considered joining up with those creeps?"

"I was worried about protecting you. I wasn't in the meeting fifteen minutes before I realized I didn't belong." He turned to me. "These guys, and the few women I saw, have a hit squad mentality. You may need to quit your job."

"Why should she?" Maggie demanded.

"To protect the innocent," I answered. Neil did a double take. "Yes, Neil, I'm not an idiot. I thought about other people getting hurt when Stony came after me tonight. But Mick, the guide I work with? He says that's not the Covenant MO. They don't *want* outsider witnesses."

"They may make an exception for you. You're not exactly a typical vampire."

Maggie held up a hand. "Wait just a damn minute. Before you quit a job you worked your butt off to get, shouldn't you see what the tour company has to say? You said a supervisor has already been informed, and they'll have the incident report in the morning. Your next shift is tomorrow, right? Then Thursday?"

I nodded. Maggie was like a general in the heat of battle when she got wound up. Even her dad, an officer and a gentleman who lives in town and has shown me his army ribbons and medals, calls her his warrior.

"Then give them time to consider before you take any action. You're not at fault, and you sure as hell shouldn't act like you are. And as far as these vigilantes go—" She stopped, took a breath, and speared Neil with a narrow-eyed glance. "We'll get a restraining order, hire a bodyguard if we have to. I will not have my friends coerced or threatened, and that's final."

"Ma'am, yes, ma'am," I said smartly, just like Radar might to Hot Lips.

She blinked, then grinned. "I went off, didn't I?"

"Like a bomb," Neil said.

"Well, injustice pisses me off. And the point remains that you don't quit unless Old Coast Ghosts forces the issue. Which they won't. Tourism is the lifeblood of this town, and you've been a transfusion for that company. The competition would snap you up in a minute, and the owners know it."

I could've done without Maggie's blood analogy, but she was

probably right. In the ghost tour business, I was more an asset than a liability. So long as a patron didn't get hurt.

And, hey, a bodyguard was a great idea. A hunk who'd be forced to spend lots of time with me? It had potential. A guy like George Clooney—

Maggie snapped her fingers in my face. "Earth to Cesca. What are you grinning about?"

"Doesn't look like anything I want to hear," Neil grumped. "Talk to you tomorrow, Mags."

He leaned to kiss Maggie's cheek, then paused when she tipped her head ever so slightly in my direction. He straightened and turned to me.

"Um, Fresca. Surf's supposed to be flat tomorrow, but there's a nor'easter coming. We could try the waves Thursday morning early. At Crescent," he said, meaning Crescent Beach. "That is, if you're interested."

Wow, Neil was inviting me to surf with him? Maggie must've turned the poor man inside out in bed. "What time?"

"Dawn? Should be high tide, too."

"Bitchin', dude," I said and gave him the hang loose sign.

He rolled his eyes but cracked a smile. "And, Fresca."

"What?" I asked. "Don't be late?"

"Keep your cell phone charged and on you in case you need it. You'll be a hell of a surfer if you live long enough."

Maggie's bedrooms aren't mere rooms, they're suites. Mine is to the right of the hall; Maggie's is to the left. She'd had the bed and bath ceilings in both suites dropped to nine feet to hide the ductwork and pipes. In my room, she'd painted the ceilings a medium soft tan with a lighter tan on the walls. Crisp white crown molding trimmed the ceilings and was repeated in the oversized baseboards. The bathroom was big enough to host a table of bridge, and it connected to a closet just as large with so many built-ins I didn't need a chest of drawers.

I don't fry in the sun, but long exposure will make me nauseated and cause skin sores. Much the way I've learned a lupus patient reacts to ultraviolet light. Maggie, bless her, installed room-darkening shades beneath the sage drapes on the massive north- and west-facing windows to keep me from getting sun sick. The neutral paint color kept the room feeling light, even with the dark oak and cherry antiques Maggie favored.

Maggie told me I could change things, but I knew she had lovingly decorated the suite before I came along. Besides, I watch enough home improvement shows to know that warm neutrals appeal to buyers. I didn't want to repaint before Maggie put the condo on the market. The Victorian home and my own new digs in back of the big house would be ready soon enough.

I hung my Empire gown in the closet, snapped on a shower cap, and let hot water shower away my tension. Or one kind of it.

Another kind of tension, fueled by erotic dreams I'd been having of me, a man, and a pulsating showerhead, built until my breasts ached for the dream lover's touch. *"Shameful,"* I could almost hear my mother say.

I jerked the dial to cold, iced down my libido, and toweled briskly. Once I'd brushed out my hair, I pulled on cobalt blue sweatpants and my favorite gray T-shirt with a surfer on the front. There, now I was refreshed, back to my normal unsexy self, and ready to hit the books.

Just as I sat at the Empire lady's desk of inlaid cherry and opened my laptop, Maggie knocked and poked her head in the door.

"Hey, can I talk to you a minute?"

I gestured at the Victorian fainting couch with its mound of pillows in greens, blues, and golds. "You make up with Neil?"

She grinned and sat. "I'll make him suffer a little longer. I still can't believe he went to a Covenant meeting."

"He loves you."

She arched one perfect brow. "But he *didn't* trust my judgment about you, did he?"

"He doesn't ask for directions either, but that doesn't make him evil."

"No, just a man."

We grinned at each other, then Maggie heaved a sigh. "I owe you an apology, Cesca. Not for Neil," she rushed on when I opened my mouth to object. "For acting like an overprotective mother."

She looked at one of the many Victorian lady prints on the walls, and I let her gather her thoughts.

"Neil says I hover, and I know I do. It's just, I'm forty-one years old. Neil is thirty-nine. We don't plan to have children, so you're the daughter I'll never have."

I scooted my chair around and plopped my bare feet on the end of the chaise. "No sweat, Ma."

She shook a finger at me but smiled. "Call me that again, and I'll take away your surfboard. Now, really, tell me the truth. Am I driving you nuts?"

"Maggie, you've been great." If she drove me berserk four times an hour, I wouldn't tell her so. I wouldn't hurt her like that. "I even like some of the mothering," I added for good measure.

"Such as?"

I flashed to Janie touching my arm, to Mick patting my shoulder.

"For one thing," I said, testing the words as I went, "you're the only person in my afterlife who hugs me."

She did the one-brow arch thing. "Are you feeling the need to be hugged?"

I swallowed, not ready to admit to need. "I came from a family of huggers," I said lightly. "I guess I miss it sometimes."

"Vampires weren't big on hugging, huh?"

I snorted. "Not in a good way."

She gave me a long, quiet look. "Does seeing me with Neil bother you?"

I tensed but tried not to show it. "Heck, no. I think you two are adorable."

"Can it, Cesca. I've seen something in your eyes. Like longing." She tilted her head. "Are you missing male companionship?"

"Me?" I squeaked, my feet hitting the hardwood floor as I sat up straight. "Maggie, everything's fine. Perfectly normal."

She nailed me with another searching gaze. "Cesca, normal isn't a static state. It's fluid. It's adjusting to what life throws at us."

"Well, sure, but I like my routine, and I'm always busy. A man would mess that up. Besides—"

I broke off, picturing Maggie and Neil. Janie and Mick. Even the newlyweds, screwy as they were.

Holding hands. Kisses in the dark. Those erotic shower dreams. Was it hot in here?

"Besides what?" Maggie asked gently.

I swallowed. Was I ready to say it out loud?

I took my courage in hand. "I don't think it's possible to miss what I've never had."

"Meaning a man?"

"Yes." If I was coming out of denial about my yearnings, might as well do it all the way. "To be blunt, sex. How can I be horny if I've never had sex?"

"Because you're a vibrant woman with wants and needs and hormones, that's how." She chuckled. "I should've had this talk with you a long time ago."

She was kidding, but suddenly, I wasn't. "Let's have it now."

"Are you serious?" She sat up straighter on the couch. "Your mother didn't tell you about sex?"

I rolled my eyes. "I'm two hundred and twenty-seven years old. What my mother told me is beyond archaic."

"What brought this up tonight?"

I stood and paced to the Regency four-poster bed. "Besides having some really hot dreams lately, tonight Janie offered to fix me up. I told her no way, but the truth is—"

I stopped, faced Maggie, and spat it out fast. "The truth is, I want to know what it's like to be with a man, but good guys don't want to date vampires, and I can't exactly go down to the marina, flip out condoms like an accordion wallet of family photos, and say, 'Hey, sailor, wanna have a good time?' "

Maggie held it for a second, then laughed so hard she sounded asthmatic.

"You're right," she said, panting to get her breath. "That's not the best approach. I take it you turned down Janie's fix up offer?"

"In spades." I paced back to the desk. "I think I should hire an escort. Would it cost extra for deflowering?"

"You could ask for a price list. Standard sex, deflowering sex, debauchery, orgies."

"No orgies," I said. "It's way too expensive to hire the cast of thousands."

She shook her head in mock disgust. "For a wealthy vampire princess, you can be a real tightwad."

"True, but seeing as how we're talking about my virginity, let's not call me tight. Let's call me frugal."

"Whatever, hiring an escort to initiate you is not a good idea. Too cold-blooded, if you'll forgive the expression." She tapped her chin. "I shouldn't suggest this, but why not enthrall some nice guy and have your way with him?"

"I tried that about two weeks ago, but I stink at enthralling. I couldn't keep a straight face."

"You laughed at him?"

I waved a dismissive hand. "No biggie. He was telling a joke and never suspected a thing."

"Honey, believe me, if you're horny enough, you won't laugh. You'll be chewing nails to get it on."

"Great, I'm horny, but not horny enough."

"You really want my advice?"

"When even Mick knows I'm a virgin, I *need* your advice."

"Fine. Wait for the right guy to come along. Someone you want to be with, someone you can trust."

"Trust not to stake me, you mean?"

She shrugged. "That and trust to care about you. Not the novelty of dating a vampire. *You.*"

"I might chew every nail in Home Depot by then."

"Oh, I don't know." She pushed off the fainting couch and started for the door. "Now that you've been honest about what

you want and said it out loud, synchronicity can work like—"
She snapped her fingers. "—magic."

She shot me a dazzling smile as she sailed out, but I don't
think she heard the eerie *rrryyyow* echo from the plaza.

Or saw the whiskered feline face floating outside my
window.

FOUR

From the front porch of his shanty cabin in a perfect circle of trees, Cosmil sat in a willow wood rocker keeping watch for the panther.

A passerby would perceive an old gentleman in dark trousers, a loose tunic, and house slippers, but there were no passersby. In addition to the night's fog, the dense woods and faeries saw to his privacy, never mind the concealing spell and wards he'd reset just today.

Only the faintest snap of a twig preceded the panther before she emerged from the live oaks and cabbage palms snarled in grapevines and kudzu. Her trotting gait looked lazy, but energy hummed around her.

"Pandora," Cosmil greeted as the big cat leapt the bowed steps to the rickety porch.

The vampire princess sensed the magick. She thought of Triton.

Cosmil clearly read the cat's thoughts and smiled. "Excellent. Francesca will trust that sense, and by extension, you. When Triton comes…"

Cosmil did not finish the thought aloud. The spoken word was even more powerful than thought, and its energy more easily detected. Cosmil could not risk detection. Not now.

Pandora sat with a thump and licked a paw. *You are correct about the danger to her.*

"The vampire killer?"

Aye, and another as well. A seeker.

Cosmil tensed. Omens had foretold the killer but no seeker. Fetid frog legs, he must know if this seeker meant her harm.

He leaned forward in the rocker, level with Pandora's amber eyes. "Did you read what is sought?"

Pandora tipped her head at him. *Justice.*

"Is that all?"

Pandora sniffed. *The vampire princess does not smell dead, but she is not quite human.*

Pandora had sidestepped the question, but that only meant she had no more to tell.

Cosmil gave her a wry smile. "Neither are we, my friend."

Of all the good he had accomplished over the ages as a wizard, Cosmil had also made mistakes. Miscalculations in spells that had led to the conception and birth of magical creatures he'd protect for the rest of his life. Pandora was the result of one such birth.

Triton was the result of another.

The time foretold had come. Triton must return to the ocean of his birth and reunite with his long-lost friend Francesca so that each might come into their full powers. As it was, Triton had delayed the trip long after he knew of Francesca's rescue—in spite of Cosmil's spells of gentle persuasion.

The boy had grown more stubborn with age, but also more cautious. For that, Cosmil could not fault him.

Especially not now as a dark force rose, an entity Cosmil called The Void when he dared name it at all. Like bilious black smoke, The Void concealed its identity while it fed on the powers of magical beings. The more unique those beings, the more power it derived.

Cosmil would move the moon itself to protect Triton and Francesca, for only through their reunion and the coming of their full powers might they help defeat The Void. There was time yet, six months, perhaps. But the sooner Triton returned...

Cosmil tugged on the sleeve of his black tunic and turned into the doorway of the house, considering which potions of high magick to prepare. Triton would not travel until after his shapeshift at the new moon, but he must arrive without incident.

Pandora watched him go through slitted eyes, then bounded off the steps and loped to her favorite tree. She settled on a high, forked limb, one paw dangling, and closed her eyes.

FIVE

Old, scary vampire me is a 'fraidy cat?

Yep, I admit it.

The super meow of Super Cat—and her whiskered image appearing then vanishing at my window—made me jumpy all night. Every sound remotely feline, every shadow at the window, frayed another nerve and chased erotic thoughts to the far corner of my mind.

I kept after my design homework, but I was sidetracked more than I wanted to be. That the design program kept glitching on me didn't help matters. I love technology, hate techno tantrums.

I usually only drink one six-ounce bottle of Starbloods a day, shortly after I wake up each afternoon. Tonight I downed one more during the early hours just to stay focused and ease my frustration. All that, um, protein wouldn't keep me from conking out when I was ready to hit the rack, but it steadied me enough that I finished my Craftsman cabinet drawing.

The nourishment also eased the ache in my right arm where Stony had abused it. Odd that the spot bothered me at all, but what did I know about implant chips? Maybe it had worked itself too close to the skin surface.

The weirdness wasn't just about the computer or Cat. As a plain psychic human, I'd had similar feelings. Those jumping-out-of-my-skin something's-happening-but-I-don't-know-what feelings that drove me just as nuts now as they had then. I blamed it on full moons, new moons, changing seasons, you name it.

In truth, moon phases made my abilities stronger when I was human. As a vampire, my powers go haywire during full moons, deader than me during new moons. Don't have a clue why the change, but it sure hadn't made King Normand a happy vampire. I'd explained that psychics weren't omniscient, but Normand the Nutcase had expected a perfect protégé princess, not a resentful rebel.

And though he was a royal pain, I never believed he was a real nobleman, much less a king. He'd hitched a ride on French ships with the soldiers who'd tried to hold Fort Caroline in what is now Jacksonville. When the Spanish slaughtered the French soldiers, King Normand moved south with his enclave of vampires and mortal slaves to settle outside the city gates. The Spanish soldiers, and later the troops of the British period, would've killed Normand sooner if they could've. My rotten luck they didn't.

I steered my thoughts away from Normand and back to tonight's mind reading. Unprecedented since I'd become a vamp, so why had it happened? I'd read somewhere that the moon was moving away from Earth at the rate of 1.2 centimeters a year. Could that bit of distance lessen the moon's influence over my psychic abilities? Wished I knew.

Nothing is as scary in the light as it is in the dark. The sunshiny Tuesday morning dawned, and thoughts of the past and weird Cat faded. Picking up my sweet Chevy SSR with its aqua metallic paint job lifted my spirits, and so did stopping at Home Depot. Not to chew nails. To pick up a chandelier Maggie ordered and to ogle the playground of gizmos and gadgets.

I returned to the penthouse and parked in the lot behind our building. Mostly it's bank parking, but each tenant gets one uncovered space. Since parking is hell anywhere downtown, I gladly paid for an additional slot. I mustered enough energy to brush my teeth before I fell into bed.

I slept dreamlessly and far later than usual, all the way to five thirty. Maggie breezed in looking as fresh in her blue gray business suit as she had this morning. She plopped her purse on the kitchen island just as I finished rinsing out a single Starbloods bottle.

She raised that brow at me. Or maybe it was at my butter yellow terry cloth robe and fuzzy dolphin house slippers—the kind with memory foam. I'm usually dressed by now.

"You look like something the cat dragged in. Have trouble sleeping?"

I startled at the C word but recovered and shook my head.

"That's an advantage of being underdead. No insomnia." I dropped the bottle in my own recycling bin. "What are you and Neil doing tonight? Is he still groveling?"

Maggie wagged her hand so-so. "If he shows up with dark chocolate or raspberry fudge, we may stay in. Did Home Depot have my chandelier?"

I nodded toward corner of the dining room. "Right there."

"Hot damn," she said, rubbing her hands together. "It's playtime!"

She immersed herself digging into the box, and I went back to my room. Now that I was awake, the first order of business was to double-check my Craftsman cabinet design. I tweaked it for twenty minutes before I was satisfied and e-mailed it to my instructor. The same prof's new lecture was posted online, so I hunkered down to read first the lecture, then the textbook. After that, I reviewed my notes for the landscape class and dreamed of the garden I'd create for my little carriage house.

Since I tend to go off in the ethers thinking about design, I set an egg timer for seven thirty. A quick shower and I tackled my hair.

I hate to admit it, but if you've seen *The Princess Diaries*, you've seen my hair. My flatiron won't work Hollywood miracles. Would a straightening product help? Industrial strength? I could cut it, but I'd had hair to the middle of my back for so long, would I feel freer with short hair or just terribly naked? Growing it back probably wouldn't be an option. I'd had Maggie's cosmetologist, Julie, wax my eyebrows, and not one stray hair had grown back to ruin their shape. Maybe I should try a short wig for a while?

I swept my mop up in a thick bun but didn't bother with all the hair spray. I'd live with the tendrils sticking out. It hadn't been as humid today. Maybe there'd be no fog tonight.

Once again dressed in my Regency gown and ballet-style slipper shoes, I grabbed my shawl, key, and cell phone, this time putting them in a reticule one of Maggie's friends had helped me crochet. Maggie was on the phone when I left, so I waved and headed out.

New night, new tour, same meeting place—the tour substation by the waterwheel, where a band was again in full swing at the Mill Top Tavern.

And, yikes, many of the same faces from last night. I'd wanted to be a successful tour guide, but having this many of Monday's group show up again? Too weird.

The newlyweds were back, and so was Gomer. Standing off to my right, Yolette in another semi–see-through outfit regaled Gomer with tales of Paris, while Etienne stood by looking bored. Gomer nodded at Yolette and drawled "Gol-lee" every now and then, but his gray eyes looked glazed. He wore different colors tonight but the same kind of clothes—a flannel shirt and polyester pants, with the sleeves, pant legs, and shirttails still too short.

To my left, Shalimar chatted with two middle-aged ladies I didn't recognize from the night before. None of them wore the teal Jag Queen visors tonight, just knit pants that looked warm and snugly, and T-shirts that read ST. AUGUSTINE.

Stony had dressed in black again and hovered about ten feet away from both little groups. He looked tense, alert, and determined, his eyes narrowing first on me, then shifting to Yolette.

I didn't feel flattered that these people had shown up again. I felt stalked.

Especially when Etienne spotted me. He hurried over, seized my hand, and pressed a kiss on my palm. Yolette, I noticed, paused in pelting Gomer with her monologue to shoot a death-ray glare at Etienne's back.

"Ah, Francesca, *enchanté*," he said. "*Comment le charmant de vous regarde.*"

I plucked *charmant* out of his effusively delivered comment and knew he'd said I looked charming or some such thing. I wasn't bamboozled.

"Thanks," I said, pulling my hand out of his grip and resisting the urge to wipe it on my skirt.

"We share more delights tonight, *oui?*" He smiled as if I found him clever and suave.

"If you find ghosts delightful," I said repressively.

"I find you the delight, *ma petite*," he bantered, stepping closer.

I frowned and stepped back. "Etienne, I don't flirt with married men."

"Ah, but Yolette and I," he said, sliding nearer again, "we have the open marriage."

"Well, it's closed to me, and right now I have to collect tickets."

For a heartbeat he looked annoyed. Then his brow smoothed. "But of course," he said, flourishing two tickets as he bowed from the waist ever so slightly.

I'd accidentally read minds the night before and was tempted to purposely try it now. I might be able to psyche out what Etienne was up to other than making Yolette jealous enough to strip my hide. And making Stony stare daggers at us. But did I really want to know what either man was thinking? Probably not.

I *was* glad to have my cell phone—on vibrate mode, and ready to dial 911, if things so much as looked like they might get out of hand. Being responsible for mortals was not to be taken lightly, especially when my vamp powers were only so-so.

I really didn't want to get close enough to Stony to take his ticket. Didn't care if he had one. I did want Etienne to stop following on my heels, so I inched toward the other five women who made up the tour.

In various styles and colors of jeans, jackets, and tennis shoes, the thirty- to forty-somethings stood not far from Stony talking about—assuming my vampire hearing wasn't on the fritz—bumping people off. Poison seemed to be the weapon of choice, though one especially sweet-looking lady wanted to use a kitchen knife on her victim.

Who knew guiding ghost tours would be so dangerous?

I must have made a noise, because Knifer looked up and caught me staring. With a grin and a wave of her hand at the others, she said, "Don't mind us, we're mystery writers. We get that reaction all the time when we talk plotting in public."

Ya think? I almost said it aloud, but good manners prevailed. Then it hit me. Mystery writers. I love mysteries, and these women write them? Oh, joy! I'd discover new titles to search for, new authors to read!

I might've gushed about then, but it was time to start. I'd gush after the tour.

"Welcome to the Old Coast Ghost Walk. I'm Cesca, your guide. Please give me your tickets, and we'll get started."

"Are you really a vampire?" one of the writers asked. Her blonde flyaway hair shone an ethereal silver in the streetlights, and she poised a pen over a pocket-sized spiral notebook.

"Of course she is," Shalimar answered, then gave me a little wave. "Hi, Cesca, I brought more friends to meet you. This is Barb and Darcy."

"Thank you, Mrs.—" I racked my memory, but Janie and I hadn't finished connecting all the Jag Queens' faces with names.

"Millie Hayward, dear. Call me Millie."

"Well, I'm honored you came back tonight with more friends, Millie."

I smiled at the two new women, both gray-haired and grand-motherly while Shalimar Millie grinned and gave me their tickets. "I hope you'll all enjoy the tour."

"Do you mind if we record you?" another of the writers asked, this one with short salt-and-pepper hair that cupped her head like a cap. "We don't want to miss anything in our notes."

I hesitated because the tour company had taped audio and video tours that were for sale. But with Stony glowering in the background, maybe he'd behave if tapes were rolling. Couldn't hurt, might help.

"That will be fine," I said and took their tickets, too.

I turned to bite the bullet and get Stony's ticket, but Gomer—I couldn't recall his real name either—strolled up. "Here, Miss Cesca," he drawled, passing two tickets to me. "That's all of us."

"*Non! Beaucoup trop.* We are too many," Yolette said, elbowing Gomer out of the way to plant herself in front of me. "He—" She flapped a hand at Stony. "—should not be allowed to go. He is *dangereux.*"

Shalimar Millie glared at Yolette with a look that could maim if not kill. Objecting to her manners? Who knew? Much as I agreed and sympathized with Yolette on this one, I couldn't ban Stony.

"Did you file a police report?" I ask calmly.

"*Non*, I did not."

I spread my hands, my reticule dangling from my right wrist. "Then I'm afraid there's nothing I can do except see that you get your money back if you want to skip the tour tonight."

"And let this pig run me off?" Yolette tossed her head again. "*Non*, I will stay."

Uh-oh. If Stony was grouchy before, he was livid now. Fists clenched and red-faced, he was growling under his breath.

I plastered on a smile and launched the tour.

"Ladies and gentlemen, tonight we were supposed to go into two haunted buildings. However, I was informed that the buildings will be locked this evening."

A blatant lie, but walking around shadowed streets with this crew would be bad enough. I wasn't about to take them into dimly lit buildings.

"If you signed up for this tour specifically to see the inside of those buildings, I apologize for the inconvenience. We will see the outside of the same buildings where there are also ghosts. If that's not acceptable, I'll take your names and see that the tour company gives you another tour for free."

I paused to see if anyone—namely the writers—would take me up on a tour voucher, but no one did. With a small shrug, I opened the substation storage locker and grabbed a new lantern off the shelf. I could smack Stony with it if he gave me any trouble. That is, if Shalimar Millie didn't pull a gun on him first.

With that happy thought, I started my spiel.

"Our first stop tonight will be the Huguenot Cemetery," I said as I led my group across Orange Street. "This cemetery is a Protestant burial ground, as opposed to the Catholic Tolomato Cemetery, which we'll see later. It was opened in 1821, shortly after Florida became a territory of the United States, and the same year a yellow fever epidemic swept through the town. The most famous ghostly resident is Judge John B. Stickney.

The judge was a widower with three children, who came to St. Augustine after the Civil War and became a prominent citizen. He died of typhoid fever after a business trip to Washington, D.C., in 1882."

I went on to finish the story of the judge and mentioned some of the other ghosts who reside in that particular cemetery before herding my group to the next stop. The oldest pharmacy, one of the buildings we were supposed to have gone into, took only a few minutes to highlight before we moved on to the Tolomato Cemetery and beyond.

I kept a sharp eye out for any trouble, but once I'd put a bug in Etienne's ear to back off, the groups seemed to have arranged themselves into camps. The writers followed me in a clump, three of them furiously taking notes, while the two with digital recorders added their comments to my running dialogue or fired questions as fast as I could answer them.

Etienne strolled with Shalimar Millie and her friends and ignored Yolette, who flounced along ahead of him, pointedly out of his reach. Yolette tossed her hair and generally looked down her nose at all of us. Not even a hint of honeymoon pheromones in the air tonight, though I thought there was the lightest scent of blood. One of the writers had a Band-Aid on her thumb. Paper cut, perhaps?

Stony was busy at the back of the pack answering Gomer's questions about fishing. When I tuned in to eavesdrop once, Stony's gravelly voice answered one of Gomer's questions. Something about trips to go deep sea fishing was all I bothered to catch.

Ahhh, wouldn't it be nice if Stony had a hobby that kept him off my back?

*　*　*

Compared to the night before, I darn near double-timed my group through the tour. I knew it, and I didn't care.

The ghosts are traditionally more active during the summer and during stormy weather, but tonight they were in a frenzy. My opinion of the activity level? The group tension transmitted itself to the ghosts. Every tourist saw and felt multiple phenomena—apparitions, orbs, and cold spots. Even old Stony looked distracted and pale a few times, though he didn't say a word.

When we arrived back at the tour starting point, I was exhausted and praying—yes praying, I can do that—that everyone would leave quickly.

Yolette was the first to grant my prayer. She sashayed off toward Orange Street when Etienne seized my hand and placed a kiss on it again. Ick and double ick, because his lips left a faint smell of blood behind. Had she belted him one in the kisser and I missed it? Darned shame if I did, but I let the thought slide away as Etienne strolled off after Yolette.

Stony stabbed me with a look that could stake and followed Etienne. I might've been alarmed for the couple, but I was sick of all three of them. Doesn't make me a good person, but it does make me human.

Gomer was the next to leave with a drawling "Bye, ma'am" and a wave. I did feel better when he strolled off in the same direction the newlyweds and Stony had taken, sure that he'd report it if Stony got violent. See? I'm not totally heartless.

Shalimar Millie looked tired and troubled as she and her friends left, and I hoped the fast pace I'd set tonight hadn't done her any harm. They headed in the same direction as the rest, toward the tourist center parking garage.

When just the writers remained, I chatted with them for a while. I learned two of them were published—the two with the recorders—and three were aspiring. After getting their names and titles of their books, I offered to get them passes for another tour that would take them into the haunted buildings. Since they were all visiting from Texas and on a limited budget, they accepted and thanked me.

I stowed the lantern in the locker and headed back to Maggie's, dialing the tour office as I went. No time like the present to mention those free passes. I'd e-mail a full report and another request for the writers' passes later. If the tour company refused, I'd pay for them myself. Maybe I'd get an extra three for Shalimar Millie and her friends. If I ever saw the ladies again, I'd have the tickets handy.

Two problem tours on my first two nights as a guide. Gee, I could hardly wait for Thursday. I almost wished the tour company *would* fire me. Or at least give me hazardous duty pay.

Exhausted as I was, I decided to walk back along the seawall. Seeing the sailboats at anchor and breathing the cool air would calm me before I studied.

I cut through to Castillo Drive, passing the Mill Top Tavern, where music still pulsed in the night. Just as I reached the sidewalk running past the Castillo de San Marcos—the old fort—someone shouted my name. Gomer, I saw when I turned, loping up to join me. There went my time to unwind.

"Hey, Miss Cesca."

"Hey, Gom—" I stopped so short, I gave my tongue whiplash. "I'm sorry, I've, um, forgotten your name."

"It's Holland, ma'am," he drawled, a hint of a grin curving his lips as if he knew what I'd almost said. "Holland Peters, but everybody calls me Holland."

Holland. Unusual, and now that he said it, I remembered it from Monday's witness list. "Good name," I said, smiling.

"Yes'm. It runs in my family."

I suppressed a chuckle. "Where are you from, Holland?"

"Well, I was born—" He pronounced it bore-un. "—in North Carolina, but I've traveled all over the South."

"Oh? Doing what?"

"You know, this and that. Fixin' cars, loadin' trucks, deliverin' furniture." He shrugged. "Mind if a walk with you a ways?"

Evasive about where he's from and what he does. Noted. Was I in danger? Doubtful. I glanced at the gently rocking boats in the bay. The curse of good manners is that it's hard to say no to polite requests. And, hey, I could have worse company. I wrapped my shawl a bit tighter.

"Let's walk, Holland."

"Thank you, ma'am."

He was quiet as we headed south on the waterfront sidewalk toward the Bridge of Lions. To my left, the seawall was lined with posts called bollards, each bollard connected by nautical-sized chain. The chains weren't enough of a barrier to keep someone from ending up in the Matanzas Bay, but Holland wasn't crowding me. If anything, he straddled his side of the walkway.

"Um, Miss Cesca," he finally said, "I thought you'd want to know, that French couple got off all right. I mean, the weird man followed them, but the house they're rentin' is in some fancy neighborhood, so they should be safe."

I blinked. "How do you know?"

"They told me," he said simply. "People tell me things, and I pay attention."

Uh-huh. "That was nice of you. I'm glad to know they'll be safe."

"Yes'm. But I wanted to make sure you were safe, too."

I slanted a glance at him. "I thought you said Stony—I mean, the weird guy—left."

Holland nodded eagerly. "He did, ma'am, but he could have friends watchin' you. Or he could come back." He shrugged again. "I wouldn't want anything to happen to you."

Why did that sound like a veiled threat? Hmmm. Paranoia? I walked just a little faster and asked, "Why would you care if Stony or one of his friends got me?"

He stopped trotting at my side, mouth open in shock. "Because you're a nice lady."

"You think I'm a lady?"

"Of course." A stride brought him level with me again. "And my ma would tan my hide if I let a lady walk home by herself. Especially after someone threatened her."

I gazed into apparently guileless gray eyes. Psychic shutdown or not, my BS meter was spiking like crazy. Half truths and secrets. That's what I sensed from him. Then again, I still felt relatively safe, and I was curious enough to see what else Holland might tell me.

"Well, then, thank you for seeing me home." I paced off again, trailing my hand on the thick ship's chain strung along the seawall. "So, are you visiting in town or do you live here?"

"I live over in Palatka for now."

"You take the ghost tours often?"

"Oh, no, ma'am. I wanted to see you."

I looked up sharply. "Why?"

"You lived history," he said, sweeping his right arm to indicate the city. "You were here before Henry Flagler was even born, much less before he changed this place with the railroads and big fancy hotels and churches and all."

Couldn't argue that I predated Henry Flagler and the improvements he'd brought to St. Augustine, but I didn't buy Holland as a big history buff.

"And you came back tonight just to see me again?"

He looked away. "No, ma'am. Not exactly."

We'd reached the corner, and paused for the traffic light to change. He didn't tower over me, but I had to look up. "Why don't you just spill it, Holland?"

"The man you call Stony—good one, by the way."

"Yes?" Pulling teeth here.

"Fact is, ma'am, he's been in Palatka and Hastings talkin' up this Covenant thing. Talkin' about killin' humans who have dealin's with vampires, too."

"Do the authorities know?"

"I don't know, but I ain't the one to report him."

"Yet you're warning me."

"Seein's how he came after you last night, yeah."

The light changed, and we crossed in silence. I had no trouble believing that Stony was recruiting, but it didn't ring true that Holland feared the man. Not from the way he acted during the tour tonight. So who was Holland, really?

I almost took a shot at reading him, but as we stood at the corner of Charlotte and Cathedral, a half block from home, I spotted Maggie on her hands and knees on the sidewalk. She cradled one arm as if it were broken. Cat—giant, brain-rattling-meow Cat—sat next to her, rubbing its face on the gray sweats Maggie wore.

I didn't think about moving, I was just there in a flash, hunkered beside her.

"Maggie!"

She rose so fast, we bumped heads.

"Ouch. Maggie, are you hurt? Is your arm broken?"

She rubbed her forehead. "Just my dignity. Some damn big cat wouldn't move away from the door while I unlocked it, then the darn door stuck, and I strained my wrist trying to keep from dropping everything."

I looked around us. Two bundles of paint sample strips fanned out on the sidewalk along with bulky fabric samples bound together with O-rings. Rolled papers I recognized as architectural drawings stuck out of the mix. Cat was gone.

"At least you didn't break anything," I breathed with relief, snagging her keys from the sidewalk. I'd puzzle over Cat later.

"May I help?" a masculine voice over us asked. Holland. I'd forgotten about him.

We both assisted Maggie to her feet, and I made quick introductions while he bent to pick up and pass Maggie the fabric swatches and rolled-up drawings. When he leaned over again to get the paint sample bundles, a wind gust from the bay caught his short shirttail and flipped it up over the waistband of his polyester pants.

Where a butt crack might have been, I saw something worse.

In the small of his back, a matte black metal grip stuck out of his waistband.

Holland "Gomer" Peters carried a gun.

SIX

Surprised? Shocked? Full-scale flipping out?

Bingo, I was flipping. Way out.

Irrational, maybe, but who expects Gomer to be packing heat? Okay, he's not Gomer. And, okay, the Jag Queens toted, but that was different. They wouldn't shoot me, or Maggie either.

Would Holland shoot us? I hadn't feared him until I saw the gun. Now his half truths and secrets seemed sinister.

He almost caught me staring as he straightened with the last of Maggie's things, but I stretched my mouth into what I hoped was a bright smile.

"Here, I'll take those." I snagged the paint samples from him. "Don't want Maggie to strain that wrist more, do we?"

"Uh, no, ma'am."

"Well, thanks for the escort home, Holland." I turned to my roomie and nudged her toward the tenants' door. "Let's dump this stuff and check your wrist, Maggie." When he moved to open the door, I rushed on. "Thanks, again, and, uh, have a good night."

"You, too, Miss Cesca, Miss Maggie. Y'all take care now."

I closed the heavy glass door, checked the automatic lock, and hustled Maggie to the elevator around the corner. Out of Holland's line of sight *and* line of fire. Sure, if he'd wanted to shoot me, he could've done it anytime, but, hey, logic didn't count when I was having a nice, healthy panic attack.

"Cesca, what the hell are you doing? What's the rush?"

The elevator doors stuttered open, and I hip-bumped her into the car, thinking fast. "We need to get ice on that wrist before it swells too much. And aspirin. You probably want some aspirin, right?"

"I want to know what the problem is."

I entered the penthouse code on the elevator panel and pressed our floor button rapid-fire five times. "Gomer. I mean Holland," I corrected as the car chugged upward. "His real name is Holland. I told you and Neil about him. He was on my tour last night, and he came back tonight."

"Wow, you must've made a good impression. You have a date?"

I snorted. "Hardly."

"Why not? He looks a little goofy, but he seemed nice, and I saw you staring at his butt. Did you get cold feet?"

I didn't want to worry her, but Holland had seen Maggie and now knew where we lived. She had to be on guard.

We reached the sixth floor, and I lurched to the carved cypress penthouse door. "I wasn't staring at his butt," I told her as the lock slid open. "I was staring at his gun."

"Excuse me?"

"His gun, Maggie. He had a gun stashed at the small of his back. Just like in the movies."

"Maybe he's a cop," she said as we dumped her samples and drawings on the couch.

"Cops wear their guns in holsters."

She considered a minute. "Not if they're undercover."

"Undercover?" I rolled the idea around, replayed his actions, his words. All right. It was possible.

Except that Holland didn't want to report Stony to the cops. His way of sidestepping because he *was* undercover?

"Cesca."

"Yeah, yeah, I'm thinking. I guess you could be right."

"Tell me what happened tonight."

I did, from the tourists who showed up to Holland walking me home and our conversation. I fixed an ice bag for her wrist while I talked.

"Did you get any particular vibes from this Holland guy?" she asked when I finished.

"Psychically, no, but he's lying about something."

"Did you ever sense danger directed at you?"

"No, but seeing the gun gave me second thoughts. He just doesn't feel right."

"Sounds like this guy is on something like a hate-crimes task force. An undercover fed," my ever-practical Maggie said, taking the ice to the sink. "The best thing to do is stay alert when you're out, and keep your phone charged and with you."

"You need to do the same. Neil's gonna have a fit when he finds out Holland knows where we live."

"No, he won't, because we aren't telling him. He'll just get his shorts in a bunch and drive me crazy, and I don't have time for that right now. Speaking of which, I need to get to work."

"Tonight?"

She nodded and crossed to the couch to snag her samples with her good arm. "The Jax Beach restoration client—the one who's fired four interior designers—changed her mind about colors and fabrics. Again."

"So you're stepping in?"

"I have to. Until she settles on colors, I can't order the kitchen tile."

"Want some help?" I carried a second load of materials to the kitchen table.

She cocked her head. "No homework? No tests tonight?"

"Nope. My landscape test is tomorrow night. I'll take it after bridge club."

"In that case, go change, and let's get crackin'."

Cosmil stood in the plaza across from Francesca's building beside the remnants of an old town well. Pandora in her house-cat form sat on her haunches at his side, her tail swishing the grass.

The man who'd walked with Francesca crossed the street to the plaza and paced between two benches as he pushed buttons on his cellular phone. Only yards away, it was not difficult for Cosmil and Pandora to overhear.

"I saw Miss Cesca home like you asked, but she spotted my gun. I'm sure of it."

A woman's voice floated through the airwaves, but the words were indistinct.

"Yes'm, she got away from me as fast as she could. She's not likely to trust me now."

The woman spoke again, briefly.

"All right. Maybe I'll tell her I'm a PI, but it'll have to wait. I have another case to take care of in Daytona."

With a last "Yes'm," the man disconnected his call, gave his phone a resigned look, and punched another set of numbers.

Cosmil heard one word, "Report," before casting a shield around Pandora and himself to protect them from the malefic energy lashing through the line.

"I've searched the beach house, but not the car."

An angry voice whipped through the phone.

"No opportunity. I'll try again and search the other man's place tomorrow." He paused, listened. "The Marinelli woman has nothin' to do with it. Yes, damn it, I'm certain." He paused again to listen. "Then send someone else to do the job. I'm doin' what you want and nothin' more."

A growl so loud emanated from the phone, Pandora raised her hackles and flattened her ears.

A spate of angry, unintelligible words shot through the device, then silence. The man folded the phone closed, cursed, and strode out of the plaza to disappear around the corner.

Cosmil glided to the sidewalk and looked up. Low lights shone through the sixth-floor windows where Francesca and the other woman lived.

I can find that man and kill him quickly.

Cosmil glanced at Pandora, then back at the light. "No need. He is not the threat, and Francesca is safe enough for now. We will not interfere." Francesca's silhouette passed by the window. "Not yet."

The second voice. Who was it?

Cosmil grimaced. "One of the true monsters, my friend. Come, I have spells to prepare."

We worked only an hour on the new presentation board. Maggie refused to labor any longer on it—not when she was sure the client would change her mind a half-dozen more times. I refilled her ice bag, insisted she take a pain reliever, and sent her to bed.

After I repacked Maggie's materials, I soaked in a long, hot bath and thought about Holland. Maybe he *was* on an under-cover sting of the Covenant. If so, whatever evidence he was looking for, I hoped he got it soon. Either way, I'd be calling the cops if Holland came near Maggie or me again.

I slipped on a St. Augustine nightshirt and memory foam dolphin slippers and e-mailed the tour company about passes for the writers, with three more for Shalimar Millie and her friends.

I tried to study, but after helping Maggie, I was too wired with design ideas. After doodling and sketching for a while, a flip through the on-screen TV guide revealed a mini-marathon of the *Highlander* series. Adrian Paul could take my mind off just about anything, and, yes, by watching him fight the good battles, I fought my own. The slash and scrape and ring of steel on steel reminded me of swordplaying with Triton eons ago.

I veered away from lingering thoughts of the boy and man who'd been my childhood playmate, then girlhood crush, and finally my dearest friend. Missing him was a raw ache in my soul, and I was stressed enough.

Instead, I puzzled over Cat and why she'd been nearby

tonight. Again. Why so much weirdness happening when I was just really getting my afterlife together? What happened to normal and predictable? I tell you, I couldn't wait for the new moon to pass. I'd never missed my ability to purposely psyche out information like I had in the past two days. Even when I only got sporadic bits and pieces of answers, it was better than this exhausting game of guessing what the heck was going on.

Good thing tomorrow was Wednesday bridge club. I needed the relaxing competition of a rousing game.

For the first time in ages, I was asleep as dawn broke.

Bridge ran promptly from seven to nine with socializing at six thirty. By five forty-five, I was dressed in black jeans and my scoop-neck cobalt knit shirt with black sandals. A dab of makeup, my hair in a braid, and I was ready.

We were meeting at Shelly Jergason's in Crescent Beach. I stopped for gas on the way, cringing at the price and the fumes that rose from the tank.

Shelly, in fact, had invited me to join the club, and we'd met because of the Vampire Protection Act. One of the strict provisions was that vamps had to take a Human Lifestyle Appreciation class, then participate in some sort of community activity. A garden club, library guild—the organization didn't matter as long as we interacted with mortals.

I'd met Shelly at the Historical Society and mentioned in passing that I was learning to play bridge on the Internet—a game that evolved from whist, so it wasn't that hard for me. Next thing I knew, she called me to substitute a few times, and when one of the ladies went back to nursing on the night shift, I joined as a full-fledged member.

Traffic was light, so I arrived at Shelly's early. Jenna Jones blew in right behind me in her red power suit, her mouth in high gear as usual.

"You would not be*lieve* the new clients I'm trying to find houses for!" Jenna paused dramatically in Shelly's huge kitchen, then dropped her purse on a rattan barstool and fluffed her short hair. "And the creepiest thing happened on the way back from my closing in Palatka. I swear it must be the full moon."

"New moon," Maybelle Banks corrected. She's the grand dame of the group. Sixty, dabbles in astrology, and cracks a wry wit.

"What?" Jenna asked with a blank look at Maybelle.

"It's the new moon," Maybelle said, "not the full."

"Whatever!" Jenna said. "I've shown this one woman every darned house on the island, and she's not—" She made quote marks with her fingers. "—feeling any of them. And the man I'm searching for! He's in California now. Says he grew up here but can't decide if he wants a place downtown or on the beach. When I mentioned property on Vilano, he had no idea what I was talking about. Vilano Beach has been called Vilano for a long damn time, and this guy doesn't sound over forty. How can he not know where Vilano is?"

Goose bumps broke out on my arms as Jenna ranted about her California client, but I had no clue why. The nearly dark moon messing with me again? The Gift resurging?

"That explains your difficult clients," Shelly piped in, "but what's creepy about Palatka? There's not much but farm country between here and there."

"Exactly!" Jenna exclaimed yet again. "I stopped to look at

a property another client asked about. Some land with a shack on it. Well, I found the road tunneling through this tangle of trees and vines, but when I got to a clearing, there's no shack, no nothing but empty land in a ring of trees."

We all waited expectantly. Shelly ran out of patience first. "And?"

"When I turned the car around, I happened to glance in the rearview mirror, and the shack was *there!*"

"Faeries," Maybelle deadpanned. "They don't want the place sold, so they hide the shack when you're looking straight on for it, reveal it when you're not."

Jenna blinked. "Are you shitting me?"

Maybelle half smiled and patted Jenna's shoulder. "Honey, you need a day off."

"More like a month. Have some wine, and chill out, Jen," Nadine Houseman advised and handed her a glass of Chablis. Nadine is medium height, in her fifties, and is the perennial chairwoman. She sees a problem, she solves the problem.

Jenna accepted the goblet with a cute glass dolphin ring on the stem—the kind meant to help tell glasses apart at a party. If I ever hostess bridge, I need to get some of—

"Cesca!"

I blinked at Jenna. "What?"

"Is Maggie ready to put the condo on the market?" Jenna demanded, apparently for the second time.

"Oh for heaven's sake, Jenna," Shelly said. "Stop nagging Cesca about the condo. If you really want to make some money, sell that oceanfront house up the block. Those owners rent to the craziest people."

"More spring breakers?" kindergarten teacher Missy Cox asked.

"No, a couple who yell at each other in some foreign language half the time. And talk about rude? They 'borrowed' the Berrys' rowboat without asking permission. Gene was furious."

"Who was furious about what?" Kathy Barker asked as she breezed into the kitchen with Daphne Dupree behind her. Kathy's an artist, Daphne a pastry chef, and they both carried white bakery boxes. I smelled chocolate and lemon already.

"Never mind," Shelly said, as the ladies set the boxes on the island counter. "Let's talk about good stuff. Cesca, you first. How did your tours go this week?"

I doubted these ladies would hear differently, so I smiled and fudged. "Great. We had ghost sightings up the wazoo."

Missy laughed. "One of my students was in your tour Monday. A little pistol named Robbie."

"You're kidding," I said, smiling. "He's adorable."

"Not when he talks that loud in a closed classroom all day, but he sure was high on you and the animal ghosts."

"We have animal ghosts in town?" Kathy asked and shuddered.

"We do," I said. "Your turn, Kathy. How was the art festival in Deland?"

"I won a first place ribbon and even sold enough to make the show worthwhile. Daphne has good news, too."

Daphne nodded. "Bridezilla Barbie's wedding is over, and the cake from hell was a success," she said to a chorus of woo-hoos. "And we're celebrating," she continued, "with lemon cake and chocolate coconut bars. Eat up before we deal the first hand."

While Maybelle and Nadine shared cute things their grand-children had done, I sampled both goodies, grabbed my sweet tea, heavy on the ice, and was ready to play when Shelly called us to order. One table was set in Shelly's dining room, the other in her small den.

Maybe it was the moon phase, maybe it was Jenna's energy, but I had the heebie-jeebies all the time I played at the same table with her. It didn't help my concentration that my cards were so-so until the end of the night. But when luck turned, it turned inside out. Shelly and I bid and made a grand slam in hearts—doubled—and I got to play the hand. What a rush.

On a victory high, I car-danced to the Beach Boys' greatest hits as I zipped home in my precious SSR. Maggie was out—presumably with Neil—so I changed clothes and sprawled on the living room sofa to watch HGTV, then switched to TV Land to catch *Night Court*.

Maggie came in at half past midnight, dropped her purse on the Victorian side table, and flopped on the sofa with me.

"How was bridge?"

I clicked the TV off. "Shelly and I bid and made a doubled grand slam. How'd the new design go over?"

"I quit. Told that woman she had to decide what she wanted before anyone could finish the job. You should've seen her Botoxic face. Scary." She paused and shuddered. "On the up side, I have a new client in Gainesville, and I can focus on our Victorian more."

"That reminds me. Jenna Jones, the Realtor in bridge club, may call you about the condo."

"To buy it, list it, or show it?"

"List it or show it, I'd imagine." I clasped my arms around my knees. "I told her I didn't think the Victorian was close enough to finished that you'd want to put the condo on the market."

"It's not, but it may be in another month, depending on how much lead time I want to sell before we move. What do you think of Jenna?"

"She talks about house hunts and closings all the time, so it sounds like she sells like tourists buy T-shirts."

"But?"

"Is there such a thing as being overanimated?"

Maggie laughed. "Thanks for the heads-up. You already take your landscape test?"

"Not yet. It's matching garden designs with period home styles."

"Timed or open-book?" Maggie asked around a yawn.

"Timed, but I know my stuff. Then I have a new book to start before I meet Neil to surf."

"You feeling any better about Holland having a gun?"

"No, but out of sight, out of mind. I'm restless, though."

"The new moon or the storm?" She does know me well.

I shrugged. "Both, I guess. I may go out for a walk later. Or ride my bike."

"Take the cell, and be careful. That Holland guy may be harmless, but Stony isn't."

"No sweat. I have super senses."

"Yes, when you use them."

"Stop fretting. As long as Stony keeps eating garlic and jalapeños, I'll smell him coming."

* * *

I took my test but couldn't settle into anything else. Not the lecture I'd printed to review, or my new mystery novel either. Deciding it was time to blow the cobwebs out of my brain, I pulled a light gray hooded sweatshirt out of the closet. It matched my sweatpants and didn't clash with my tennies. What kind of fashion do you want at two in the morning? I snagged my cell, key, and my aqua zippered change purse with the five-odd dollars I keep handy. Hey, even a vampire needs emergency money.

With all I needed in my deep sweatpants pockets, I maneuvered my bicycle out of the storage area in the outer foyer and rode the elevator down to the lobby.

At night the wind usually dies down, but it had risen more in the hours I'd been home from bridge. It blew from the east-northeast over the bay and into town, which made it cooler than it had been earlier. The surf should be bitchin' when I met Neil at dawn. Rip currents might be stronger, but I could handle that.

I rode north toward the area now called uptown. Past the ancient Castillo de San Marcos, a fort of massive coquina stones that the British had barely dented when they bombarded it. Past the Huguenot Cemetery and Nombre de Dios, site of another cemetery, a chapel shrine, and a 208-foot cross erected where the first Spaniards had purportedly landed.

Maggie's under-construction Victorian was on a side street near the Fountain of Youth complex, but I didn't go by it. I'd spent enough time underground there, listening to other people live their lives. To tell the truth, I wasn't sure I'd like living aboveground not fifty feet from where I'd been buried, but Maggie was excited we'd still be neighbors. It would be an insult to move away, even if I could find my own safe place within five miles of her.

I rode on, reveling in the wind, the hum of bike tires on concrete, and the quiet of the small city all but shut down for the night. I cruised to San Carlos Avenue where the carousel stood in tiny Davenport park. The carousel itself dated from the late 1920s, and I loved the brightly colored horses. I turned west for a block, hit U.S. 1, and rode back south toward King Street.

The bars closed at one in the morning, most restaurants, earlier. Cars whizzed past me, but not many at this hour. Walgreens and Wal-Mart were open all night, but I hadn't brought enough cash or a credit card to seriously shop. Besides, if I went to Wal-Mart, I'd need my truck to haul stuff home.

I turned east onto King to complete my big loop and grinned at the wind lifting my hair away from my neck. I still felt antsy, though, and pedaled by the plaza half looking for Cat. No sighting, no head-splitting meow.

I wasn't tired enough to go back home, so I decided to cross the Bridge of Lions to the island. That's Anastasia Island, and it's the temporary bridge at this point. The Bridge of Lions had been deemed unsafe, but the city wanted to save it, so a temporary bridge spanned Matanzas Bay while the 1920s structure was being fixed.

The island is where I used to sneak off to as a teenager. Take one of my papa's small boats and row to the beach. Not that Matanzas Inlet was a straight shot from the ocean to the bay back then. I'd rowed around and through shoals to get to the beach, but it was worth it. Especially on a moonlit night.

The moon was dark now. Low clouds raced across the sky, and darn it, I hit a piece of glass on the sidewalk near the British Pub.

The nearest open gas station was the Gate station on 312 more than three miles away. The tire didn't seem to be losing air, and the station was only a short detour.

One of the guys on duty at Gate was a surfer I'd seen on the beach.

"How's it going?" he asked when I entered.

"Good, except I need to check my bike tires."

"That's fifty cents, and we don't have gauges."

Another guy glared at me as if air weren't worth buying, and I had to agree. I added two boxes of mints to the bill and pocketed the change and receipt. Within five minutes, I'd inspected for damage (nothing I could see), aired up a little anyway, and headed east to the St. Augustine Beach pier.

I left my bike in the covered pavilion and walked under the pier. The beach had eroded somewhat in all the hurricanes and storms of the past few years—so much for beach renourishment—but it was low tide. I sat on the fine, cool sand and let myself think about what I'd been avoiding.

Cat, Jenna's California client, and the disappearing shack. Faeries. Magick.

Triton.

Found on the beach by a Greek fisherman who adopted him, Triton was four and I was three when he came to live in the Quarter. We grew so close that we read each other's minds, shared each other's nighttime dreams, and never questioned why we shared The Gift. Or parts of it. Everyone in the Quarter expected us to marry, including me. I didn't remember a day without Triton and couldn't imagine a future without him.

Then puberty hit and, while Triton and I were playing in the ocean one new moon night, he shifted from a man to a dolphin.

That would be a shocker even in this modern age when magick is more or less accepted. Back then, let me tell you, we were freaked.

The change, we soon learned, only lasted one full day and only at the new moon each month. Good news, right? The better news was that the telepathic connection we'd shared since childhood became even stronger during his shift. Triton taught me how to follow him in my mind, to astral travel the seas with him. Talk about magical.

We kept his secret, of course, and I still would've married him and been happy. It was Triton who couldn't be happy with me. Month after month, as he searched for his own kind, my girlhood dreams died, and our friendship changed.

It changed again when the vampires caught me. I was the lookout for Triton that night and didn't sense the vampires closing in until it was too late. After I was turned, I contacted Triton on the sly a few times, but the weight of his guilt for not protecting me became a burden for both of us. When Normand threatened to kill my parents to bring me in line, Triton helped them escape. He did the same for my few other family members until he was the last close tie to my old life.

I urged Triton to leave St. Augustine, too, and we promised to stay in telepathic touch. For fifty years, I could still reach out and sense him—even from my coffin. Then one day, nothing. Total shutdown. I hadn't heard from him since.

Logic told me he was dead. Hope made me believe otherwise, but, in all my Internet searching, I couldn't find him.

Which was probably for the best, I told myself firmly as I mounted my bike and pedaled back to the penthouse. The new afterlife I was aiming to make normal would turn upside down if Triton came home.

*   *   *

Interesting fact: Surfer buns look great in wet suits.

Not that I looked at Neil's when there were ten others on the beach at dawn on Thursday morning.

We parked in the Crescent Beach parking lot by South Beach Grill and hiked down the beach access ramp toting our boards. The nor'easter wasn't full on us yet but, with the wind driving rough waves, making high tide higher, only a narrow strip of sand rose above the waterline. The hearty souls on sunrise walks took the elements in stride.

The frothing sea blew foam on the beach that tickled my ankles as it brushed by. I thought I saw a small boat out past the breakers right before we hit the water, but it could've been a stalwart pelican riding the swells. I didn't bother looking with any vampire vision. Between the blowing mist and sand, I paid more attention to being sure my leash was secured to both my board and my ankle.

We all dropped onto our boards within seconds of each other, but Neil paddled a bit south of the others, I guess to give me more learning room. Like other sports, surfing has its rules of etiquette. Even though I'd been in the water with at least six of these same guys, I wouldn't want to tick them off by accidentally dropping in on a wave or doing something else to brand me as a novice kook.

After riding three sets of waves almost until my board fins scraped bottom, Neil and I straddled our boards out in the swells, waiting for a fourth run. That's when something bumped my right foot.

I jerked my feet up, thinking, *Shark.*

Instead, a dead body surfaced smack between us.

SEVEN

Facedown. Nude. Slender back bruised. Long, dark hair floating like a living thing, hiding the body's face.

The impressions snapped through my brain before I screamed like a girl.

Or maybe that was Neil.

Or both of us.

It could've been seconds or minutes before I heard him shout and looked up.

"Grab an arm and ride her in."

I shook my head. *Not on your sweet life, bub.*

"Come on, Fresca, buck up," Neil yelled over the roar of wind and waves. "We can't leave her."

I failed to see why not, but Neil already had her right arm. I swallowed hard and flailed for the dead woman's waxy white left wrist. At Neil's signal, we flattened on our boards to let the waves carry us in far enough to stand. Balancing so we didn't crush the woman between us was iffy, but we managed.

In chest-deep water, Neil shouted for me to hold the body while he unfastened his leash. I hugged her to my board, grimacing at the feel of bare icy skin, puffy under my hands but not as bloated as I'd expected from reading mysteries. When Neil was free, I slid off my board and grabbed his longer one so it wouldn't smack into the body.

"You have your cell phone?"

"In the truck," I shouted back, feeling under the water to work my own leash free.

"Take the boards and call 911 while I drag her in to shore."

I just might've moved at vampire speed to haul the boards above the waterline, drop them on the sand, and sprint to my truck in the parking lot. My hands shook so badly, it took four tries to punch the right three digits.

Cell service can be spotty at best on the beach, so I mentally crossed my fingers as I watched early walkers and joggers help Neil.

"A body on the beach," I blurted when the operator answered. "It was in the water, but now it's on the beach. Crescent Beach."

The operator must've calmed me enough to get the information she needed, because I was off the phone and standing with Neil, the onlookers, and the other surfers when the first of the sheriff's cars arrived ten minutes later.

Believe me, I wasn't checking out surfer butt anymore.

Faceup in the sand lay Yolette, the French bride, with two punctures on her inner thigh that looked a lot like fang wounds.

Neil's an anthropologist for the state of Florida with forensic pathology training, which I haven't mentioned because it didn't matter. Now it did, because he wasn't as grossed out as the rest of us who stood around the body. He didn't hands-on examine the dead woman before the cops arrived, but he looked long and carefully enough to memorize every pore.

I was majorly grossed, but I looked, too. The bride's neck was obviously broken. Even I could see that by the way her head lolled on the sand. Her belly was bloated some, but my gaze kept returning to her right thigh.

Though I wouldn't call myself an expert on death by fang, I'd seen my share of bites in the old days. Not one so intimately placed, but still, if these *were* fang wounds, she hadn't been drained.

Lividity, I thought, mentally snapping my fingers. That was the word for the bruising on her back caused by blood pooling, but it wasn't on her front.

Neil confirmed that and more when the deputies shooed us away from the body. They dispersed the onlookers and told the witnesses to wait for the detectives. The other surfers were allowed to stow their gear, but the deputies insisted Neil's and mine stay put. Guess they'd look for trace evidence. I *had* braced the body against my board. Maybe I'd buy a new one to replace the garage-sale learner. The county cops could keep it.

The deputies didn't separate us to keep us from talking, but the other surfers clustered at the base of the boardwalk steps— pointedly away from me. Gee, and they were so friendly before. At least Neil didn't abandon me. We huddled on the boardwalk as he dried his hair with an extra beach towel I'd grabbed from my truck.

"Are those vampire marks?" he asked, his back to the beach.

I tucked my dolphin beach towel tighter into the straps of

my coral one-piece suit and cocked my head. "You think they aren't?"

He shrugged. "Not even a vampire would shoot a body then try to drink from it."

I gaped. "Yolette was shot?"

"Yolette? You know the victim?"

I nodded. "She's the bride who took my tour Monday and Tuesday night. The one who hit on me."

"Shit. That won't look good."

No, it wouldn't, and my stomach knotted with worry. I took my hair out of its ponytail, scraped it back with my fingers, and tied it up again. "Neil, go back to the shot part. I didn't see another wound."

"It's in the back of her head, just above her hairline. I felt the entry wound when I turned her over, but I didn't find an exit wound."

"Which means what?"

"Small-caliber weapon. Maybe a .22."

Gun calibers were a mystery to me, but I shuddered. "Did she look like she'd been in the water long? I mean, she's puffy, but she's not as swollen as I thought she'd be from the movies I've seen."

"Hollywood distorts forensics."

"But mystery novelists are obsessive about details. From what I've read, bodies aren't supposed to float for days and days after they're dumped—sometimes weeks—depending on water temperatures and a bunch of other stuff. Neil, that woman was alive on Tuesday night. This is Thursday morning."

I don't know if he was thinking it, but I had to wonder if she'd been dumped so the morning surfers or beachcombers would find her. Tricky, considering the tides, the storm, and the rip currents. Possible? Heck if I knew.

Two things *were* becoming eerily clear to me. Yolette had not died by accident, and I would be answering questions about the fang marks.

Fifteen minutes later, two plainclothesmen—one youngish, one middle-aged and slightly overweight with bags under his eyes—headed toward the boardwalk. The young one stopped where the other surfers stood, the older one trudged up the boardwalk stairs to us.

"Neil Benson and Francesca Marinelli?"

"Not *Chess-ka*," I corrected. "*Cess-ka*."

The man blinked, and Neil rolled his eyes.

"Okay, then. I'm Detective March of the St. Johns County Sheriff's Department. You two found the body?"

"More like it found us." Neil gestured down the beach where more official cars had now parked. "We told the other officers what happened."

"Yeah, and they should've separated you, but we'll work with what we have." The detective paused and gave me a look. "You're the vampire?"

"Yes, sir."

"You saw the marks on the body?"

"Yes, sir."

"You kill her?"

"No, sir."

"Figured it wouldn't be that easy." March actually cracked a weary smile. "Tell me what happened."

Neil recounted the time we arrived, the approximate time

we entered the water, and how long we'd surfed before the body floated up between us. I nodded a lot, nice and cooperative.

"So you towed her in," the detective said, looking up from writing in his small notebook.

Neil shrugged. "I didn't think you had much of a crime scene in the water. Not in this weather."

"You decide that from watching *CSI*?"

"No, I'm an anthropologist with forensic training."

The detective grunted. "Good for you. Here's the bonus question of the day. Either of you know the victim?"

Was that my future cell door creaking, or did the wind whistle especially loudly? Didn't matter. I had to tell him now or be under more suspicion later.

With Neil reassuringly stationed at my shoulder, I said, "I don't exactly know her, but I know who she is."

"Name?"

"Yolette." March stared at me, but I'd learned a thing or two from reading. Rule one: Don't volunteer information to fill the silence.

"Last name?"

"I don't remember."

He frowned. "Then how do you know her?"

"She took two of my ghost tours. I'm a guide."

"When was this?"

"Monday and Tuesday nights."

"Time?"

"Eight to nine forty-five and nine thirty to ten thirty."

"Tuesday's tour was shorter?"

"Yes."

"Why?"

"We, uh, didn't tour the haunted buildings."

Detective March scribbled in his notebook. "She with anyone? And, please, don't be afraid to give me more than a ten-word answer. This wind is hell on my sinuses."

Yep, March was on to my say-nothing strategy, but he'd cracked a joke. I struck a balance with my next answer.

"She was with a man I understood to be her husband. They're French, and I think they're on—were on—their honeymoon."

"The husband's name?"

"Etienne."

"You know where they were staying?"

"Some house on the beach. I don't know where."

"How'd you know it was on the beach?"

I frowned. Had Holland said so? Yes, but so had Etienne. "The husband mentioned it during a tour."

"Did you see the victim at any other time?"

I hesitated, not wanting to talk about the embarrassing scene at Scarlett's. "I saw them at Scarlett O'Hara's Monday night after the tour. They were having dinner."

"And you haven't seen the woman since Tuesday night?"

I shook my head and pulled my slipping beach towel tighter again. How sad that the honeymoon was well and truly over.

"What's your relationship?"

"Hunh?" I said, thinking he referred to Yolette.

March pointed his pen at me then Neil. "Your relationship. You two just surf buddies or what?"

Points for Neil. He didn't gag at the "or what."

"I'm teaching Cesca to surf," he said. "My girlfriend is her sponsor and roommate."

"Your girlfriend's name?"

"Maggie—Margaret—O'Halloran."

"Address?"

We'd given our names and numbers to the deputies, but March took Neil's information again, then mine. Address, home, cell and work phone numbers. My boss's name and number at the tour company.

"Oh, wait," I said, snapping my fingers. "Yolette's last name. It'll be on the incident report."

March's eyes narrowed on me as if I'd just confessed to the crime. Maybe an *aha!* moment shouldn't be shared with cops predisposed to suspect the worst.

March's voice rumbled. "What incident report?"

The hell with it. I hadn't done anything wrong, had nothing to hide. Besides, the cops needed to notify Etienne, and Yolette's killer needed catching.

"Ms. Marinelli?"

"On the Monday tour," I said, measuring my words, "this guy I'm pretty sure belongs to the Covenant made a scene. The people who were still with me when it happened gave us their names and numbers for the incident report we filed. Yolette and her husband were two of those tourists."

"Who is we?" I must've looked blank because he added, "You said the report 'we' filed. Who else are you referring to?"

"The other tour guides. Janie Freeman and Mick Burney. The supervisor was notified by phone. The written report was turned in Tuesday."

"So your boss at the company—" He looked down at his notes. "—Elise Williams will have the names and contact info?"

"She should."

"All right, thanks." March stuffed his notebook and pen in his jacket pocket. "Ms. Marinelli, when did you realize you knew the victim?"

"When I saw her face."

"And that was?"

"After I called 911 and went back to the beach."

"You didn't recognize her in the water?"

"No. We towed her in facedown."

Detective March shook his head as if looking for holes in our story, which he probably was.

"Anything else you noticed this morning? About anything?"

"I thought I saw a boat past the breakers before we got in the water."

"What kind?"

"A little one. Like a kayak." He raised a brow, and I shrugged. "Or it could've been a pelican."

"Did you see it fly off?"

"I didn't pay attention."

"Then that's it for now. We'll need you to come to the station to make and sign complete statements."

"Fine," Neil said. "I can come now, but Cesca will have to sleep first."

"That true?" March asked.

I shrugged. "I can only be up a few hours after dawn."

"All right, but don't leave town. Either of you."

"I'll have to go if I get a call on state business."

"If that happens, Mr. Benson, let us know." March frowned and looked at me. "Ms. Marinelli, when can you come in?"

"At four or five this afternoon."

"Good. Maybe the ME will have a report by then."

I nodded and shut out the mental image of cell doors slamming on me.

"Detective," Neil called as March turned to leave. "Do you still need our surfboards?"

"For now." He fished two cards from his shirt pocket and handed one to each of us. "Call, and I'll let you know about your property."

When Detective March plodded back down the boardwalk stairs, Neil raked a hand through his hair.

"Come on, let's go," he said, heading for the parking lot.

I fell into step behind him, wondering how much longer I'd be a free vampire.

"Here's the plan," he said as we walked. "You go on back to the penthouse and sleep. I'll call Maggie at work and fill her in. We'll get you an attorney."

"I need a lawyer right now?" I squeaked.

"It's just a precaution." We stopped at my truck, and he tossed the towel he'd used onto my passenger seat. "After all, you haven't done anything wrong, right?"

"Effing right."

Both his brows hiked to his hairline at my vehemence. "Effing? Fresca, you don't curse except for an occasional hell and damn. Are you scared about this?"

"Neil, there's a body with apparent vampire marks on it. I'd met the victim, I found the body, and, oh yeah, I'm a vampire. If nothing else, I'll be a scapegoat."

"But you don't own a gun."

"How hard are they to get? The Jag Queens have guns, for

heaven's sake. I don't need *Suspects for Dummies* to see where this is going."

"That's the smart mouth I know." He cuffed me on the arm— the right arm that now hurt again. "Don't worry about it. The attorney will protect your rights while we let the system work."

He waved and hopped into his jeep. I groaned. Let the system work? Sure. How many times had I read those same words in novels? Enough to know the heroine always had to climb out of hot water by solving the crime herself.

So would I...if I had to.

I awoke at three Thursday afternoon to wind, rain, and the shrill ringing of the phone. I rolled over to grab the receiver, but the answering system kicked on before I reached it.

Okay, so I was avoiding the inevitable, but my eyes were gritty and, for the first time since I'd been unearthed, I didn't feel like bouncing out of bed. Instead, I lay there remembering the morning. Was the gruesome news out? Was I, in fact, the prime suspect? I was supposed to guide a tour at nine thirty, the late shift. Did I still have a job?

The ghost tours ran rain or shine, so I didn't think a nor'easter would cancel my gig as long as tourists showed up for it. On the bright side, the bad weather would excuse my bad hair, which I probably wouldn't get completely dry before I had to meet a man about a murder.

On that happy thought, I rolled out of bed and headed for the shower. After a quick wash, I gooped leave-in conditioner on my hair and wrapped it in a towel. Then I hurried to the dorm fridge in the kitchen where I kept my Starbloods. As I had my breakfast, I listened to messages.

One from Neil: Talked to the cops. Detective March seems to be an all right guy, but our boards may not be returned for a while. Call Maggie.

Three from Maggie: Call me. I have attorneys for you, Sam Owens and Sandy Krause. Call me.

Two from Detective March: Get my butt to the sheriff's office on U.S. 1 and Lewis Speedway before five. Not his exact words in either message, but I got the gist.

A call from work told me I needed to sign a waiver form if I wasn't going to make a claim on the injury to my arm. Someone from the office or an early shift guide would leave the form at the tour substation for me to pick up tonight.

I tossed off the rest of my drink, washed and recycled the bottle, and had tackled drying my hair when the phone rang again.

"Cesca! Thank God! I was beginning to worry," Maggie said when I answered.

"I'm fine, Maggie. Getting ready to go to the sheriff's."

"Have you called the attorneys yet? You haven't, have you? All right, I'll call their office and get one of them to meet you. They owe me. I'd be there, but I'm stuck in Gainesville with this new client. Don't talk to the county cops unless at least one of the attorneys is with you. Promise?"

"Promise."

"And call me before you go to work. I want to know how the interview went."

I promised that, too, and hurried to dry my hair a little more while keenly aware that the clock was ticking. When I couldn't afford to wait any longer, I put my damp hair in a ponytail and dressed in my favorite comfy jeans, a three-quarter sleeve navy and tan sweater, and tennis shoes.

At four thirteen I blew through the double glass doors to the sheriff's office along with the wind and rain, and my umbrella with now-bent spokes. A woman with curly red hair shot out of one of the chairs against the wall. Her navy suit screamed expensive, her first words branded her as no-nonsense.

"Francesca, right? Sandy Krause, of Krause and Owens."

She held out her hand and shook mine. Didn't even flinch when she touched me. Points for her.

I didn't know exactly what to say, but those ingrained manners kicked in. "Thank you for meeting me here."

"Anything for a friend of Maggie's." She released my hand and addressed the woman at the reception counter. "Please tell Detective March that Ms. Marinelli and her counsel are here."

She turned and motioned me back to the row of chairs where she picked up a black leather briefcase and a tan London Fog trench coat.

"I'll request a few minutes with you in private before the formal interview," she said softly, "but tell me right now if you killed this woman."

"I didn't."

She gave me the laser eye. "My job during the interview is to protect your rights. If I tell you not to answer a question, don't."

"Yes, ma'am," I said and nearly saluted. If Maggie was a warrior, Sandy was a drill sergeant.

The metal door to the sheriff's inner sanctum hissed open, and Detective March stood in the threshold, his brown suit looking more rumpled than it had this morning.

"Good of you to finally get here," he said to me.

"Most vampires aren't up yet, Detective."

"Most don't surf after sunrise and find bodies, either."

I smiled. "Touché."

"Ms. Krause," he greeted Sandy.

"Detective. I've only just met my client. May I have a few minutes in private with her before we begin the interview?"

March jerked his head toward the corridor I could see stretching behind him. "We'll walk to the investigations building. Ten minutes is all I can give you to confer. My wife will shoot me if I'm any later than I'm already gonna be."

Sandy nodded, and we followed March through a maze of hallways, finally reaching a room with eight desks neatly partitioned with low movable walls. Closed doors to what I guessed were offices or conference rooms lined the perimeter of the large space.

March opened the door to a room not much bigger than a coat closet. An old metal card table with a scarred top crowded against a gray wall. Three institutional and uncomfortable-looking metal chairs sat neatly around it.

"Ten minutes, Ms. Krause."

She nodded, told me to sit, and pulled a yellow legal pad from her briefcase.

"All right. Maggie and Neil told me what they know, but that's secondhand information, and the cops have had all day to interview witnesses. Tell me what happened this morning."

I did, recounting everything as closely as I could remember it.

"That tallies with Neil's account. Now tell me about the tours on Monday and Tuesday. The trouble you had with the Covenant guy."

I hit the highlights of Stony's threats, first to me, then to

Yolette, and tried not to blush again over Yolette's pass at me while we were at Scarlett's.

"So this Stony physically attacked you. Did he hurt you?"

"My right arm was sore for a while. I think he pinched the GPS tracker under my skin."

"Any bruising?"

I shrugged apologetically. "I didn't pay attention, and I heal quickly."

"What about Tuesday?"

"Stony was back, but there was no trouble, just tension." I closed my eyes for a moment, picturing everyone. "Stony stayed in the back of the group. The victim, Yolette, followed the writers, who were right behind me."

"Etienne wasn't there?"

"He was, but he and Yolette seemed to have had a tiff. He walked with the older ladies."

"Did the victim and her husband leave together?"

"More or less. Etienne kissed my hand, and Yolette stalked off. He followed her."

"And? What did the others do?"

"Stony followed the couple, and Gomer followed him, then came back and walked me home."

"Maggie mentioned this guy. Gomer had a gun, right?"

"Plain as day, but his name is Holland Peters. I just called him Gomer."

"He show you an ID?

"No."

"Then Gomer will do for now. Where were you on Wednesday?"

"I slept during the day and played bridge that night."

"What about later? Maggie said you might have gone out after midnight."

"I rode my bicycle from about one thirty to three thirty that morning."

"Did you see the victim at any time after Tuesday night?" When I shook my head, Sandy asked, "Can anyone alibi you while you were riding the bike?"

"Yes. A guy at the Gate station." I nearly bounced in the torturous chair, excited to have something new to contribute. "I ran over some glass on Anastasia Boulevard and was afraid the front tire might be leaking. I went to Gate to air it up. I bought mints, too."

"You get a receipt?"

I nodded. "I don't have it on me, though."

"No problem, but save it. It's proof of your whereabouts if the witness doesn't remember you." She tapped a pen on the pad twice. "As I said before, the cops have had all day to con-duct interviews, so they may or may not have some surprises. I have the funny feeling they will. If I don't nod, you don't answer."

"I understand, but what about my GPS tracker? That should help prove I wasn't near Yolette again."

"The tracker can verify where you were but not where the victim was." She stood, and so did I. "We need to know her movements before the tracker records will be of use."

Confidence that I'd soon be off the suspect list dimmed, but I didn't have time to brood. We followed March to an interview room—different yet similar to the ones I'd seen on TV or read about. A rectangular table squatted just inside the door and flush to two walls. One rolling armchair sat at the far end of the table with three armless institutional chairs angled around it. At least the padding on those looked more substantial than the one I'd just left. No one-way mirrors in the room, but I'd bet cameras were hidden somewhere.

Only the tall, tanned, gorgeous guy standing in the middle of the room was a twist on the cop-shop decor. He looked a little Latino and a lot hubba-hubba. Sun-streaked brown hair swept back from a high, broad forehead, and aviator sunglasses perched on a perfect nose.

My own nose twitched at the scent of light musk. His cologne? I swear I had a hot flash as I slid into the seat March indicated next to Sandy. In dark blue jeans, a white polo shirt, and a deep olive sports jacket, Hot Hunk seemed relaxed, but I heard the air around him hum.

"Ms. Marinelli, Ms. Krause, we called a preternatural crimes special investigator out of Daytona to sit in. This is Deke Saber."

Deke. *Pant.* Saber. *Double pant.* Could his name be any sexier? If the rest of him matched the packaging—

He didn't sit but lowered his sunglasses to reveal cobalt blue eyes and stared at me for a long moment.

"*You're* the big, bad vampire?" he snorted. "You look like a coed on a bad hair day."

EIGHT

His voice was deep and mellow, but can you say attitude adjustment? So much for the inner man matching the outer one.

Chalk it up to stress, but a piece of me snapped.

"That does it," I said and slapped my hand on the table before I thought about it. Not all that hard, but Sandy and Detective March jumped. Sexy Deke Saber merely pushed his shades back in place.

"Francesca," Sandy warned.

"Yeah, I know I'm not supposed to talk without your okay, but darn it, I'm ticked. It's one thing to question me. I get *that*. I even get," I said, pointing at March, "you two playing good cop, bad cop. But it's another thing," I said, glaring at sexy Saber, "to take cheap shots at my hair."

Saber looked bored. Sandy groaned softly.

Detective March rocked back in his comfy chair and tapped a pencil on the white legal pad angled on the table. "Did Yolette criticize your hair?"

"Yolette?" I cocked my head at him. "No. Why would she?"

March shrugged, but Saber spoke as he took the last armless chair, turned it backward and straddled it. His hip holster and black gun handle flashed from beneath his sports coat. Probably to intimidate me. Hah! In his pathetic dreams.

"Who does criticize your hair?" he fired at me.

"Neil," I said, feeling a touch claustrophobic with the men on my right and Sandy on my left. "I swear I'm straightening it first chance I get."

This time Sandy stifled a chuckle. Saber didn't.

"Neil Benson? The guy you surf with? The guy you found the body with?" he asked, rapid-fire.

"Yeah, that Neil. The only Neil I know, by the way."

"You want to hurt him for insulting you, right?"

I blinked. "What the devil are you talking about?"

Saber shrugged and folded his arms over the chair back, nonchalantly as you please. "You're the one who came unglued just now. You lose your temper often?"

"For your information, that wasn't unglued, and it wasn't temper. That was righteous indignation." I looked pointedly at March. "Detective, you want to go home, and I need to be dressed and at work by eight forty-five. You have questions? Ask them."

I think his mouth twitched as he looked at his blank pad. Then he was all business.

"Let's start with this morning. You and Neil went surfing."

I looked at Sandy. Her expression was stern, but her eyes twinkled as she nodded. I went through the story again, sticking to facts and nailing March with eye contact. He stopped me a few times to question details and jotted notes like mad. Saber straddled the chair, expressionless. I wished I could snatch those darn aviator shades off and see his eyes.

"So you felt something bump your foot, looked down in the water, and saw the body," March said.

"Correct," I confirmed for what felt like the tenth time.

"Then Neil suggested towing the victim to shore."

"He didn't suggest. He told me we couldn't leave her and to take her arm and ride her in."

"And while he removed his leash, you say you hugged the body to your surfboard. Why?"

"To keep it from banging into her."

"But you didn't want to do it, right?" Saber said.

"I didn't want to touch her, if that's what you mean."

"Why not?"

"Duh. Dead person. Icky."

"You're dead."

"Correction. I have a heartbeat, a pulse, and brain waves. I might be underalive, but I'm not dead."

He frowned as if he'd never thought of vampires that way.

March cleared his throat. "We've been at this awhile. Would either of you like something to drink?" He looked directly at me. "We have artificial blood."

Sandy audibly gulped—well, audible to me. I declined with my standard response. "I don't drink in public, but I'll have a cup of ice, if you have some."

"Ice. Plain ice?"

I smiled. "It's important to stay hydrated."

Saber snorted, in disdain I suppose. An unattractive habit that—pardon the pun—made his sex appeal take a nosedive. March shook his head but went to the door and asked someone who must've been hovering for a glass of ice and bottled water.

When our refreshments were delivered, March took over again. "Let's cover the ghost tour on Monday night."

Again, I went through the events in excruciating detail, including the confrontation with Stony. I did leave out the Jag Queens pulling weapons. I didn't know the gun laws, and I didn't want to get them in trouble.

"This man you call Stony," Saber said, his tone cynical. "He verbally and physically threatened you, and you expect us to believe you didn't retaliate?"

"I told him he had bad breath."

Sandy covered another laugh with a cough.

"Describe Stony one more time," March said.

"About your height," I told March and jerked my thumb at Saber, "and his attitude. Dark hair, light eyes like blue ice. A scar on the right side of his face from about his ear to the middle of his jaw. Gravelly voice."

"What about weight? How was he dressed?"

"I'm terrible at estimating weight, but he wasn't fat. Maybe a hundred seventy pounds? Black turtleneck, black Wrangler jeans, and black tennis shoes. Not high-tops but not low-cut either."

March thumbed his legal pad and pulled a sheet free. "This the guy?"

He slid a rough artist's rendering across the table, and I picked it up. "Wow, that's close. How did you get this?"

"I spoke with Jennie Freeman and Mick Burney."

"It's Janie. Janie Freeman. Not Jennie."

"Right. Anyway, I also talked to the ladies who took the tour and the teenagers. They all confirm your version of the events, including the attack on you, and Stony sticking close to the newly-weds. We worked this up from their descriptions. Is it accurate?"

"I think his nose was a little longer and thinner. His hair might've been a little longer, too."

"Would you work with our artist to refine the drawing?"

"Now?" I pushed the paper back to him.

"Tomorrow will be fine."

"I can be here at eight."

He nodded. "Good. Now, is the tour the last time you saw those three people?"

"I told you this morning I saw them at Scarlett's, then again on the Tuesday night tour."

"What happened at Scarlett's?"

At Sandy's nod, I went through the scene from the time Cami came out with the Starbloods bottle to the time I had it taken off the couple's bill. Maybe repeating the story several times already had desensitized me, because I even got through the part about Yolette's pass with relative ease. Relative being I didn't stammer when Saber arched a haughty brow.

"So Stony threatened the victim," March said. "What did he say exactly?"

"Close as I remember, he said, 'I'll kill you before you screw a vampire in my town.' "

"He said 'in my town'? He lives here?"

"That's the impression he gave. He sounded like a sheriff in an old B Western." I smiled. "No offense."

March flashed a tired grin.

Saber pushed up from his chair, and the legs thudded on the thin carpet. "Are you homophobic?" Saber shot at me. "Did the victim's pass humiliate you?"

"Humiliate, no. Surprise, yes. I mean, a threesome on their honeymoon? Call me old-fashioned, but that's just odd."

"All right," March said, "let's go through Tuesday's tour."

I told him about the writers, about Yolette wanting Stony kicked off the tour, and about the apparent tiff between the newlyweds. Saber glowered and paced.

"So the guy you call Stony didn't cause trouble Tuesday?"

"Not a bit. He and Gomer hung at the back of the group."

"Who the hell is Gomer?" Saber snapped.

"One of the tourists reminded me of Gomer Pyle. His name is Holland Peters."

"He on both tours, too?" March asked.

I nodded. "He told me Stony had been in Palatka and Hastings recruiting for the Covenant."

March shot a glance at Saber, who shrugged and said, "First I've heard of it."

Saber pulled a small square from his inner jacket pocket and shoved it toward me. It was a snapshot of a brunette woman with a pointed chin and flashing eyes.

"You know her?" he asked. "Look carefully before you answer."

I gazed at the picture long enough to satisfy him. "I can't be absolutely sure I've never seen her on the street, but she's not familiar. Why?"

"She was murdered in Daytona Beach last Friday."

"I haven't been to Daytona."

"She was a vampire in the nest there. Ike's second-in-command. You heard from Ike lately?"

"First, nests are supposed to be illegal. Second, I've never heard from Ike, never met him, and I'll be fine if I never do."

"He hasn't contacted you at all?"

"Why should he? Vampires don't do Welcome Wagon gift baskets."

"Detectives," Sandy said, "we've been at this for close to two hours. My client has been more than open with you. She obviously had no reason to be involved in either of these women's deaths."

"But can she account for her movements since Tuesday night?" Saber asked.

"She can. What's more, the GPS tracker has recorded her movements for months now."

March cleared his throat. "The tracker should do exactly that, Counselor, but Ms. Marinelli's tracker stopped sending signals on Monday night."

"It what?" I blinked at March, touched my right upper arm. "That was three days ago! I'm supposed to be notified if I fall off the radar for more than an hour."

"Apparently there's a glitch in the system," March said.

Sandy turned to me. "No wonder your arm ached. Stony must've damaged the tracker."

"By doing what?" Saber scoffed. "Manhandling you a little?"

I gaped at him, and maybe March and Sandy did, too, because the room fell silent.

"You know," I said steadily, "I could have filed assault charges if I'd known Stony's real name. Just because I heal quickly doesn't mean I can't be hurt." I stared at Saber's sunglasses a long moment and added, "If you prick me, I will bleed."

"I've pricked you this evening, Ms. Marinelli. You plan to bleed me?"

"Hardly. Pay attention, Mr. Saber. I. Don't. Bite. People."

"Why not?"

"Because you never know where they've been."

I looked pointedly away from Saber to Sandy. "Resign as my counsel if you want, but I'm done. Detective March—" I cut my gaze to him. "I believe the phrase is charge me or let me go."

"I'm not prepared to charge you." He sighed and dug into his jacket pocket. "Here. The VPA sent this by courier."

March handed me a small disc sealed in plastic. A new Vampire Protection Agency tracker.

"Thank you," I said. "To show good faith, I'll leave you with a few facts." I leaned forward and tapped on his tablet. "You might want to write this down, since your hotshot preternatural investigator apparently hasn't filled you in.

"First, in addition to a lot of other information, the VPA has a cast of my fangs on file. Call Dave Corey at the Jacksonville office to access them. They won't match the victim's marks, because my teeth are wider."

He scribbled a note without breaking eye contact. "Go on."

"Second, Yolette was dead before those punctures were made. Vampires are predators, not scavengers. They don't shoot people, *and* break their necks, *then* munch on them."

"Shoot them?" March echoed, his eyes narrowing on me.

I realized my goof—giving them more information than they thought I had—and thought fast to cover my tracks. "If what Neil said is right, yes. He told me he felt a bullet hole in the back of her head."

"He specifically said a bullet hole?"

"I think so. No matter how she died, the point is she was dead before the fang marks were made. No blood flow. No reason to feed off her."

"Why not?" March asked. "A vamp can suck wounds, right?"

"But they don't feed that way, Detective. Blood is life. Blood of the dead is just dead. The bites are staging."

He nodded. "Anything else?"

"On the incident report form, there's a line to list injuries. Janie and Mick both knew my arm was sore, first from the grabbing and shaking, then from being jerked around in Scarlett's. I don't know if that's why the tracker stopped working, but Janie insisted we list an arm injury, and now the tour company needs me to sign a medical waiver. In spite of what *some* people think—" I glared at Saber. "—a trauma to a vampire body has consequences. However briefly it may last."

I pushed back my chair and stood. "I'll be here at eight to talk to your artist, but if you have any more questions, contact my attorney. Right now I need to get this tracker implanted and get to work."

I admit it. I sailed out of the room, out of the building, in, as the Regency novels say, high alt. Even the foul, rainy weather didn't dim my triumph, though it did make me stop to coax my umbrella open.

Sandy was snug in her trench coat when she caught up with me outside the sheriff's department doors. "You did well, overall, but don't push Saber too far."

"He deserved it."

"Certainly he did, but he's at least a state- if not federal-level cop and an unknown factor. I'll call a few colleagues in Daytona and see what they know about him." She gestured at my arm. "Can you get the tracker taken care of today?"

"If an ER doctor can work me in, I can get it done now. If not, it'll be tonight after work."

"Good. And, Francesca, don't worry. There's no way they'll railroad you for this."

Why did that have a "famous last words" ring to it?

I followed Sandy's midnight blue Beemer south on U.S. 1 until I turned into the Flagler Hospital grounds. There I caught a break because—in spite of the rain—the ER was virtually empty, and the doctor who'd inserted my first tracker was on duty. The procedure had to be documented with photos as well as a written report, so a nurse took digital pictures as the old tracker came out and the new one went in. A few stitches later, a quick test of the device, and I was outta there.

At seven fifty, the rain had stopped, but the wind gusted strongly off the bay. At times like those, I wished there was a back entrance to our building for tenants. Since there isn't, I parked in my reserved space, sprinted around the building to Cathedral Place, and ran up the stairwell.

Maggie wasn't home yet and didn't answer her cell. I left her a message about the interview with March and left another message for Dave at the VPA about the new tracker. Those duties done, I refreshed my makeup, then decided to toss down another six-ounce bottle of blood to speed-heal the new implant into place.

Tonight I'd decided on a Minorcan costume paired with a water-repellent microfiber cape with a hood. The cape wasn't period-authentic, but it was warm, and I'd had a bad day. Why add to it? With my damp hair twisted into a high bun and my teeth freshly brushed, I left for work at eight thirty.

I arrived at the same substation on St. George Street where

music pulsed from the Mill Top Tavern and Mick paced the small plaza dressed in street clothes and a windbreaker.

"God, Cesca, don't you ever check your damn cell phone?" was his cheery greeting when he spotted me. "Janie and I have tried to reach you a dozen times."

"I've been on the dead run all day."

"Dead run? Har, har." He punched me on the shoulder, the good one. "Seriously, answer your cell now and then. We were worried about you."

"You were?"

"Hell, yes. For some reason we like you."

I grinned. "Thanks. Hey, you're not on rotation tonight, are you?"

"No. I volunteered to give you this personally." He passed me a rolled piece of paper and a pen. "It's the medical waiver."

I unrolled the form, scanned it, signed it, and handed it back.

"I'll take this to the office in the morning," he said, tucking the form and pen in his windbreaker. "You talk to the cops yet?"

"For more than two hours this afternoon."

"Have they found Stony?"

I pulled my hood tighter as a gust of wind blew off the bay. "They have a sketch, but I don't know how hard they're looking for him."

"Well, Janie and I put in the good word for you."

"Thanks." I smiled and looked around. "Is anyone signed up for the late tour?"

"Yeah, nine hearty souls. You're stopping at the drugstore, right?"

He meant the building that housed the oldest drugstore, circa 1737. The building was once a house of revelry north of town, then moved and plopped atop an Indian burial ground that was part of the Tolomato Cemetery. The drugstore is one of the most haunted places in an entire downtown of haunted places, and one of the buildings I'd skipped on Tuesday's tour.

"Yep, that's on tap tonight."

"Mind if I tag along for a while? Ghosts flock to you, and I want to find the bugger that bit my arm last week."

"Fine by me, but I've had two weird tours this week. Sure you want to risk another one?"

"I'll chance it. I brought my digital Kodak. And if the ghost biter doesn't show, maybe Stony will."

"Oh, yeah, I'd love to hand his mug shot to the cops."

"Great minds think ali— What the heck?"

I turned in time to be engulfed in a Shalimar embrace.

"Francesca, you poor dear!" Shalimar Millie was back and dressed in Jacksonville Jags sweats again—minus the visor—as were two other ladies from Monday's tour. Their purses were beach bag–sized and hitched on their shoulders.

"Millie, you're all right," I said, smiling.

She pulled away, looking part confused, part indignant. "Did you think I was ill?"

"Oh, uh, no," I stammered to cover my apparent gaffe. In my admittedly limited experience, people of a certain age either complained about infirmity or denied it. "You just looked tired, or, um, worried or something on Tuesday night."

She flipped a hand in dismissal. "I simply had some unfinished family business on my mind."

"Well, I'm glad you're back."

"Oh, we plan to keep coming back." She nodded firmly. "We've adopted you."

I stared for a beat. "Excuse me?"

"We're sure that frightful man from the other night killed the Frenchwoman and is trying to pin it on you." She smiled broadly. "Until that troublemaker is caught, two or three of us will take every tour you lead. And," she added, patting her purse, "we'll be packing."

My mouth fell open. Packing? As in armed? I wanted to laugh until I realized she was perfectly serious. Then I felt my eyes widen and stuttered, "B-but, ma'am, you don't need—"

"Not, ma'am, just Millie. That's Grace Warner, and that's Kay Sims," she said, pointing to ladies who both had short silver hair and identical determination-stamped expressions.

"Millie, I appreciate your thoughtfulness, but—"

"No buts," she said, holding up her beringed hand. "Some people adopt highways. We're adopting you. We have disposable incomes, senior discounts, and we'd love to help nail that nasty man. Not that the Frenchwoman wasn't a pariah, but that wasn't *your* fault."

I had two seconds to digest Millie's announcement—and puzzle over her pariah comment—when someone tapped me on the shoulder. I nearly jumped out of my shoes as I spun around to find a twenty-something man in jeans and a Flagler College sweatshirt standing almost on top of me. When did he sneak up? *Vampire Senses Stunned by Shalimar Lady. Film at eleven.*

"Ms. Marinelli? Paul Thoreaux. Has the sheriff's department made any progress on the French Bride murder?"

"Hunh?" Quick when I'm startled, aren't I?

"Are you a suspect in the case?"

Yikes, a reporter? I glanced at the press ID clipped to his sweatshirt and gathered my sadly scattered wits.

"I don't think I can comment other than to say I had no reason to harm the bride, and the groom has my sincerest condolences."

"He says you didn't do it."

I blinked. Not the sharpest knife in the drawer tonight. "Who and what are you talking about?" I asked.

"The husband. Etienne Fournier. He says you didn't kill his wife but thinks some guy who was following them around did it."

"Stony, the Covenant guy?" I asked.

"The stalker was honest-to-God Covenant?" Reporter Paul all but wagged his tail in excitement. "Shit, they play rough, but I didn't think they bothered regular people." He darted me a glance. "No offense."

"None taken. Mr. Fournier is right. I didn't kill his wife."

"That remains to be seen," a deep, mellow voice said from my right.

I turned. In slow motion. Hoping what I heard would prove to be a trick of the wind.

It wasn't. Deke Saber sauntered toward our little group in the same clothes he'd worn this afternoon minus the sunglasses. The jacket was buttoned to hide his gun, but I saw the slight bulge at his hip. Could this day get any worse?

I didn't even try for tactful. "What are you doing here?"

"Taking in the sights," he said mildly.

"You're taking my tour?"

"Who's this guy?" Reporter Paul asked, all eagerness.

"I'm a new...acquaintance of Ms. Marinelli's," Saber said.

"She doesn't look happy to see you," Millie shot back.

"I'm hoping to grow on her." He flashed the kind of smile meant to charm the support hose off the older ladies.

Shalimar Millie didn't fall for it, bless her. "Humph. Handsome is as handsome does."

"Hell," Reporter Paul groused. "I thought you were that Stony guy. The one stalking the French couple."

"Oh, no," Millie supplied. "That man had a long scar on his face. If he tries to pull anything tonight, we'll shoot him."

Paul blinked long eyelashes.

"That's right," I jumped in. "These ladies are armed with their digital cameras tonight. So is Mick." I pointed to my colleague's goofily grinning face. "He's also a tour guide. Maybe you should talk to him."

The reporter brightened and headed toward Mick, whose goofy grin morphed into a dirty look at me.

I spun toward Millie and her merry band and shooed them back a few paces. "Ixnay on the gun-ay talk-ay, ladies," I whispered, hoping Saber couldn't hear.

"Why? I have a permit," Millie said.

"To carry concealed weapons?" I hissed in frustration.

"We're seniors. The fuzz won't bust us," Silver Kay said.

"Not unless we actually shoot someone," Grace added.

Millie shook her head at me. "My dear, you're looking awfully frazzled. Did you get a chance to, uh, eat tonight?"

"Maybe you should've had a double," Saber drawled.

I jerked around to find him closer than he should've been. *Super Hearing Fails Vampire Again.*

Millie sniffed. "Maybe you're the problem, Mr.—"

"Are you the vampire?" a new voice on my left demanded.

I glanced over my shoulder to see four women dressed in more leather than an entire herd of cows. Black leather bustiers, second-skin pants, ankle boots with three-inch heels, and long coats. Their acrylic nails—and exposed midriffs—were stark white in contrast. So were the fake fangs flashing behind bright red lips. None of them more than twenty-five or -six, they made the goth gang look mature and well-dressed by comparison. Worse, faint bite marks dotted their necks and exposed arms.

I was thinking, *Yikes,* but must've nodded.

The tallest of the foursome, long-legged and black-haired, looked me up and down. "We're going on your tour."

"To check you out for the Daytona vampirth," a blonde added, lisping the *s.* Pointing to the tallest girl first, she introduced them as Claire, Barb, and Tetha. "And I'm Thithi."

I almost said, "I'm Thethca," but caught myself when Barb and Tessa, both redheads, waggled their fingers and flashed big fangy smiles at Saber.

"Hi, Deke."

"We've missed seeing you at the club," Tessa pouted.

Yeesh. Wasn't this just peachy. Gun-toting seniors, a reporter, Saber, and now blood bunnies. That's what they had to be. Human women who wore fake fangs and got their jollies hanging out with vampires. I'd read an article about blood bunnies, but seeing them was another plane of weird. If Stony *did* show, it'd be the highlight of the evening.

Saber had mentioned Ike this afternoon. Now the blood bunnies showed up. Coincidence? I thought not.

I wanted to bang my head on the nearest coquina wall.

I plastered on a smile instead. "Welcome to the Old Coast Ghost Walk. We're a bit late getting started, so hand me your tickets, and let's get right along, shall we?"

NINE

The biting ghost didn't manifest at the oldest drugstore, but the angry spirit of Fay's House made up for it. When Fay's wrathful face loomed in the window, her mouth moving in silent curses, a fierce wind gust rose to sound as if she were calling the hellhounds on us. The other tourists didn't seem shaken, but the blood bunnies screamed like preschoolers.

A bigger person might've been sympathetic. I wasn't. I gave Fay a thumbs-up. Probably shouldn't encourage the cranky spirit, but who did these bimbos think they were, coming to check me out? More important, had this little field trip been their idea, or had the head honcho, Ike, put them up to it? If so, why? VPA Dave had told me Ike ruled his illegal but overlooked nest with an iron fang, but he'd never so much as acknowledged my existence. Until now.

The bride Yolette and Ike's second-in-command vampire were both dead. What did they have in common, other than Stony and the Covenant? I wished Saber was off investigating that angle instead of trailing me, though it *had* been fun to watch him try to avoid the blood bunnies all night. Without success.

Of course, I'd quickly and quietly reassured Millie, Kay, and Grace that the blood bunnies' fangs were as fake as their nails. Probably their boobs, too. Reporter Paul didn't seem to care, judging by the drooling way he watched the women. They batted their eyes at Paul and Mick, but they darn near draped themselves on Saber.

He scowled through the tour. I smiled.

Mick abandoned me after the drugstore visit, heartless wretch. But it was our last stop and only two short blocks from our starting point. I rattled off my closing spiel at close to eleven o'clock and waved a figurative, not-fond farewell to the blood bunnies. Reporter Paul trailed after them, poor deluded guy. Someone ought to warn him, though it wasn't gonna be me. I thanked Millie, Kay, and Grace for coming and was enfolded in another Shalimar hug before they walked jauntily off. Geez, they had more energy than I did.

Saber didn't wait five seconds after the ladies left to annoy me. More than he already had, that is. Truth is, seeing him again tonight made me breathless. Could be that his faint musky smell was giving me some vampire version of asthma. Or it could be just plain nerves.

"How many of those women carry concealed?"

I contained my start, just barely. "The blood bunnies? You'd know better than I would."

He shook his head, a small smile playing on his sensuous— yes, sensuous—mouth. He bugs me, but I'm not immune to his attributes.

"Come on. I overheard that 'Ixnay on the gun-ay talk-ay' business. You suck at pig Latin."

I shrugged, wrapped my cloak tighter, and started hoofing it south on St. George. "Tour's over. Good-bye, Saber."

He stuck his hands in his pockets and fell into step on my right. I thought about turning on the vampire speed, but nervous as I was, I might fall on my face. I walked energetically instead. Saber kept pace.

"I'm not planning to run the senior citizens in, you know. You can talk to me."

"Why would I want to do that?"

"Because I'm interested in you."

"You are?" My heartbeat jumped. The only man who'd intrigued me in centuries was interested in me?

"Sure. I may be a preternatural expert, but I can always learn something. You're a new breed of vampire to me."

Feeling more sexless than ever, I kicked myself for thinking he meant anything personal. "So I'm, what, some kind of science experiment?"

"Your smart brain might want to remind your smart mouth that I'm also investigating a case you're connected to." He paused a beat. "Like it or not."

I stopped short, planted my fists on my hips. "In other words, you want to continue the interrogation."

"If you're willing."

"You think I fell off the dumb wagon? My attorney will have a fit if I talk to you without her present."

"You held your own this afternoon."

"And, surprise! I'm doing it now." I stomped off again, nursing a bruised ego.

"Tell you what. I won't ask you about the murder. We'll just chat."

"Chat? Who are you, and what have you done with the jerk from the sheriff's office?"

He flashed a smile, and laugh lines crinkled around his amazing blue eyes. Who knew he had laugh lines? Who knew he laughed?

"You like being a vampire?"

"Since I don't have a choice, I like it a lot better now than I used to."

"Because of the whole villagers-uprising-to-burn-you-out thing?"

I blinked at him. Nah, he couldn't know about that unless he'd read the newspaper article. "Actually, because I don't have to live with vampires and play their politics."

"I wouldn't think a princess vampire had to play politics."

I groaned. "You did see that article, huh?"

"Looked it up online. Seems like you had it pretty good."

"Oh, sure, I did. The ranking vampires in Normand's court just loved it when the king made me his princess and second-in-command. Yeah, they partied for days over that."

"Aw, did the poor vampire princess not have any friends?"

Triton flashed in my mind's eye, but that's not what made me stop again. Dark of the moon, iffy psychic senses and all, the hair on my nape stiffened. Magick scraped against my skin.

I scanned my surroundings. We stood at the intersection of St. George and Hypolita. In the iron-gated park to my left—nothing. At the pub up the block, three men smoked in the doorway. A tour train idled at the stop sign. In the Columbia Restaurant courtyard to my right, a man with dreadlocks played the flute. Late for a street performer to be out, but not unheard of.

Wait. The tour train didn't fit. Both companies quit running by five every evening, unless perhaps it was a special tour. But only the driver was on board.

I peered at his fiftyish, careworn face and the shaggy gray hair peppered with blue black strands. He met my gaze with an intensity that gave me goose bumps, then shifted gears and drove on through the intersection. When the last car passed, Cat—giant Cat—sat by a bollard on the other side of St. George Street as if it had hopped off the train.

"Oh, so it's you," I muttered.

"*Rrryyyow,*" Cat answered, tail whipping side to side.

"Shit," Saber swore. "That's the biggest damn cat I've ever seen. Must need a hell of a litter box."

Cat gave Saber a long, unfriendly look, snorted, and rose to trot south on St. George as if leading the way home.

I rubbed my temples and followed.

"You act like you have a headache," Saber commented.

"I think I do."

"Vampires don't get diseases, they don't get sick, and they sure as hell don't get headaches."

"See, that's your problem, Saber. You see me only as a vampire. I'm also female, and we can get headaches any time we darn well please."

Did I screech the end of that statement *juuust* a little? Tough. He was jumping on my last frayed nerve.

I glanced at my Timex with the illuminated dial feature I didn't need. Four more blocks to walk. If I hurried, I could catch *Night Court.* I'd feel *much* better then.

"Why do you wear a nightglow watch? You can't have bad eyesight."

"My sponsor gave it to me," I said and picked up my pace.

"Right, Maggie." He strode beside me in blessed silence for a minute. "I read Detective March's interview with Neil Benson."

"Uh-huh."

"He calls you Fresca?"

"Sometimes."

At Treasury Street, Cat veered left, and so did Saber. Since I was on his left, he plowed smack into me. He reached to steady himself or me, I wasn't sure which. His arms tightened around me, his body brushed mine, and, big, *big*, uh-oh.

Besides feeling his gun pressing into my hip, a lower part of him stirred. Damn it. I *soooo* didn't need this. A distant, vague attraction I could deal with. My erogenous zones doing the happy dance? No. Oh, definitely no. Not when I was a science experiment to the guy.

"What are you doing?" I said, aiming for haughty instead of hot-to-trot.

"Following your cat."

"She's not mine. If she were, I'd have sicced her on you. You wanna let go now?"

He gave me a wicked grin but stepped away. I continued down St. George Street without another word.

"Wait. You're walking past the cathedral?" he asked with a smidgen of concern as he leapt to catch up again. Cat did, too, prancing out in front of us.

"Why not? You think I'll burst into flames?" I heaved a purposely dramatic sigh. "For a preternatural crimes expert, you have an awfully narrow view of preternatural people."

"You're not a typical vampire."

"So I've been told."

"By Mick?"

"No, by Neil."

"You have a thing going with him?"

"Yuck, no. He's Maggie's man." I turned left on Cathedral Place into a face full of wind and the tangy smell of the bay. Only a half block to home.

"What *is* your relationship with Neil?"

"We surf sometimes, and we get along for Maggie's sake."

"You surfing tomorrow morning?"

"Duh. No. Detective March has my board. *And* I have to work with the sketch artist at eight."

"What are you doing the rest of tonight?"

"Taking my design course online, reading, maybe watching a movie." I needed to chill out, for sure.

"What about tomorrow night?"

"I'm taking dance lessons. The salsa, since I know you're going to ask."

"You sound like you plan every second of your life."

I shrugged. "I like knowing what to expect every day."

"What else do you do on your nights off?"

"Play bridge. Take classes. Shop at Wal-Mart."

"Wal-Mart?" From the corner of my eye, I saw him shake his head. "Like I said, you're *not* a typical vampire."

Cat trotted right past my door tonight. I stopped, and she let out a low *rrryyyow*. I paid no attention because, yippy-skippy, I could ditch Saber now.

"Fun as this has not been," I said, pulling my key from my

pocket, "twenty questions time is up. I hope you find Stony or whoever killed Yolette."

"*Rrryyyow,*" Cat growled louder and leapt back to pounce on the hem of my cloak.

"Is this a kiss-off?"

"You're the investigator. Draw your own conclusions."

Still growling, Cat bit my cloak and pulled hard. Off balance, I stumbled a few steps. Fortunately, not into Saber. Cat spat the material out, turned toward the bay again, stopped, and looked over her shoulder. I had the insane urge to say, "What is it, Lassie?"

Saber more or less did. "I'd swear that animal wants you to follow her."

"Maybe," I said, poking my key in the lock, "but it's not happening."

I was tired, stressed and, where Saber was concerned, too interested for my own good. Plus, maybe I'd watched one too many mysteries, but Cat was spooking me out more than she had on Monday. I couldn't stop her from showing up, but I sure as heck didn't have to follow her.

Cat stalked back and *rrryyyow*ed pitifully as she sat near the stoop.

"Come on, Princess, where's your sense of adventure?"

"It's Cesca and, hello, finding a dead body is enough adventure for one day."

He glanced down at Cat. "Is she always this prickly?"

I swear Cat shrugged her shoulders. "*Rrryyyow.*"

As the door shut, I heard him say, "See you tomorrow." Oddly, it sounded more like a promise than a threat, but that would be civil bordering on mannerly. Saber was only setting a trap. He had to be, after the way he'd acted at the sheriff's office. That or he had one hell of a Jekyll-Hyde complex.

"I talked to Sandy tonight," Maggie said, after giving me an exuberant hug as soon as I walked in the penthouse.

Ever supportive, that's my friend. Dressed in mint green sweats, she pulled me to the couch with Neil looking on from the kitchen.

"She said you were brilliant in the interview. Composed and thorough in your answers."

I shrugged out of my cloak and toed off damp slippers before sitting beside her. "Did she say anything else? Like when things would get back to normal?"

"Not exactly," she said, suddenly more somber. "She *will* try to be there while you work with the artist in the morning, but she has to be in court at nine. She also got the scoop on Deke Saber."

My stomach flip-flopped with renewed nerves. "What scoop?"

"He's a former creature hunter," Neil said flatly as he moved into the living room. "He's credited with killing more werecreatures and vampires than anyone in the country."

"Uh-oh." My fluttering stomach clenched. Talk about the wrong man to let under my skin.

Maggie took my hand. "Don't worry. He's a consultant now, not a hunter."

"Then he must've been fishing tonight, because he showed up on my tour."

Maggie stared, and Neil plopped on the coffee table in front of us. "Did he interrogate you?" Neil asked.

"Not precisely, but I couldn't shake him afterward. He walked home with me."

"That should be police harassment. Sandy can slap a suit on him first thing tomorrow."

"I doubt that would stop Saber," I said before Maggie wound into full-rant indignation.

"Why didn't you—" Neil snapped his fingers. "—warp speed yourself home?"

Neil didn't know I was a speed novice, and I wasn't fessing up, so I shrugged. "Seemed kinda pointless since he knows where I live."

Plus I'd rather win a battle of wits than speed any day, especially now that I knew what Saber was. Should I let on tomorrow? Maybe he wouldn't even be at the sheriff's office at eight. I might work with the sketch artist and never see Saber.

Until the next time he popped up unexpectedly.

An experiment shouldn't feel warm and fuzzy about seeing the mad scientist again, so why did I?

"Well, if he corners you again," Maggie was saying, "talk to Sandy immediately."

I agreed and changed the subject. "You two have fun tonight?"

Maggie and Neil exchanged one of those glances that spoke volumes. I thought of Saber's body brushing mine, but that was just lust. Sex was intimate, but Maggie and Neil had more than sex and a much deeper intimacy.

"Hey, Fresca," Neil said, snapping his fingers in my face. "Are you laying off surfing till you get your board back?"

"Actually, I think I'll buy a new board."

"The queen of cheap is buying a new board?" He gripped his chest. "You mean brand-new? Retail?"

I snagged a decorative pillow and smacked him. He might've smacked me back, but the phone rang. No one calls Maggie after ten at night except her dad, so we all blinked at the white cordless unit before Maggie answered. A moment later, that one eyebrow arched halfway to her hairline.

"Wait a sec," she said and turned to me. "It's that Saber character. I'm putting you on the speaker so we can be witnesses to this." She punched the speaker button, and I said hello.

"Marinelli, is your truck parked in the bank lot?"

I glanced at Maggie. "What?"

"Damn it, where is your truck parked?"

"It's in the lot. Why?"

"You'd better get down here."

The lot was only partially lit by security lights, and shadows danced across the asphalt. Saber stood by the bed of my SSR. I could tell my truck wasn't its pristine aqua blue metallic color anymore but couldn't see exactly how bad the damage was until I drew level with him. Black spray paint spelled the word DIE on my tailgate, and that was only a fraction of the destruction.

"Damn." I reached to touch a shattered taillight.

Saber didn't stop me. Instead, he said, "I've called the city police and sheriff's office. The city cops are rolling. We'll need to photograph and fingerprint the truck."

Fingerprints. I didn't want to blow the chance of catching the vandal, so I took Saber's hint and clasped my hands tightly behind me. Good thing, because shock warred with righteous rage as I circled my baby to inspect her damage.

Crimson paint smelling faintly of blood covered the cab,

windshield, and hood in streaks and dripped onto the pavement. Where the paint didn't cover them, deep scratches etched both entire sides. I couldn't tell whether they were words, symbols, or random marks, but each ugly gouge pushed my blood pressure higher. Though the windows were intact, the headlights and taillights were all smashed.

By the time I'd made the circuit around my SSR, a city cop car pulled up to block the parking lot entrance. Neil stood beside Saber and looked grim, while Maggie stepped up to hug me.

"Oh, Cesca honey, I'm so sorry."

I accepted her comfort, but my gaze never left Saber's.

"How did you find this mess?" I asked him when Maggie let me go.

He shrugged. "When you went inside, I followed that cat. It headed straight for your truck."

Maggie planted her hands on her hips. "Who cares about a damned cat? When are you going to catch Stony? He has to be behind it. He killed that woman, and now he's terrorizing Cesca."

"Now, Maggie," I said, putting my arm around her in hopes of stemming a tirade, "this is vandalism. A very bad case of vandalism," I added darkly, "but not terrorism. And here come the nice policemen to help us."

Make that police persons. A male officer of about forty paired with a much younger female who did all the talking.

"Who called in the complaint?"

"Deke Saber, state special investigator." His ID already in hand, he flashed it and went on. "I made the call, and this is the owner."

"Your name, ma'am?" the female asked.

I moved away from Maggie and gave the officer my full name, address, and both the house and my cell numbers. When they insisted on seeing my driver's license, Neil volunteered to run upstairs for it.

"Approximately how long has your vehicle been parked here?"

"Since a little before eight this evening," I said dully.

"Any idea who might have done this?"

I glanced at Saber. "I have an excellent idea, but I don't know his name."

"Officers," Saber said, "I told dispatch there's reason to believe this incident is indirectly connected to a murder the sheriff's office is investigating."

The cops exchanged a glance. "The French Bride murder?" the female cop asked.

Great, the reporter had used the same catchphrase for the case. Now if they could just catch the guy responsible.

The male officer's eyes narrowed on me, then Saber. "You're the vampire killer, right? That why the state is in on this case? Because she's one of them?"

Oh, good, another fan. I was grateful Maggie didn't make a snide comment from the sidelines, but beside me, Saber scowled.

"I'm a preternatural crimes expert, and the case has international implications. I'm here to eliminate possible suspects."

The cop didn't look chastised but grunted something that could've been "Yessir."

Neil came back with my license and, after making note of the number and expiration date, the officers and Saber looked my truck over together. I hardly had time to eavesdrop when they were back.

"We'll file a report, ma'am. You can get of copy of it next week." She handed me two sheets of standard white paper folded in half, one tucked in the other. "This is a victim's rights booklet. My name and the case number are here on the front."

I nodded and clenched the pamphlet in both hands. "Thank you, Officer, but what about the truck?"

Frankly, I didn't want my trashed baby to be sitting in the parking lot in the morning for the bank and office employees to see. Not to mention the locals and tourists. Friday was a busy day downtown.

"The county's taking care of it," Saber said. "All the tow trucks are tied up on other calls, but they'll page me when one is on the way."

I wondered if he thought I'd done this myself and was determined to set him straight.

As soon as the St. Augustine city officers left, I whirled on Saber.

"If you think I did that myself—"

"I don't."

"—I'll—" I stopped short and glanced at Maggie and Neil to be sure they heard us. "You don't think I did this?"

"No, especially after seeing you look over the damage."

His voice rumbled with such uncharacteristic gentleness, I wondered what I'd revealed.

"It's just a truck," I said offhandedly so he wouldn't see any deeper.

"It's your independence."

So much for not seeing deeper. I looked at Neil, who stood solemnly by Maggie. She jerked her head toward our building.

"What?" I mouthed.

She blew her blonde bangs in exasperation and marched up to Saber. I stepped behind him, out of her way.

Maggie eyed him up and down. "I want a straight answer. Do you think Cesca killed that woman?"

I sucked in a breath. Saber ran a hand through his hair and spoke directly to Maggie.

"Officially, she's still a suspect. Unofficially, I can't buy it."

"Why not?" I asked, surprised. Had he planned to let *me* know this anytime soon?

He gave me an over-the-shoulder glance. "I don't think you have a motive, but I do have more questions."

Lips pursed, Maggie nodded as if she'd made up her mind about something.

Boy, had she.

"It's too cold to do this outside," she said. "Come up to the condo with us."

From my point behind Saber's left shoulder, I shook my head hard enough to rattle my brains. Maggie—and Neil—ignored me, but Saber turned to face me. I stilled so fast, I darn near concussed myself.

"Do you mind if I come up?"

All right, I had to admit I liked him for asking. But there I was in a manners dilemma again. I'd had a hell of a day, my precious, freshly painted truck was trashed, and Saber was coming up for, what? Tea?

Cornered and resigned, I said, "Let's go."

We trooped into the building, stood silent in the elevator. In the penthouse, Maggie ushered Saber to the dining table and put water in the electric kettle. Tea. I was right. Geez.

Saber was mannerly enough to compliment Maggie on her home and make conversation with Neil about the state archaeology department. Neil's face lost some of its tension as he talked about the digs he'd been part of. Maggie appeared to relax, too, as she set out mugs and tea bags, sugar, and milk.

I wasn't calm at all. Saber's unbuttoned jacket gave me an occasional flash of his weapon, and my body tingled in memory of our accidental hug. Yet there he sat, nonchalantly chatting while my day went from bad to worse.

I smoothed the victim's rights pamphlet on the table, picked at the bent corner, and gritted my teeth to keep from jumping out of my skin. By the time the teakettle shut off, I couldn't keep quiet a minute longer.

"What do you want to ask us, Saber?"

He cut his gaze from Neil to me. "First, I need to tell you it's doubtful we'll get any prints. There was no trail of paint to follow. No apparent footprints. If it'd been me, I'd have had a garbage bag handy to toss the paint cans in, and I'm guessing that's what happened here. The city police and county deputies can check around, alert sanitation workers to keep an eye out, but the guy could have ditched the stuff anywhere."

I'd figured the same thing. Still, it sucked. "Peachy. Guess I can toss the victim rights booklet."

"Sorry to disappoint you, but you strike me as the type to want the truth."

"Yeah, and I hate that about myself," I muttered as Maggie served the tea with a plate of Fig Newtons. Yum. Comfort food.

When she handed me a steaming cup and I snagged a Newton, Saber looked surprised.

"You, uh, ingest food?"

"Saber," I said, deliberately taking a small bite of cookie and talking around it, "if you're gonna call yourself a vampire expert, you really have to catch up to the times."

His mouth quirked in that too-attractive way. "I'm trying."

Neil chuckled, and Maggie hid a grin behind her mug. I had three sips of tea and another bite of cookie—mostly to show Saber I could—before Neil caught my eye.

"You realize," he said, looking steadily at me, "no matter who did this—Stony or someone else—he knew you drove an SSR, and he knew where you parked."

"Which means he knows where Maggie and I live."

Neil pushed his mug away. "I don't think you and Maggie are safe here."

Maggie snorted. "Neil, the guy doesn't have a key to the building, he doesn't have the code to the elevator, and I have my dad's army service revolver. Just let him try anything."

I blinked at her across the table. "*You* have a gun, too?"

"Yes, and I'm teaching you to shoot this weekend."

Saber choked on a sip of tea. Neil groaned softly.

"It won't do any good to learn," I said. "The Vampire Protection Agency frowns on me having a weapon."

"Screw the VPA. You have the right to protect yourself."

"I agree with you, in theory, Mags," Neil said, "but this sicko can come after either of you anywhere, anytime, and it won't be with a can of paint. He's erratic, and that makes him even more dangerous."

Maggie took his hand. "Honey, I understand your concern, but I need to start the design for my new client, and Cesca has work and activities. We can't put our lives on hold until the cops lock this guy up."

Neil shot Saber a measuring glance. "No, and I don't guess Mr. Special Investigator here can move Cesca into protective custody, can you?"

I froze. My little voice screaming, *Nonononono* was rewarded when Saber shook his head.

"I doubt the county keeps safe houses fit for a vampire." He grabbed a cookie and took a healthy bite of it.

"Then how about this." Neil turned his hand to clasp Maggie's. "I have to teach a graduate seminar all day on Saturday in Tallahassee. You said you wanted to check out some warehouses there, Mags. You could come with me. Make a weekend of it, and give the cops time to track down Stony while you're safe out of town."

"No. I won't leave Cesca alone."

"She won't be alone. Not if Saber moves into the penthouse to guard his suspect."

TEN

~

"What?" Maggie and I yelped together while Saber coughed a fine spray of Fig Newton on the table.

I pounded Saber's back, the pulse in my throat doing triple time. Was Neil nuts?

"Are you nuts?" Maggie snapped. "You want to go off and leave Cesca alone with a vampire killer?"

"He's a consultant, Mags," Neil countered, unperturbed. "You said that yourself, and he's a law officer. He's equipped to protect her."

"He could shoot her!"

"Wait a minute," I said, but for naught. Neil and Maggie went right on quibbling.

"He's not going to shoot an innocent citizen," Neil argued. "Besides, Cesca could break him in two without turning a hair. And with her hair, that's saying a lot."

Saber coughed again, but I caught his eyes laughing and crossed my arms to keep from punching him.

"Cesca is nonviolent, and she's as vulnerable as anyone when she's asleep."

"Safe room, Mags," he said referring to a reinforced space at the end of the hall. Maggie had it built in case she couldn't evacuate in a hurricane. "She can rack out in the safe room."

"After all the time she was buried, you want to stick her in a closet?"

"Hey, she'll be dead to the world in there. She can lock herself in and get out whenever she wants."

I cleared my throat. "May I interrupt?"

"No," they said in unison and went back to wrangling.

Saber leaned sideways toward me. "They do this often?"

"It's the Neil and Maggie show."

"I'll get that page about the tow truck soon."

I nodded. He needed to go, and I needed to convince Maggie Neil was right. Partly so, anyway.

I put two fingers to my mouth and whistled. Dogs probably howled a mile away, but it did the trick.

"Maggie," I said, "Neil's right about your safety. It's fine if you go away for the weekend. You've done it before."

"Not when you were being threatened."

"I can take care of myself. I'll skip dance class, call work to reschedule, and lie low while you're gone."

"You will not. You say that, but you'll do as you please."

"No, I promise. And," I added, suddenly inspired, "I can ask Janie to stay with me."

"I still think Saber should do it," Neil put in.

"No way," I said, shaking my head. "He can't bodyguard *and* investigate me. It's a conflict of interest."

"See?" Maggie triumphantly shot at Neil.

"It's not procedure," Saber drawled, setting his mug on the table, "but I can get around that. Look, I don't think you're stupid enough to kill a woman and then bite her, even if you had a motive." He paused a beat. "The thing I can't figure out is why the killer would bother to implicate you."

"Simple misdirection?" I suggested. When he looked surprised, I added, "I read a lot of mysteries."

"Which leads to the next question. What do you know that you haven't told us yet? Not because you mean to withhold information," he hurried on when I frowned, "but because we haven't asked the right questions."

"What's left to tell you?" Maggie demanded. "Stony did it. He hates vampires. He'd implicate Cesca in a heartbeat. Leaving her alone with you won't find him any faster."

Saber blew out a breath and leaned back in the chair. "What makes you all so sure it's Stony?"

"Who else could it be?" Maggie asked impatiently.

"The guy Cesca calls Gomer," Saber threw out. "We haven't located him yet."

I frowned. "You haven't found Holland Peters?"

Saber shook his head. "And tonight those women connected to the Daytona vampires showed up."

"What women?" Neil asked.

"These four weirdo women who hang out with the Daytona Beach vamps were on my tour tonight," I said to Neil, then grinned at Maggie. "They wore these leather getups—you should've seen them."

"Could they have vandalized the truck?" Neil asked Saber.

"Doubtful, but the timing of their visit is suspicious. There was a similar murder in Daytona last Friday. We're looking into connections between them."

Interesting that he didn't say the other victim was a vampire, but I stayed focused.

"Who else do you suspect? I assume you've checked out Yolette's husband?"

"Still checking, as a matter of fact, but there's also Mick."

"Mick. The tour guide Mick?" I asked.

"He worked in a vampire bar in Daytona Beach."

"Sure, as a bouncer a long time ago. He told Janie and me about it."

"Did he tell you," Saber said slowly, "that a vampire kidnapped his girlfriend?"

I pictured how gentle Mick was with Janie and must've gasped. "Oh, no."

"What happened?" Maggie prompted.

"Mick tried defending the girl, but he was beaten and left for dead. The girl was turned." Saber paused, and I bit my lip. "A week after Mick left the hospital, the vampire and the girlfriend were killed in a house explosion."

"Was Mick charged?" I asked softly.

"No, but the cops may have looked the other way."

"Still, Mick didn't have any more reason to kill Yolette than I did."

"Who else is on your suspect list?" Neil asked.

"You were, briefly. So was Maggie, because there was a chance one of you would kill to protect Cesca."

I blew out an exasperated breath. "I don't need protection from Maggie or Neil. I'm a vampire, for heaven's sake."

"Not a normal one."

"I'm perfectly normal," I snapped.

"Your powers are pathetic."

"He's right, Fresca," Neil said.

I looked to Maggie for help, but she shrugged. Guess Neil and Maggie had noticed I don't use my powers after all. I almost admitted I don't *choose* to use them, but I refocused.

"Who else is on your stupid list?" I asked.

"Millie."

I stared. "Shalimar Millie? That sweet lady? Have you lost your mind?"

"She didn't like the victim."

"Well, no, but..."

I stopped talking and started remembering. Yolette said her first husband's aunt wore Shalimar, and that he'd been allergic. Or was it Yolette who had the allergy? I'd assumed the dead husband had been a Frenchman, but—

Saber's phone beeped, distracting me. He checked it, shoved it back in his jeans pocket, and rose.

"The tow truck's a few blocks away. You thought of something, didn't you?"

"It's probably not important."

"Write it down anyway," Saber ordered as he buttoned his sport coat and headed for the door. "Write a narrative for me about the tours on those two nights, even if you've been over it with us. Conversations, actions, movements, observations. Bring it tomorrow, and I'll take a look while you're with the artist.

Which reminds me," he added, his hand on the doorknob. "You need a ride in the morning?"

"I'll bring her," Maggie said firmly.

"Fine. Thanks for the tea."

Saber left, and the three of us exchanged glances.

"We still haven't settled the trip issue," Neil said.

"Oh, yes, we have." I got up, snatched my mug and Saber's, and took them to the sink. "Maggie, go with Neil. If you don't, if you're out doing business and I'm holed up, you'll be the target for sure, and I can't have that."

"Why the hell not?"

I spoke over the rush of water from the faucet. "Think about it. If something happens to you, who's gonna be my sponsor? Neil? No. He rags on my hair, so sooner or later, I'd have to kill him, and then where would I be?"

"Hey," Neil objected.

"Neil, you know I'm right, and Maggie, you do, too. Go to Tallahassee."

She bit her lip. "You'll call Janie to stay with you?"

"Yes, and if she can't or won't, I'm good. I have *Magnum* DVDs coming in the mail tomorrow, a James Garner movie marathon, a *Night Court* marathon, homework, books to read—" I waved a hand. "I'll even clean the penthouse."

Finally she laughed. "You are desperate."

"Let's call it persuasive."

"I'll phone in, you know. At random times."

"I'll answer."

She hesitated a minute more. "Okay, I'll go."

"We need to leave by nine, honey," Neil put in.

"That's cool," I said before Maggie could object. "I'll catch a ride back from the sheriff's with Saber. Make him stop for donuts and really freak him out."

Neil laughed, and Maggie shook her head. "Be careful of him, Cesca. He seems to be on your side now, but I wouldn't push him too far."

Cosmil hovered under one of the dozens of ancient oaks in the plaza watching Pandora in her panther size as she descended from branch to branch. She landed with a soft plop on the ground before him, but a disguise spell insured that anyone passing saw only a large house cat and an old man.

"Did you get close enough to overhear them?" Cosmil asked.

The vampire princess will be alone for two days.

"And the man called Saber? Will she be safe from him?"

He will not kill her.

"Can you track the vandal?"

Pandora shook her head. *I smelled only blood and sand. The scent stopped at the street.*

The vandal had left by car then. Cosmil frowned at the puzzle, but it was not his priority. Triton had shape-shifted into dolphin form with the dark moon to roam the coastline of the Pacific one last time. In twenty-four hours, when he shifted back to human form, he would rest for two days before his business affairs concluded. At the time he traveled east, he would be most vulnerable to detection.

If only Cosmil could unmask The Void, he might call on allies to contain it. He would perform the revealing spell one more time but save his highest energy and magick to cloak Triton's movements. Meanwhile, Francesca must be guarded.

"Keep watch," he murmured. "Let no harm befall them."

As the panther bounded back up the tree, Cosmil's body shimmered and disappeared.

I settled down to work on the tour details for Saber, breaking now and then to finish reading my design course lectures. I have a good memory, but reconstructing the two tours was harder than I thought it would be. I *was* pleased that absolutely nothing Mick had said or done pointed to him as the killer. Certainly not of a total stranger.

Millie? She'd seemed disapproving of the couple from the get-go. There was the confrontation about Millie's perfume overuse. There was the oddity about Yolette's first husband's death. Etienne had said it was an accident, but I'd heard *Murder* loud and clear in my head with no idea whose thought I'd plucked from the airwaves. Was the little set-to cause for Millie to kill Yolette? I couldn't see it.

Now, Holland? He was a giant question mark. He carried a gun and was not what he seemed, but was he a killer?

When I'd written as much as I could, I rewarded myself by watching *Bringing Up Baby*. Afterward, I looked over my tour notes again, but pictures of Saber kept intruding. That faint musk scent I smelled when Saber was near puzzled me. It was so much fainter than most men's cologne and aftershave, and I wasn't even sure it was coming from his body. His laundry detergent? Maybe I'd ask about it if we—

Wait! What was I thinking? I planned to spend as little time with Saber as possible. The fact that he made my pulse race a *little* faster was beside the point. Until the cops found Stony, they had squat. I'd deal with Saber long enough to be cleared, and that would be that. He could find a science project somewhere else.

At six o'clock Friday morning, I brushed my teeth, showered, and washed my hair. I left the flatiron heating longer than usual and actually got my hair smoothed. Well, all right, not smooth as in straight, but I didn't look like Janis Joplin on a bad hair day. Pleased, I spent just a touch more time on my makeup and dressed in jeans, a lightweight emerald green sweater, and sandals. Not that I was fixing myself up for Saber or anything.

The nor'easter had blown itself out, leaving the March morning comfortably breezy. Maggie dropped me at the St. Johns County Sheriff's Office just before eight, having lectured me about being cautious all the way from the penthouse. Man, did I have more sympathy for teenagers with carping parents! Still, I hugged her and told her to have fun before flying out of the car and into the office.

I waited only a few minutes for Detective March to escort me to the back. Today his suit was blue with a white shirt. He already looked slightly rumpled, and the day had just started.

"Your attorney's not coming?" he asked as we walked through the bullpen.

"She might stop in, but she has court at nine."

"How long before you have to sleep?"

"Nine thirty at the latest, or I'm dead to the world."

He didn't laugh. No sense of vampire humor, I guess.

"You said the rendering I showed you yesterday was close?"

Gads, had it only been yesterday afternoon? "Very."

"Then this shouldn't take much time, but don't leave until you sign your statement. In here."

He opened the door to the same side room Sandy and I had used to consult, and introduced me to the artist. A trim, middle-aged woman, Billie Ormand sat at the utilitarian table with a laptop and went right to work. We'd been at it maybe ten minutes when Saber came in with a cup of coffee for Billie and ice for me.

I have to admit I was impressed he remembered the ice. Thoughtful was the last word I'd have used to describe him yesterday.

But he did look good in jeans, an ocean blue polo shirt, and a sports jacket. Tired but good. I wondered how late he'd worked.

When he left, Billie winked. "Hot guy."

I smiled and tossed an ice cube in my mouth.

In another fifteen minutes, we had an image that could've been a photograph of Stony. Billie called March in, and Saber came along.

"Good work, ladies. I'll get this in circulation and run it against the database. Saber, the statement Ms. Marinelli needs to sign is on my desk. She's free to go after that."

"I have two questions," Saber said as I read then signed the statement. "Did you write the narrative about the tours?"

I pulled the eight single-spaced printed sheets from my purse and handed them over almost before he finished asking.

"Thanks. You have a ride home?"

"No, would you mind?"

Did he seem to brighten? "Let me check out with March."

He did, and we were at the lobby threshold when Etienne

Fournier barged through the double doors to the reception desk.

"I must speak with the Detective March, *immédiatement*," he demanded as dramatically as Yolette would have. "*Vite, vite.*"

I wondered what the hurry was and if he truly didn't blame me for his bride's death. Maybe I shouldn't be here when he turned around.

I tugged on Saber's sleeve to drag him out while Etienne was distracted, but Etienne spotted us and rushed to me.

"Ah, Ms. Marinelli, Francesca!" He grabbed my right hand and pressed a kiss on it. "I am so sorry it was you who found my *pauvre* Yolette. And yet *non*. You saved her from disappearing altogether. To have her vanish and never know what had happened? I should be devastated."

Saber's warmth at my back steadied me. "I'm terribly sorry for your loss, Mr. Fournier," I said as I gently pulled my hand away.

"*C'est une tragédie!* I loved her so. She was, how you say, my soul mate." He paused with his hand on his heart. "But I do not blame you. You could not hurt her. I know this. You are not ruthless like so many of your kind."

My kind being vampire, I assumed. A backhanded compliment, but I glommed in on the not blaming me part.

"Thank you, Mr. Fournier. I hope the authorities catch the killer quickly."

"*Oui*, they are sure to now. I," he said grandly, "have information."

"What information?" Saber asked.

"I see him. *Cet homme horrible.*"

The horrible man? He'd seen Stony?

"You mean the man who was stalking you?" Saber said. "You saw him?"

"When and where?" March's voice boomed from behind me.

I jumped out of the way as he charged through the doorway to Etienne. In the excitement, I hadn't heard him coming.

"I see him at his home. I think it is his home. He carries *une valise* into a house."

"Where is the house?" March ground out.

"I do not know the street name but on the edge of the town it is. Not far from here. I rush to tell you."

"Come with me," March ordered Etienne. "Saber, you want in on this?"

Saber glanced at me.

"Go get him. I'll call a cab."

Saber shoved the tour narrative at me, muttered "Later," and followed the two men. I stuffed the sheaf of papers in my purse and grabbed my handy cell phone. Thirty minutes later—close to collapse—I walked into the penthouse and fell in bed.

I jerked awake at four fifteen, still in my jeans and sweater. Eeeks, had Maggie called? Is that what startled me? I hopped up to check but found no messages from Maggie. Or Saber, for that matter.

Should I track down him or Detective March and ask how the capture went? I had a right to know. If Stony was behind bars, then I could go about my merry business, including dance class tonight and tour guiding tomorrow.

I got my daily requirement of Starbloods down while I cleaned out my purse. The eight-page tour narrative I left on the dining table. Didn't need those now with Stony caught. I brushed my teeth and was washing the morning's makeup off when the phone rang. I sprinted to my bedside to snag the extension.

"You caught it on the first ring," Maggie said, sounding both relieved and suspicious. "What's up?"

"Good news. Stony turned up today."

She shrieked, and I jerked the phone away from my poor ear, but I grinned all the same.

"So tell me. What happened?"

I relayed Etienne's entrance and announcement, and March and Saber's rushing off.

"Are you sure they caught him?"

"No, but I'm calling the sheriff's office before five."

She reminded me of the time, ordered me to "Get to it," and disconnected. Before I could punch in the sheriff's number, the phone rang again. Deke Saber on the caller ID.

My pulse jumped as I answered.

"Good, you're awake. We need you to come out to the office and ID the guy we picked up this morning."

"I can be there in—" I calculated hair time. "—forty minutes if I can get a cab quick."

"Make it five. I'm parked a few doors from you near the Greek restaurant. Black Saturn Vue."

The line went dead. Damn. Saber was back to being Mr. Hyde and pushing my blood pressure all the way to measurable range.

I ran to the bathroom to slap on face powder, whip on mascara, and pop my hair in a ponytail. I jammed my feet into my shoes but didn't change from my blue jeans and emerald sweater. They were only the tiniest bit wrinkled from sleeping in them and, besides, who was I trying to impress?

I wrenched open the SUV passenger door six minutes later

and ducked into the seat. Saber looked different, and it took only a second to see why. He didn't wear a jacket to hide the holster on his hip.

He caught me staring and gave me a quick once-over before he wheeled into traffic. "Sleep in your clothes?"

I ground my teeth at the crack, but stayed focused. "Why do I need to ID Stony? Is he denying being on my tours?"

"We just need to know if he's the same man who threatened you and the Fournier woman."

"What's his real name?"

"Can't tell you."

Huh? My blood pressure spiked again, this time in pure irritation. "What happened? Did he put up a fight? Did you find anything incriminating?"

"I can't say."

I watched his profile as he wove through the narrow streets, saw a muscle jump in his jaw, and figured he must be clenching his teeth. Was he tense or ticked? Whatever it was, my stomach knotted with nerves.

I tried another question. "You've held him all day waiting for me to wake up?"

"No comment."

"That's bogus."

He cursed, I thought at me, but it was aimed at a driver who cut in front of us. "The narrative you gave me this morning. I need it."

"Then take me back. It's on the table."

"Damn!"

"Look, you commanded me to be at your car in five minutes. You caught Stony. I didn't think you needed the darn thing."

Saber raised a brow. "Get up on the wrong side of the crypt?"

"Just drive. Let's get this over with."

At the sheriff's office, Saber pulled on his jacket as we entered through the main building. We wound through the corridors and straight to the desk where Detective March sat.

"Ms. Marinelli," March said as he rose and indicated a chair beside his desk. I sat and faced him catty-corner, while Saber leaned against the partition behind March.

"You know Etienne Fournier came in this morning with a tip," he said rather ponderously, straightening his tie over his rumpled white shirtfront.

I nodded.

"We want you to tell us if the man we located is the same one you call Stony, then we want to talk with you again. Would you like your attorney present?"

My stomach full-on cramped this time. Gut instinct was telling me something, but what did I have to fear?

I considered a moment then said, "I can call her office, but she's probably gone for the day."

He pushed the phone toward me and leaned back in his swivel chair, hands clasped on his belly. I took Sandy's card from my wallet and punched in the number. As expected, she'd left, and so had everyone else. There was an emergency number, and I jotted it on her card, but I didn't see the point of dragging her or her associate in on a Friday afternoon. How bad could this be?

"I got the answering system, Detective March. Tell you what. To move things along, I waive my right to have my lawyer here for now but reserve the right to change my mind."

He smiled politely and gave me a single nod. "Fair enough. Let's do it."

My pulse thudded, albeit slowly. Unlike books and movies, this was a real, live lineup and a moment of truth. I started to rise until March opened a folder and placed six photos on the desk.

"Ms. Marinelli," he said, "please look carefully and point out the man who threatened you and the victim."

"This is the lineup?" I asked.

He didn't smile. "We're doing a printed lineup. Do you recognize any of these men as the one you call Stony?"

I spotted Stony immediately. The snarly lips, the scar, the weirdly light eyes. I tapped the photo. "That's him."

"You're absolutely sure that's the guy?" March asked.

I glanced up at Saber, then back at March. "Unless Stony has a down-to-the-scar identical twin, I'm sure."

March sighed. "Then we have a problem, Ms. Marinelli. The man you identified has an ironclad alibi."

ELEVEN

How could I be innocent, but suddenly feel guilty?

No alibi, that's how.

I was so stunned by the revelation that Stony had an ironclad one, I followed March into an interview room in a fog.

Until I saw the clear plastic cup of ice on the table, a good inch of water melted in the bottom. Then I got it. No wonder March asked me about having my attorney present. He'd known this was more than a trip to ID Stony. Saber had, too, the swine.

Was this another interview or an interrogation? I wasn't sure of the difference, but strongly considered calling a halt right then and there and phoning the emergency number I'd scribbled on Sandy's card. I decided to go with the flow unless things took a bad turn.

Dumb move, right? A too-stupid-to-live move that Maggie and Sandy would have my head for if they found out about it. Thing is, I'd held my own so far, and I hated waiting until who knew when for a lawyer to show. Besides, I really wanted to get to my dance class at eight. That was my normal routine. That was control. The sooner we got down to business, the better.

We took the same seats we had last time I was here. Was that just yesterday? After the routine of recording the date, time, and names of three of us present in the room, March followed procedure to the letter and asked if I'd still talk with them without my attorney present.

My bravado faded, and I tried not to audibly gulp as I answered, "For now."

"Very well," he said. "The man you identified as threatening you and Yolette Fournier is Victor Gorman. You recognize the name, Ms. Marinelli?"

"I don't," I said, but my voice sounded a touch shaky. Shakier than I wanted it to. "He really has an alibi?"

March didn't answer me. Instead, he opened a file folder on the table. "For the record, tell me again about your run-ins with Mr. Gorman."

Ire and self-preservation flared. "Detective, let's be clear that he created the run-ins."

March gave me a rather condescending nod, and I went through the events of Monday and Tuesday again, including the confrontation at Scarlett's.

"Tell me what you did on Wednesday night," he said next.

"Played bridge until nine and went home."

"Where?" March pressed.

"Where was bridge club? At Shelly Jergason's house in Crescent Beach."

"Where were the Fourniers staying?" Saber asked, arms still crossed on his chest.

I angled my chair so I could more easily look at both March and Saber. "According to Gomer—I mean Holland Peters— they were staying in some fancy neighborhood, but he didn't say where."

March leaned marginally closer. "When did you have that information?"

I tapped my chin, even though I wanted to squirm. Didn't take psychic senses to feel where this was headed.

"Holland told me on Tuesday night. He said the Fourniers told him. He also said Stony followed the Fourniers to their car on Tuesday night after the tour, and that he, Holland that is, followed Stony."

"Where were the Fourniers parked?" Saber shot.

"I don't know. They all headed toward the visitor's center parking garage."

"Must've been quite a parade," March said. "Saber asked this once. I'm asking again. Where exactly were the Fourniers staying, Ms. Marinelli?"

I shook my head. "I don't have a clue. If Holland knew, he didn't tell me."

"The fact is," March said tersely, "the Fourniers were rent-ing a house in your friend Shelly Jergason's neighborhood."

"They were?"

"And Ms. Jergason remembers mentioning these people at your bridge club."

My jaw dropped. "The people that yelled at each other? That was the Fourniers?"

"Cut the act, Ms. Marinelli. How long have you known Holland Peters?" Saber fired at me.

"I don't *know* him," I said, panic warring with patience. "It's more like know *of* him. Holland—who I still called Gomer then because I didn't know his name—was on the Monday and Tuesday tours. When everyone else left Tuesday, I talked to the mystery writers who took the tour, then started walking home. He found me and asked to walk with me. We saw Maggie, my roommate, at the door to my building. When Holland leaned over to help her pick up the stuff she'd dropped, I saw the gun stuck in his waistband at the small of his back. That made me nervous, so I hustled Maggie inside, and that's the last I saw of him."

"He hasn't called you?" March asked.

"Why would he?"

"Why would he walk you home?" Saber snapped.

I shrugged. "He said he wanted to be sure I got home all right. That Stony might come back or one of Stony's buds might be watching me."

Saber persisted. "So he told you he was protecting you?"

"Actually, he said something like his mother would have his hide if he let a lady who'd been threatened walk home alone."

"Gallant of him," Saber sneered. "Did you feel safer?"

"Not particularly, but I didn't feel *un*safe until I saw his gun."

"What kind was it?" March asked.

I shrugged. "I don't know modern guns."

March arched a brow. "When did you last handle a firearm?"

Soon as he asked, the memory blossomed. Unworthy of me as it was, I leaned back in the uncomfortable chair to enjoy the moment.

"The very last time was about October 1792. Or was it '93? No, '92, when I was twelve. A friend and I got into the dueling pistols an Englishman had given my father." I paused a dramatic moment, inwardly snickering at the incredulous expression on March's face. "Boy, was my father angry. Before that, in 1790, when I was ten, there was the Spanish soldier's musket incident. But, really, neither weapon went off."

March cleared his throat. "So for the record, you have never handled a modern firearm?"

"I have not."

"What did you do this past Halloween?" Saber asked.

I blinked at the left-field question. "Huh?"

"Did you attend a party with your roommate? A function in town? How did you spend the evening?"

"I think I watched a *Dresden Files* marathon."

"You didn't dress up?" Saber pressed. "You know, a wig, a cape, fake fangs?"

"I don't extend my real fangs," I said, narrow-eyed. "I wouldn't be caught dead with campy fake ones."

When neither of them fired another tag-team question, I leaned forward, hands clasped on the table, and eyed Detective March.

"I've played nice—without my attorney, I might add—now it's your turn. Does Stony really have an alibi?"

March's gaze held steady. "It's Victor Gorman, and yes, his alibi checks out. He was in Key West from Wednesday morning until this morning."

I blinked. "He's not the one who trashed my truck?"

"Correct."

I tried wrapping my head around the idea that Stony could

be innocent. "I know Key West is like ten hours from here, but it's not completely impossible for him to come back."

"Except," March said, "he was with family members deep sea fishing by day and apparently drinking by night."

He said the last so wryly, I figured the drinking made some impression on the town. Which is hard to do in Key West. That place is wild, or so I hear.

Fishing. Fishing rang a tiny bell, but I couldn't place it.

I felt like the falsely accused heroine in a cozy novel, except that the hot seat wasn't remotely cozy.

"So," I said slowly, "I'm getting the third degree again because my alibi went kaflooey when my tracker did, and the Fourniers happened to be renting a house in the same neighborhood I was in on Wednesday night. Am I right so far?"

March nodded.

"Then again," I continued, "if you're holding this guy, it's been over six hours. Which means you probably found something at his house for you to keep him this long."

"Mr. Gorman is accusing you of setting him up," March said.

"Well, of course he—" I stopped short. To set someone up you need—The light dawned, and I snapped my fingers. "Evidence. You can't set up someone for a crime without it."

Saber remained expressionless, but March cocked his head at me. "What makes you think that?"

"Detective, it's a classic mystery plot element."

He allowed himself a small smile. "We did find a few things—in his house and in the Dumpster of a restaurant nearby."

I spread my hands. "So what am I supposed to have planted?" Then it hit me. "Wait. Fake fangs and a gun. That's why you asked me about them. You found them at Stony's."

"Victor Gorman," March said.

"Whatever. Am I right?"

"Among other things, yes."

"Did you get the cast of my fangs from the state yet?"

"We did, and they don't match the bite mark, but," March said sternly, "that only clears you of biting the victim. Not of shooting her or breaking her neck."

"You honestly think I shot Yolette—a relative stranger—when I don't know squat about guns, *then* broke her neck, *then* bit her with fake fangs, and finally dumped her body in the ocean all to set up a man who made a threat?"

March shot Saber a glance, then looked back at me. "You have that backward," March said.

"I have what backward?" I snapped.

"The victim didn't die from the gunshot. She died from the broken neck."

I felt my eyes widen.

"The Daytona victim's neck was broken, too," Saber added.

"Bu-but it's hard to break a neck, isn't it?"

"How would you know?" Saber asked.

"Mostly TV."

"*CSI?*" March scoffed.

"*Bones,*" I answered, remembering a specific episode of the series. "You have to be a ninja or a special forces guy—or drop someone on their head or something."

"Or have vampire strength?" Saber taunted.

"For your information," I snarled, "I don't use my vampire strength, and the only thing I ever purposely broke was a cooking bowl of my mother's. I was three."

"Uh-huh," Saber drawled. "Let's get back to Gorman. You

told us yesterday afternoon that you would file an assault complaint if you knew his name."

His snide tone fired my temper. "No, I said I *could* have, as in having grounds to do it. Besides, since when is filing an assault complaint equal to setting a guy up for murder?" I snapped my fingers. "Oh, I know. It's not."

"We also found paint cans in the Dumpster," March said, watching me closely.

I sat straighter. "The kind of paint on my truck?"

"That hasn't been ascertained yet."

"I did not vandalize my own truck," I said through gritted teeth. "I just had her repainted and detailed, and it wasn't cheap. And you," I added, pointing at Saber, "told me last night you didn't believe I'd done it. Why would you change your mind?"

Saber gave me a long look. "You have plenty of money. A small fortune, judging by the balance in your bank accounts. You could get that truck fixed ten times over and not feel the pinch."

"Except that I happen to have even more sense than I do money. I take care of my things. I save for the long afterlife I plan to enjoy."

I didn't know what fixing my SSR would cost but consoled myself thinking that it could've been worse. It could've been bombed and set to go off with me in it. Or with people going in and out of the bank parking lot. Yep, it could've been much worse.

"Who knows what kind a vehicle you drive?" March asked.

I answered slowly, thinking. "Let's see, Maggie, Neil, the paint and body shop guys. The bridge club ladies."

"Janie? Mick?" Saber prompted.

"Yes, I'm pretty sure they know."

"What about Holland?" March asked.

"Not unless he saw me driving it." I looked at Saber. "You haven't located him yet?"

"The only Holland Peters we've found," March answered, "died five years ago in Tulsa."

My jaw dropped again. "Why would he give me a false name?"

"I don't know," March said, "but we need a description."

I gave as accurate a description of Gomer (*so* not Holland Peters) as I could—right down to a small mole on the left side of his jaw. I hadn't remembered that until I pictured him in detail.

I also remembered why fishing had rung a faint bell. While Gomer had hung at the back of Tuesday's tour with Stony, I'd eavesdropped every little while. Not that you could call it a conversation, but I overheard Stony say something about trips to deep-sea fish. Specific times or places I didn't hear, but Gomer would've. Who else could have heard the exchange? And, big, huge, this-one's-for-all-the-money question, who would kill Yolette, implicate me, and frame Stony?

"Ms. Marinelli," March said, rather loudly since he was right next to me.

"Yes, what?"

"I understand your roommate and her boyfriend left for the weekend."

"That's right."

"And you've not rented a car?"

"What, are you offering a loaner?"

He rolled his eyes, the first true flash of humor I'd seen from him today.

"I'm offering a deal. I can't hold Mr. Gorman. No matter what else he has or hasn't done, we don't believe his threats against you are idle. In fact, he admitted hearing about the murder and coming back early specifically to hunt you down. For your safety, I've requested that Special Investigator Saber stay with you for the time being."

"Oh, but I'm calling a girlfriend to stay with me."

"Janie Freeman?"

I nodded.

March shook his head. "It won't do. Ms. Freeman is a witness, and she won't be any help protecting you if the need arises."

He turned off the tape recorder and closed the file with my name on it. "You need to be guarded."

"What you mean is, I'm still a suspect."

He inclined his head. "Take it as you like. Either Saber stays with you or you can be a guest of the county."

I didn't know if he could make that threat stick, but I do know when not to push my luck.

Afterlife is full of challenges. I was stuck with Saber, but I'd deal with his surly attitude. I'd hunker down in my room and have as little as possible to do with him.

No chance for my libido to go haywire.

Much.

In the parking lot on the way to his SUV, Saber told me he'd already checked out of his hotel and would take me straight to the penthouse. As we settled into his Vue, I glanced at the digital clock on the dashboard. Seven o'clock. Good. Traffic might have thinned by now, which meant less time stuck only touching distance away from the man. And, if he'd cooperate, I'd still make dance class. I'd like to be in control of *some*thing again.

"I don't suppose," he said as we cut off U.S. 1 to take the downtown route, "you have food in the fridge."

"Probably not. Maggie eats out and makes sandwiches a lot." I stole a glance at his profile. "You could go eat while I'm taking my salsa class."

He shook his head. "I'm not leaving you alone."

"No problem. The class is taught in a restaurant. You like Spanish food?"

We stopped at the light where A1A cut over to Vilano Beach, like the twentieth car in line. So much for traffic thinning.

Saber edged his aviator shades down his nose and looked over the rims at me. "You're not even going to try to make this assignment easy, are you?"

I shrugged. "Where's the hardship in eating out?"

"That's not what I meant."

"You're the one who agreed to play jailer."

"Bodyguard."

"Whatever. You could've pulled rank on March and refused."

"I figured," he said as the light turned and the cars in front of us accelerated, "you'd rather have me around over going to jail or being with a complete stranger."

"I've got news for you, Saber. You're strange enough."

"There's the pot calling the kettle black."

I crossed my arms over the seat belt strap. "I'm not the least bit strange. I'm just trying to have a normal afterlife."

"You're a vampire. There's nothing normal about it. Vampires don't take dance lessons. They don't play bridge. They don't, for God's sake, surf."

Everybody's a critic. I ground my teeth as he braked again. Now we were tenth in line. "What's your point, Saber?"

"You're not mortal, Francesca," he said, his eyes again hidden behind the aviator shades. "Stop trying to blend."

His use of my given name slowed my tongue for one second before I lit into him.

"I am *not* trying to blend. I've never hidden what I am. Hell, I have to be registered like a stinking sex offender," I fumed. "As for dancing, playing bridge, and surfing, maybe I'm ahead of my time. Maybe I want something more out of life than hanging out in nightclubs and being all woo-woo vampiric."

"Maybe you're afraid of being what you are."

"What's that supposed to mean?"

"You've been out in the world since when?"

"Last August. So what?"

"How many times have you intentionally used your vampire speed?"

"Once."

"And your vampire strength?"

"Twice on stuck jar lids."

"And what other powers do you use?"

"None."

"Wrong. You walk in the sun."

I snorted. "That's not a power. It's just a—"

"Do all the other vampires walk in the sun?"

"Hell, I don't know. I haven't known any in centuries."

"Day-walking is a power. Your vampire senses are a power,

and you have at least a half-dozen others you haven't tapped. You're a vampire. Be who you are."

I balled up a fist to smack him, but checked the impulse as the line of cars moved again. I *was* being me, and I didn't care what Saber thought. He was less than nothing to me. A man I wouldn't have met if it hadn't been for Yolette's murder. Sure he was wrong, but why argue with a mule?

Well fine. Saber didn't get me, and I didn't get him. That would just make it easier to ignore him altogether. Ignore the way his tanned hands gripped the steering wheel. Ignore the way his thigh muscles bunched when he hit the brake. Ignore the virility that rolled off him, and remember that he was just a temporary annoyance.

Finally we arrived home, Saber taking Maggie's parking space. I hopped out before he turned off the engine and headed around the corner to the building entrance.

"Don't even think of locking me out," he called as he pulled the strap of a black nylon duffel bag over his shoulder and strode after me.

"Then hurry it up. I need to change for class."

"Funny," he said as we both stepped through the door, "I don't remember saying I'd take you to this class."

I stopped and turned on him. "Saber, you keep pointing out that I am a vampire, a fact I'm well aware of, thank you. How hard would it be for me to throw you into next year?"

He stepped close enough to be almost toe-to-toe. "You might be able to pull that off, but I *am* armed. With silver ammo."

I snorted. "Apparently my speed can trump your silver bullets, so let's get something straight. Barring danger to others or myself, I'll do what I want when I want. You don't want to drive me to class? I'll get there on my own."

"And if I tell you there is danger at any time?"

"If I don't think you're lying, I'll defer to you. We clear?"

He shrugged, but I took that as a yes and marched off toward the elevators. I punched in the code, not bothering to hide it from him, and we rode up in silence. Once in the penthouse, I told him to drop his stuff in the living room. No way was I letting him step a foot in Maggie's room without asking her first. Yikes! She was going to have a cow when I told her Saber was staying after all.

I checked messages, and sure enough Maggie had called. I snagged the extension and dialed the number on the way to my room. No answer, but voice mail clicked on, and I left a brief, highly edited message saying Saber was with me, I was going to dance class, and I'd call her when I returned.

I chucked my clothes and stepped in the shower for ten minutes. The steaming water eased my stress less than I hoped because it triggered memories of that erotic dream. Damn the timing. I gave myself a stern lecture that my libido and Saber didn't mix as I dried off and donned the red bra and panties I'd broken down and bought myself for Valentine's Day.

I applied a little more makeup, rearranged my ponytail, and slipped into one of the few dressy outfits I own: a filmy red, pink, and green hibiscus-patterned skirt and a red scoop-neck blouse with short sleeves. Red was a power color, right? Well, I was going all out tonight. I dug my red pumps with the two-inch heels out of the closet and was ready.

Back in the living room, Saber sat parked in front of the

TV watching ESPN. Did his eyes flick to me as I came in? Who cared? I was ignoring him, right? I crossed to the table where I'd tossed my purse, pulled out a credit card, a twenty dollar bill, and my key.

"I'm ready," I said and headed for the door.

Saber pushed the Off button on the remote, stood slowly, and turned to me. In the time it took him to look me over from head to toe to head again, I could've changed clothes another three times. Maybe I *should've* changed, because I didn't want to like the way his cobalt blue eyes gleamed. In appreciation, I thought, until he opened his mouth.

"Is this a fancy restaurant you're dragging me to?"

I rolled my eyes. "This is a tourist town, Saber. Nothing is that fancy except the Casa Monica Hotel."

"Then why are you—" He flipped a hand at me. "—dressed up? You have a boyfriend we don't know about?"

"I wish," I muttered. "Can we go already?"

TWELVE

Café Cascada was usually packed on a Friday night, the multiple fountains with their mini-waterfalls a tinkling background music to dining. Tonight, it seemed quieter, the lighting seemed dimmer, more intimate.

Danielle, part-time hostess, part-time dance instructor, greeted us before Saber and I got all the way in the door. Looking gorgeous in her full, iridescent blue skirt and off-white peasant blouse, her flame-colored hair loose around her shoulders, she beamed at us.

"Francesca, you brought a dance partner tonight. How delightful!"

"No, no, Danielle," I denied, "he's just here to eat."

"Not to dance?" She gave Saber a blatantly feminine appraisal—one I wished I could pull off—and stepped closer to him. "What a shame. You look like you can move."

He waggled his brows. "I can."

I restrained myself from doing an eye roll.

"He's hungry, Danielle. For food. He hasn't eaten all day." I shoved Saber toward a table—which was rather like shoving my truck—but I got him to a table for two.

"Go ahead, Saber," I said, motioning to the chair. "Sit, eat, have some wine. The class won't last too long."

Danielle, who had followed, pulled the chair out for him, something I'd never see her do for other guests. He rewarded her by aiming a dazzling smile over his shoulder. At me he smirked.

I escaped—okay, flounced—through the arched doorway into a slightly smaller room ringed with dining tables for two and four. The middle of the floor was left open for dancing, but it looked to be a tiny group compared to most Fridays.

The Franklins, a middle-aged couple, sipped their usual sangrias. Two blonde women I didn't recognize, who couldn't have been much over twenty, sported tight jeans and tighter sweaters. They drank something dark from clear glasses—rum and cola, I thought, though the rich aromas of the restaurant almost overrode the smell of the liquor.

When the salsa music started, Danielle made her entrance in a swirl of skirts. We reviewed the steps, spending more time on review because this was the blondes' first class, and because a few diners who had finished joined the fun.

After fifteen or twenty minutes, we began dancing in earnest, and I lost myself and all sense of time in the music and movement and energy of the dance. Mr. Franklin gamely took turns partnering the three of us singles, but we didn't mind practicing the steps on our own. We laughed, swayed our hips, and twirled to the driving rhythm. I was having a blast, until I twirled smack into Saber.

I knew I hit him hard enough to send him reeling. He didn't.

Instead, I bounced off his body, and he reached out to steady me, his hands on my upper arms. My mostly bare upper arms that now crawled with goose bumps.

I reached for my hair as if to straighten my ponytail, and his hands fell away, but his mischievous grin stayed put.

"Finished with dinner already?" I asked, a little more breathless than I wanted to sound.

"Decided to catch the floor show," he said, "up close and personal."

I blinked. His looks, which had struck me as vaguely Latino the first time I saw him, now seemed more so. Even his startling cobalt blue eyes spoke of Latin passion and seemed to challenge me. I felt suddenly hot, the salsa music thrummed in my body, and a nanosecond later, he stepped into me. He gripped my waist and hand, and moved to the rhythm.

Body memory is a wonderful thing. It lets you move in ways you know by instinct—or by practice—while your brain is screaming "Oh. My. God."

My brain screamed that and more, but I didn't break free of Saber. I didn't want to. I simply let myself follow his lead, even when he changed the dance from salsa to merengue.

I went from hot to flash point when he plastered us pelvis-to-pelvis and rocked to the driving beat. His blatantly sensual gaze held me in thrall. The brush of our bodies made me forget to breathe, but I met him step for timeless step. When I was nothing but molten cells, he dipped me so low, my hair brushed the floor. I didn't even realize he held my leg behind the knee until applause started and he caressed the bare skin up my thigh as he helped me stand again.

"Wonderful, wonderful," Danielle exclaimed from behind me.

I scrambled out of Saber's arms and turned, breathing harder than I thought was possible for me. At my back, Saber didn't sound the slightest bit winded.

"Really," Danielle continued, "I've never seen the merengue danced with such passion. You two could win a competition."

Saber gave her a little bow. "Thanks for letting me horn in on your class, Danielle."

She grinned broadly and patted his arm. "Anytime, honey."

She dismissed class and reminded us that she wouldn't be teaching next week. The Franklins looked disappointed, the coeds, crushed. They shot drooling gazes at Saber.

"Ready to go home?" he asked, taking my elbow to escort me from the restaurant.

Home with Saber? After an intimate dance that made my erotic dreams look like patty-cake? Ay-yi-yi. He might be my jailer, but there was no way I was ready to be completely alone with him right now. What could we do with the rest of the night?

Oh, wait! Wal-Mart. Nothing remotely erotic about Wal-Mart, right? Not much erotic about Target or Kmart or a dozen other stores, either, but Wal-Mart was open 24-7!

Now if I could just get him to take me there.

"Don't tell me a manly man like you can't be seen at Wal-Mart. Heck, Saber, nobody in town knows you."

Oh yes, he'd driven me to the store, but he'd groused about it the whole way.

I took a shopping cart from the nice cart lady at the door, looked over my shoulder and said, "Let's go."

Since Maggie really didn't keep much food in the refrigerator—or the cabinets for that matter—I headed to the grocery department first.

"We have Saturday and part of Sunday to get through. What do you want to eat?" I asked.

"Will it bother you if I broil a steak?"

"Broil away."

I pointed him toward the meat counter and followed at a distance with the cart—the distance because the smell of meat turns my stomach, even in a store. The odor of cooking meat is worse, but what could I expect when the villagers had deep-roasted vampires, and I'd had to smell it? On the other hand, I love the aroma of charcoal. Go figure.

After he grabbed the biggest T-bone in the case, Saber moved on to the vegetables, where he picked up a bag of pretossed salad and baking potatoes. Next we moved to dairy, where he snagged real butter, sour cream, and a package of cubed cheddar cheese. As we moved up and down the other aisles, he added two kinds of steak sauce to the cart along with salad dressing and a box of animal crackers. The dressing was French, a sharp reminder of why we were together in the first place. The animal crackers? Maybe he ate creatures now instead of hunting them, but the choice was rather endearing.

When he was satisfied with his grocery selections, I wheeled the cart toward the clothing section.

"You're not buying Wal-Mart clothes, are you?"

"Actually, I'm looking at purses, but what do you have against Wal-Mart fashions?"

He shook his head. "Vampires don't wear Wal-Mart."

"They don't know what they're missing," I said as I paused

and eyed the purses. A quick look told me they didn't have the
color I was looking for. I'd try Bealls Outlet another time.

I wheeled through the women's department to a major aisle
and turned right to head toward the back of the store.

"Didn't like the purses?" Saber asked, trailing behind me.

"I need a different color."

"So now what are you looking for?"

"The classic movies they have on DVD."

"And then what?"

"Oh, I don't know," I said, waving a hand. "I might price an
external hard drive for my computer. Wander through the small
appliances. Pick up self-tanning lotion and hair straightener."

"Your hair is fine the way it is."

My heart stuttered a beat. "It is?"

"Yes, and stop fishing for compliments. You're milking this
Wal-Mart trip to annoy me, aren't you?"

I stopped the cart, my back to the sporting goods section.

"You know, now I understand why women hate to take men
shopping. Sheesh! What are you in such a hurry to do? Is bas-
ketball on tonight? 'March Madness'?"

"I want to review the narrative with you," he said, all business. "A woman is dead, and you're involved, however inno-
cently. You saw something or heard something that might help
find the killer."

"So you *don't* think I did it?"

"No."

"Oh," I said, biting my lip and feeling ashamed. "And if I
didn't remember to write this particular thing?"

"We'll go over and over those two days until we find the key.
Unless you want March to put your butt in prison."

"Prison, hell," a gravelly voice said behind me. "You ought to be executed."

I whirled to find Stony—Victor Gorman—not five feet away and closing fast. He was dressed like a black ops guy from TV, but with less gear. Worse, he carried a box of gun cartridges in one hand and a bow—as in bow and arrow—in the other.

"You have some goddamn nerve setting me up," Gorman growled. "I could kill you right now and be glad to die for the cause."

Saber stepped in front of me, and I let him. "Mr. Gorman, I'll remind you I'm a state investigator and caution you to watch what you say."

Gorman gave Saber the evil eye and pointed the tip of the bow at him. "What the hell are you doin' here with...that. You used ta kill these things, and now you're shoppin' with 'em?"

I leaned around Saber. "Hey, I have excellent taste."

"You're not helping," Saber warned me, then turned back to Gorman. "In light of your new threats, if Ms. Marinelli turns up with so much as a stubbed toe, I'll be sure we haul you in for it. Do you understand me?"

"Ms. Marinelli?" He sneered and raked my sole dressy outfit with a look of disgust. "Dress 'er up any way you want, but she's a fuckin' parasite. I got the right to free speech, and you can't tell me different." He shifted his cold blue eyes to me. "You're gonna pay for killin' that Frenchie, bitch. I know where to find you."

With a last glare, he spun and stalked back to the sporting goods counter. If Wal-Mart carried missile launchers, he was fired up enough to walk out with a dozen.

Saber faced me and put his hands on his hips, but I was way ahead of him.

I made a NASCAR-worthy one eighty with the shopping cart and headed to checkout.

I changed while Saber put the groceries away. We hadn't talked much on the way back, but I knew Saber was ticked from the way his hands had clenched the steering wheel. If he'd been using vampire strength, he would've crushed it to dust.

The confrontation had shaken me, but I was calm by the time I called Maggie again. She took the news of Saber staying at the penthouse in stride when I told her he was protecting me from Gorman. Fine, she said. The linens on her bed were clean because she'd anticipated Janie using her room. All in all, not the ordeal I thought the conversation would be.

In my jeans and St. Augustine T-shirt, I walked barefoot into the dining area to join Saber at the table, where he sat reading my notes. His eyes held no warmth, no appraisal now. Nothing to make my tummy flutter, but it did anyway. Maybe it was just his holstered weapon on the table.

"Find the missing links?" I asked, hoping against hope he had. Especially when I noticed a chair set squarely beside his.

"No, but I have a list of questions."

He turned the page of a white legal pad, headed it *Suspects*, and wrote Victor Gorman's name first.

I tapped the page as I sat. "I thought you'd cleared him."

He shrugged. "In light of the threats he made tonight, he's staying on the list. Let's start with what he said and did, and how the others reacted."

I closed my eyes and started from the beginning—from the first time I noticed him until he stormed out of Scarlett's—while Saber took notes.

"So the French couple indicated that Gorman had been following them even before they all showed up for the tour."

"Right. Yolette said he was spoiling their honeymoon, and I told her they should report it to the police."

"Which she didn't."

"No. I specifically asked on Tuesday when Yolette threw a fit about Gorman being on the tour again."

"Cover the time after Gorman left the tour on Monday."

Again I closed my eyes to picture the scene. "We walked back to the substation chatting. I asked why Yolette and Etienne came to St. Augustine for their wedding trip, then Millie asked if they were staying in a B and B downtown."

"And that's when you knew where to find them."

"No," I snapped. "I never knew where to find them, and I didn't want to."

"Then what exactly did they say?"

"They were staying in a modern place on the beach where they watched the sunrise."

"That's it?"

"You want to hear this or argue with me over every detail?"

"Go on."

"That's about the time Yolette made a crack about Millie's perfume. She said it was strong, and that her first husband—no wait, her *late* husband—had an aunt who overused Shalimar."

"Was Millie insulted?"

"She was when Yolette said it had made the dead husband

sick." I paused. "In fact, Millie looked more than insulted. She looked—"

"Angry?"

"Stricken. Insulted, but sort of sad at the same time."

"Then what?"

"Millie asked how Yolette's husband died, and Etienne said it was an accident." I looked at the table, then back at him. "But in my head I heard, *Murder.*"

He gave me the narrowed eyes. "In your head?"

I took a deep breath and blew it out. "I'm psychic, okay? I mean when I'm not blocked by the dark of the moon, I can hear thoughts, or I have flashes about people or have the occasional vision. Not constantly, but more if I focus. That night it was close to a new moon, but the energy of the group must've been so weird that I picked up the odd thing here and there."

"Why can't you do this all the time?"

"Beats me. It's like a channel with various amounts of static at various times. Something will burst through, then static again."

"So when you picked up *Murder,* who was thinking it?"

"That's the thing. I don't know." I got up to pace around the table. "I thought it was Millie at first, just because she was the one who asked about the dead husband. But the voice sounded more masculine in my head."

"So Etienne said it was an accident and you, what? Simultaneously heard *Murder* in your head? Heard it afterwards?"

I stopped pacing. "It was more simultaneous."

"Can you smell lies, Cesca?"

I shook my head. "Not exactly. I can smell a change in body

odor when people are under stress. Sometimes that means they're lying, sometimes it's just nerves."

"So you didn't detect that either of the Fourniers were lying."

"No, but people lie effortlessly all the time."

He rubbed his face. "Point taken. What about the guy you call Gomer? Where was he?"

"Watching the Fourniers." I closed my eyes and tried to picture him. "He was tense, but that's all I remember."

"And you didn't see him at Scarlett's later?"

"No. I didn't sense him around at all, but then I didn't sense the Fourniers or Stony in the restaurant either."

"Did Gomer seem to know anyone on the tour? Hang around anyone?"

"He stuck close to the wiseguys—the men who sounded like *Sopranos* characters. Gorman stayed close to the Fourniers. The rest of the tourists stayed in the groups they came in."

"How about Tuesday? Your notes say the Fourniers seemed to have had a fight."

"They weren't lovey-dovey like on Monday, and Yolette was in a real snit about something."

"How did Etienne act?"

"Like he didn't care. He flirted with me, but I gave him the brush-off. Then he walked with Millie and her ladies, Yolette walked in front of them right behind the writer group. Gomer walked with Gorman."

"Did you overhear any conversations?"

"Nothing that struck me until Detective March said Gorman had been fishing. Then I remembered hearing Gomer and

Gorman talking about deep-sea fishing, and Gorman mentioned a trip."

"He tell Gomer where or when?"

I shook my head. "Not that I heard. When I tuned in to them, I was listening for trouble, not a vacation report."

Saber jotted more notes, then tore a fresh sheet of paper from the pad and handed it to me. "Grab a pen and help me summarize this."

Can you say please? I thought but snagged a pen from the junk drawer. This all seemed jumbled to me. Maybe writing the key points would crystallize the information.

"Let's start with Gorman," Saber said, as I wrote. "Hates vampires. Made overt threats against Cesca and the Fourniers. Confirmed member of the Covenant. Weapons found in his home, two being tested for ballistics match. May have known where victim was staying, but alibi in Key West during times of both the murder and vandalism."

Saber glanced up from his notes. "Need me to slow down?"

"Nope, I'm fine. Who's next?"

"Gomer aka Holland Peters. Gave false name to Cesca. Knew Fourniers were staying in a house on the beach, but did he know where? Carries concealed. May have known details of Gorman's fishing trip. Motive to kill Yolette? Motive to vandalize truck? Why lie about identity?"

Saber paused and shuffled his papers.

"Next we have Millie. Didn't like Fourniers and seemed to disapprove of Yolette. Yolette insulted her. Any connection to Yolette's dead husband? Carries concealed. Motive to kill? If related to the dead husband, could be revenge, but for what? Did

Millie know where couple was staying? Did she know Yolette would be on honeymoon in St. Augustine? If so, how?"

"It does stretch coincidence to be on the same tour by pure dumb luck," I said.

"By light-years," Saber agreed. "Let's do Mick next."

"It's a waste of energy and paper to list him."

"Cesca."

"All right. Shoot."

"Mick. Didn't seem to like or dislike the Fourniers. Unlikely he knew where they were staying. Has a bad history with vampires but appears friendly with Cesca. Has gun permit but doesn't appear to carry. Might kill to protect Cesca or Janie."

Saber paused. "Did you get all that?"

"No, I played tic-tac-toe instead."

He flashed a grin and tapped my paper. "We're almost done. Etienne Fournier. Opportunity a given. Means possible, though no weapons found when house searched. Motive? Bears looking into. Yolette ticked with him on Tuesday night. Why? Did he have anything to do with death of first husband? Did she?"

I finished and looked up. "Shouldn't we list what we know about Yolette herself?"

"Go for it."

"Yolette," I wrote as I talked. "Widowed, maybe by accident, maybe by murder. Etienne second husband. Or were there more? How long had she known him? Claims they had sex with vampires. Did she and the now-dead husband also have sex with vampires? Claims Gorman followed them around the city prior to Monday. How long had they been here? Peeved with Etienne on Tuesday. Why? Run-in with Millie. Could Yolette's dead husband be Millie's nephew? Yolette said she never met the aunt. Would Millie know who Yolette is? Know that Yolette would be in St. Augustine?"

When I finished the list, I looked at Saber. "So what now?"

"Until we get a lead on Gomer, I talk to March about digging deeper into the Fourniers and Millie."

"Why not do a little digging ourselves? There are lots of resources online."

"We can try it." He cleared his throat. "I want to go back to something else, though."

"For Pete's sake, what? I've told you everything."

"You haven't," he said steadily, "told me how you became a vampire."

I went still for a split second, then said lightly, "You mean what was a nice girl like me doing with a nasty bunch of monsters?"

He shrugged. "Something like that."

"Well, it's not like I raised my hand and said, 'Bite me, bite me.'" I flipped a hand as if to bat away the question. "It's ancient history. Why do you care?"

"Because you're so damned determined to be an unvampire, and I want to know why." He caught my hand and tugged me into the chair beside him. "What did the monsters do to you, Cesca?"

THIRTEEN

I didn't want to go there, to the dark time when I'd lost control of my life and my future. I'd despised being a victim, but I hadn't been strong enough to end my own half-life in order to escape the demi-hell that had been Normand's court.

Now Saber was asking questions I'd hoped he wouldn't. Unlike the newspaper reporter who'd written of Maggie's rescuing me, Saber would pester and probe until I spilled my guts enough to make him happy.

Or he thought I'd spilled my guts. But I was in charge, and I went for flippant and light like I always do.

"Other than change my entire life, not much. No beating, no raping." I paused. "Actually, I was bored stiff most of those three years."

"You're dodging me. You were psychic before they caught you, right? Normand—" He pronounced it as the French would. "—knew you. He had his eye on you all along. Am I right?"

"He and an old suitor of mine, yeah," I admitted. "How did you know?"

He kept his gaze level. "I've studied vampires for a long time. Even the modern ones like to have a psychic or witch or sensitive of some kind around. It's a power thing, and if the person won't cooperate willingly, the vamps threaten families and friends." He paused. "That happen in your case?"

I nodded. "I gave a few command performance readings when I was the mortal me, but the king always let me go home. He cooked his own goose when he turned me, though. Being underalive screwed with The Gift."

His mouth twitched. "Bet he was ticked."

"And then some," I agreed. Old Normand had been so angry, he'd turned redder than the blood he drank.

"Who was the old suitor?"

I sighed and considered barricading myself in the bathroom, but I'd have to come out sooner or later—to face myself if not Saber. Maybe it was time to talk. Maybe the dark time wouldn't seem so bleak if I did. And maybe a cup of peach tea would help.

"We all went to school together," I said as I got up to put water in the electric teakettle, Saber turning to watch. "In fact, we went to the oldest schoolhouse down on St. George Street. Triton was the adopted son of a Greek fisherman, and Marco was the son of a soldier who came in the second Spanish period. Triton and I had known each other since we were three or so, and we were so close we read each other's minds."

"You loved him?" Saber asked.

"Yes, and Marco was jealous. He courted me—he and a few others who weren't terrified of The Gift. I couldn't stand any of them. I would've married Triton in a heartbeat, but there were, um, obstacles."

"Family objections? Religious differences?"

"No, our families expected us to marry."

I set the kettle on its warmer and leaned a hip against the counter, editing the story I'd give Saber as I went along. I wasn't about to tell him Triton had shape-shifted into a dolphin every new moon. Saber would think I was making it up or completely nutso. Besides, the truth about Triton was none of his business.

"So," Saber broke into my thoughts with his rumbling voice, "you loved Triton, and the families didn't object. Why didn't you marry him?"

"He thought of me as a sister, not a wife," I answered lightly. "Anyway, my parents didn't force me to marry, so I turned my suitors down flat. Marco was the last of them, and I was almost twenty then. He swore he'd make me pay, and I blew him off. About a month later, the king sent for me again, and there was Marco. He was one of them."

"Marco set the trap to capture you?"

"Yes, but not until a month after my twentieth birthday."

"About the time Normand would consider you mature, but not over the hill." Saber was quiet a minute, then asked, "Did Normand give you to Marco?"

"No, and it's one of the few things I can thank him for. The king himself turned me, then kept me darn near cloistered. After a while I realized that I woke up hours before the rest of them. I figured out how to get out of Normand's house and back in before anyone else was awake, but it took me almost a year to work up the nerve to leave the grounds."

"Bet you scared the shit out of people."

I kept looking at Saber but saw my terrified mother and sisters-in-law, the horror in their faces and their screams to spare them and the children. After that, I stuck to contacting Triton to pass him information about the vampires. A few months later, I begged him to get my family out of town.

"The vampires," Saber continued, "they didn't figure out you were a day-walker?"

"I was careful and, if I do say so myself, pretty crafty. By the second year, Marco suspected. He was busy working himself up to be Normand's main enforcer. Which was fitting, since Marco was good at pushing the other people around."

"Vampires."

"Huh?"

"They weren't people anymore."

"Whatever," I said as the kettle shut off with a snap.

I plopped tea bags in mugs—peach for me, Earl Grey for Saber since he'd had it Thursday. I poured the water, fuming that Saber didn't think of me as people. I sure wasn't chopped liver.

I set napkins and the mugs on the table and settled in my chair. "The point I was making is that Marco finally convinced the king that he should be my mate. His plan was for me to lure soldiers, turn them, and increase the king's power base."

"Bet that went over well."

I remembered the scene. "Oh, yeah. It was the first time I wanted to use my vampire speed and strength and snap Marco's nasty neck. Normand refused to give me to Marco for months, I think to play with Marco's head. A power trip thing. Then Marco told him about my daylight escapes."

"He knew for sure?"

I nodded.

"How'd he find out?"

"Talking to the townspeople. Marco had decided to knock off Normand and take over. He'd been riling up the men in town and the soldiers at the fort. Someone saw me and told him."

"Did your Gift warn you about this plot?"

"Not until the night the king decided to punish me for my excursions. We were coming off a new moon, but I had a vision. The villagers were coming to slaughter and burn us out. All of us. Marco had betrayed Normand, but the townspeople double-crossed Marco. I didn't tell the king any of it."

"Why not?" he asked softly.

I took a sip of cooling tea. "Because I hated him for making me a vampire."

"So you, what?"

"I let him lock me in the casket, let his slaves wrap it in silver chain, and then I waited for the mob."

"You were raised Catholic, right? You couldn't kill yourself, but the mob could do it."

"Except they didn't find me."

I heard the screams in my head, the cries for mercy, even the cries for death as bodies burned. The fire roared above the ground, and I'd felt the earth scorch.

"Was Marco destroyed?"

"I guess so. He knew I was buried with Normand's treasure, and he would've wanted that, even if he killed me to get it." I hesitated. "For a while after Maggie found me, I was terrified Marco would come gunning for me. Since he hasn't, I have to think he's dead."

Saber was quiet for a full minute—had to be a record—and I let the memories fade.

"Two hundred years without feeding? You should have been insane when Maggie found you. You should've torn her to shreds. How did you survive?"

The question wasn't snide—well, not much. I thought he was reaching out to understand me. I sighed and reached back.

"You know what astral traveling is?" I asked.

"More or less."

"That's how I survived. I projected myself to the outside world and fed on energy."

He looked surprised, then disgusted. "You drained people psychically?"

So much for reaching out, except to smack him. That sounded good. Or dumping hot tea on his head.

"For your information, I never *drained* anyone. I looked for angry people to feed on because they had energy to burn. A few of them even got nicer afterward." I paused a beat. "Of course, during World War II, I tried to get to Hitler. He was too far away, so I went for the guys in the U-boats off the coast."

He shook his head. "I almost bought that."

"Hey, you asked, I'm answering. Believe what you want."

I took another swallow of tea and stared him down.

"Why don't you use your vamp powers?"

"Like what? Vampire speed? Maybe it makes me dizzy."

"Why do you drive a car and ride a bicycle?"

"Because I like things with wheels?"

"Can you fly?"

"You have Tinkerbell in your pocket with pixie dust handy? I promise you I can think happy little thoughts. Like having you out of my afterlife." I stood and fisted my hands on my hips. "Why are you so bent, Saber? Why do I have to conform to your narrow-minded view of vampires?"

"Because I—"

He broke off, his cobalt eyes darkening as he rose to face me. He radiated a tumble of anger and frustration and—

Pheromones. I smelled pheromones.

One musky scent was strong and seductive and Saber's.

Another, that faint scent of musk, the one I'd smelled every time I'd been with him, lay under the strong scent. And if it wasn't his, it had to be...

Mine?

I inhaled a desperately deep breath and oh my gosh! It *was* my scent. I had pheromones for Saber!

My little voice screamed, *Run*, and I backpedaled, forgetting the chair right behind me. My legs hit the seat, my butt hit the chair back, and I fell flat on my back, smacking my head on the hardwood floor for good measure.

Stars dotted my vision, distorting the expression on Saber's face as he stood over me.

"I don't know what brought that on," he said, "but it proves one thing."

"Wh-what?" I asked, still stunned.

"You can't fly."

Embarrassing as it was to take a fall for a man like Saber, at least I proved something to him. Not the no-fly thing; the vampires-can-get-hurt thing. I had a bump the size of an egg on the back of my head for a full half hour. Saber even put an ice pack on it after he noticed my eyes weren't tracking just right.

I'll give him this. Other than his first crack, he didn't rub my clumsiness in my face. He merely gave me a hand up, righted the chair, and asked to use my laptop.

Of course, I wasn't about to let him snoop in my room or my computer files. Not that I had anything to hide—except a giant stuffed dolphin on my bed—but it was the principle of the thing. On the other hand, I wasn't sitting beside him again, too close for comfort. So, at nearly one in the morning, he sat at the dining table surfing for information on the Fourniers and Millie, while I tried to read the lecture on mid-century modern design I'd printed. I say tried, because my real task was trying to get over scenting my own pheromones.

Me attracted to Saber in more than the most superficial gee-ain't-he-gorgeous way? How scary is that?

He irritated me—a fly buzzing the picnic of my afterlife just begging to be swatted. Oh, I felt some lust, all right, but I couldn't imagine being tangled in the sheets with Saber. Heck, if I weren't vampire enough to make him happy, I sure wouldn't be woman enough. He'd be ragging me at the first hint of my inexperience.

"You committing that page to memory for life?"

I startled and looked up to find him watching me. I wondered how long—and if I'd been making faces thinking about sex with him.

"Did you find anything online?"

"You were born June 23, 1780, wear a size four, and have an IQ of one sixty-two, based on testing and observation of your learning curve, which—" He squinted at the computer screen. "—the psychological tester called phenomenal."

I did the intelligent, mature thing. I crossed my eyes at him. "I meant did you trace Yolette's first husband."

"Yolette Marie Girard Fournier wasn't married in the States. No marriage license application on file."

"Girard? How did you get her maiden name?"

"Her passport."

"Ah, of course. Did you trace Millie?"

"Not far enough. I got a street and unit address, so I figure she lives in a condo."

"Wow, single homes don't have unit numbers? They teach you that in detective school?"

"You have an unvampire headache from your fall, or are you just being bitchy?"

"Where does Millie live?"

"In Captain's Harbor. I got her deceased husband's name, found his obit and their marriage application."

"But you can't trace her relatives?"

"I'll pick up there tomorrow while you work with the artist on the sketch of Gomer."

"She might be on my tour again tomorrow. We could question her then."

"We could, huh? Is that the royal we, Princess? Didn't you tell Maggie you wouldn't give a weekend tour?"

"You'll be there, and Millie already likes me."

"No. You're not trained in interrogation techniques."

"So coach me," I said before I clearly thought that through. Spend more time with Saber? Maybe not.

He gave me a long look, one that warmed and darkened his eyes. My skin tingled, and the faint bouquet of my own phero-mones tickled my nose again. Time for a subject change.

"Fine, question her yourself, but you have to admit it's a good opportunity to do it casually." I tapped my lecture printout on the table to straighten the pages and rose. "If you're finished with my computer, I have a chair to design."

"One more question."

"What?" I said through clenched teeth.

"If I fall asleep, you promise you won't leave the condo?"

"I'm not going anywhere tonight."

"What are you doing after you finish your design?"

"Watching my *Magnum* marath— Oh, wait. I forgot to pick up the mail. I'll be right back."

I dashed into my room to get my keys and back out to find Saber waiting at the door.

"What, I can't get the mail by myself?"

"You can, but you're not going to. I'm coming with you."

Please don't, I wanted to say, but I rode the elevator down with him, staying as far away as I could without being too obvious.

The mailboxes were around the corner from the elevator near the tenant entrance, where they were convenient for the mailman. I sped toward them but stopped short when I heard the unearthly caterwauling.

"What the hell?" Saber said behind me.

In unison, we sprinted to the leaded-glass door and looked out to find Cat yowling and pacing around a man crumpled facedown on the tiled landing outside. A man whose face was turned from us but who was dressed pseudo black ops, like Victor Gorman had been just hours ago.

The smell of blood was thick and sharp and far too strong.

* * *

I try to face the challenges of afterlife head-on, but, except for the first month out of my box, I'd never had a week as confusing as this one. Or one less fun.

I guess I'd been in denial about the faint musky scent being my own pheromones, and I'd still like to deny that. I sure hadn't given much thought to Cat suddenly showing up—and showing up so often.

Now it was time to pay attention.

So, while I waited in the Flagler Hospital ER for Saber and Detective March to bring word about Gorman's condition, I considered it. Or rather, her.

Cat had prowled around Gorman's prone body twice more before she gazed straight into my eyes and that sense of magick had scraped my skin like extra coarse sandpaper. This was obviously no common house cat, but was Cat a shifter like Triton—sometimes in human form, sometimes in animal form? Or could magical animals themselves change sizes the way I was certain Cat had that first night in the fog? I didn't know enough about shape-shifting in general to hazard much of a guess, but I could boot up my computer and find answers pretty darn soon.

If I got out of the hospital before I had to meet the sketch artist at the sheriff's office.

Not five minutes later, I heard footsteps, Saber's voice and March's along with the St. Augustine officer who'd been assigned to wait to talk with Gorman.

I jumped up from my seat as they trooped in, and Saber motioned me to the deserted hallway.

"Well?" I prompted, looking in turn at each of their haggard faces.

March looked at the St. Augustine uniformed officer, whose name badge read MICHAELS and got a small nod.

"Gorman will make it," March said, "but he won't be talking to us tonight."

I let out a breath I didn't know I'd held. "How bad is he?"

"He has a pretty good concussion," Saber answered, "cracked ribs, contusions, and possible spleen damage."

"Geez, who would do that?" I said, shaking my head. "None of this makes sense."

"Ms. Marinelli," Officer Michaels said, "Special Investigator Saber went over Gorman's behavior at Wal-Mart. Is there any way he could've been breaking into the building?"

I shrugged. "I doubt it. If he did get in, he'd have to have a code for the elevator to go to the penthouse level, *and* a key to the condo door. Unless he had a battering ram handy."

The youngish officer cocked his head. "Did you say anything about going out? Could he have been waiting for you?"

"No. The only reason I was downstairs at all was because I forgot to pick up my mail. Like I said, it makes no sense."

"Tell me about it," March said dryly. "Look, you and Saber go back to your place. He'll bring you to the station to see the sketch artist at eight, then maybe you can both get some sleep."

I glanced at Saber, and it hit me that, with Gorman no longer a threat, he didn't have to bodyguard me. Did I want to bring that up? I sighed. No.

Being rid of Saber might make me pheromone-free, but I was too tired, too stressed, and too confused to rock the boat—leaky as it was. If I felt that way, Saber and March had to be dead on their feet.

Sometimes you just have to go with the afterlife flow.

Cosmil stood in the perfect circle of trees. Above his open, out-stretched hands, a glass sphere so ancient its origins were lost in time hovered in the air. At his feet, Earth pulsed her ancient rhythm into his body. The change was complete. Triton was man again this night, this moment. The sphere captured his long stride from the waves and up the beach to his home, where jagged coastal hills loomed in the background. The sphere kept Triton's image sharp as he showered and dressed, then crossed to the luggage open on the bed. Atop precisely folded clothing lay a brochure and an airline ticket.

The brochure read *Anastasia Isle Antiques*—the St. Augustine business Triton had purchased with spacious living quarters on the second floor. Cosmil knew Triton would change the store name and would ship many artifacts from his West Coast store to the new one. How long Triton would continue to operate the shop once he was fully empowered was a question for the future.

The airline ticket was dated Wednesday next. The day most conducive to Cosmil shielding Triton's movement and the ripples it would send into the magical world.

Cosmil sent a small effort of will into the sphere, and Triton moved to a salvaged captain's desk where a contract of sale awaited his signature. Pink *Sign Here* tabs fanned down the sides of the pages. A fanciful pen in the shape of a mermaid and a gold dolphin charm rested on the scarred wood of the desk.

Triton hesitated, then pocketed the charm and signed and initialed the papers.

And it harmed none, Cosmil had seen the completion of a phase of Triton's business affairs. The sphere lowered slowly into his hands, and he wrapped it in fine brocade shot with silver thread. As he stooped to gently set the sphere in its carved olive wood case, Pandora trotted into the clearing.

Blood. Cosmil smelled blood.

The vampire killer was set upon and wounded.

"By whom? The investigator?"

Pandora sat and licked a massive paw. *I did not see the attack, but it was not him I scented. Only the blood.*

"And Francesca?"

Safe. Pandora cocked her head at the olive wood case. *Was the identity of The Void revealed?*

"No, but Triton returned from the sea and will be home soon."

Get him here safely, Old Wizard. The stench of blood and danger grow stronger.

FOURTEEN

I didn't know how much time it would take Saber to shower, shave, clean his gun, or whatever else he did in the morning, so I pounded on Maggie's suite door at seven fifteen Saturday.

"We have forty-five minutes to get to the sheriff's office," I called through the wood panel.

I knew he didn't get more than three hours of sleep, but the amount of growling and grunting from the other side of the door convinced me that Saber, even after a good night's sleep, was not a morning person.

We stopped at the Dunkin' Donuts on San Marcos for Saber's coffee fix. He must've really needed it, because he didn't bat an eye when I ordered a French cruller. It was almost worrisome when he didn't react, so I gave him the pastry after I pinched off some for myself. He *humphed* and polished off the cruller so fast I doubt he tasted it. I savored my bite.

I met with the same sketch artist, Billie Ormand, at eight on the dot, while Saber worked on the computer to find Millie's family. Detective March wasn't in yet, which didn't surprise me. In the middle of the night at the hospital, it looked like he'd thrown a coat on over a pajama top and pants he'd slept in for three days running.

Billie and I were finished with Gomer's likeness by eight thirty. The likeness would be distributed all over Florida and southern Georgia first, then nationwide. Wherever Gomer was, I hoped the sketch turned him up fast.

Saber had also been successful, judging by the gleam in his still bloodshot eyes as we left the sheriff's office. Either that or the sugar and caffeine had kicked in.

"So, what'd you find out?" I asked as soon as we were buckled in his Saturn Vue. He took the back way, Lewis Speedway, but I didn't care about the route home. I wanted the scoop.

"The short of it is I traced Millie's family. Her nephew, James Peters, age twenty-seven, was traveling in France when he met and married Yolette Girard, age thirty. He died about two years ago."

"How?" I probed, so eager I nearly bounced in my seat. Now we were getting somewhere!

"At the fangs of a vampire involved in a sexual three-for-all with James and Yolette. According to Yolette, the vampire got too rough during sex, but there was some question about the death that was never resolved."

I rolled the information in my head for a second. "James Peters and Holland Peters. Is that significant?"

He arched a brow. "Good catch. Holland was James's dad, Millie's sister's husband. He died two years before James's marriage."

"But why did Gomer use that name?"

"He could be a con man, or he could know Millie."

I digested that for a second and didn't like where Saber would probably take it.

"What about Millie's sister? Is she still living?"

"No. Sarah Upton Peters died a year to the day after the death of her only child. Cancer."

I sighed. "Poor Millie. To lose her nephew and sister in a year must've been devastating."

"And a possible motive for murder."

There it was. Saber suspected Millie. "You really think Millie blamed Yolette for James's death?"

"Wouldn't you?"

"But Millie couldn't know Yolette would turn up in St. Augustine," I argued.

"She could if she hired a private investigator to keep track of Yolette. He'd report the marriage and the trip."

I thought that over. Maggie said Gomer might've been an undercover cop, but we didn't think of him being a PI.

Millie a murderer? I still couldn't see that.

"You said a vampire was blamed for killing James. Female?"

"Yeah."

"What happened to her? Was she executed?"

"She disappeared, and the trail went cold within a week of James's death. Until now."

He pulled a piece of paper, folded in quarters, from his inner jacket pocket and handed it to me. "Recognize her?"

I stared at the grainy image, trying to place her. Long, dark hair. Flashing eyes. Very pointed chin. Then I remembered the photo he'd shown me Thursday afternoon.

"This is the same woman who was killed in Daytona Beach."

"Right. Rachelle."

The paper rattled as I refolded it. "But, Saber, Millie couldn't have killed Rachelle."

He blinked. "Why not?"

"You've seen Millie. She couldn't get close enough to a vampire to do harm in a million years."

"She's been close to you."

"Not in a threatening way. If she pulled a gun on me, I'd be gone in a flash."

He snorted.

"Okay, maybe flash is a stretch, but Millie wouldn't be a match for a whole nest of vampires."

"She might've hired an assassin."

"Look, I know she's not poor, but—"

"She's wealthy, Cesca. Her family was one of the original oil families in Oklahoma. They made a bundle and parlayed it into a lot more. James had a trust fund."

I thought about all the reasons why people commit murder. "Did Yolette inherit?"

"The inheritance laws in France are a good deal different than they are here, but they recognize prenup agreements. I figure Yolette inherited if she had a prenup with James, though some may have reverted to his mother."

A wealthy young man who left his bride a boatload of money. Etienne had made a comment about Yolette's wealth that I didn't pay much attention to at the time. Something about being able to indulge in her little whims—like the *Highlander* TV series paraphernalia and coming to St. Augustine for their wedding trip. Etienne's tone had sounded bragging and snobbish, and I'd forgotten it because, frankly, who cared?

Now I cared. If Etienne inherited, and we followed the money, Etienne was our murderer. Unless of course Yolette had not changed her will or had a prenup or whatever was needed in French law to keep him from inheriting.

But there was always life insurance, right? Did they do life insurance in France?

I eyed Saber as he made the turn onto Charlotte that led to the bank building parking lot. "So are we talking to Millie, or is March doing it?"

"We?" he said with a raised brow.

"We," I said firmly. "I landed in the middle of this, and Millie's our best lead right now. If you're going, I'm going. I want to hear what she has to say firsthand."

"What happened to talking to her tonight on the tour?"

"Are you saying you want to wait?"

"Only until I catch some sleep," he said, parking the SUV.

"You're not going to sneak out on me?"

"No, because you're right about her knowing and trusting you. March gave me the go-ahead to talk to Mrs. Hayward, and I'll take you as long as you let me do the talking."

I didn't argue, but I didn't agree, either. Saber was so beat, he didn't notice. In the condo, he fell fully clothed onto Maggie's bed.

I had to crash soon, too. I left my purse and keys on the dining table and went to lay out my clothes for later in the afternoon. One less chance for Saber to get the jump on me.

I came fully awake at three in the afternoon and leapt out of bed. Had Saber gone to Millie's without me?

I rushed to the kitchen in a thigh-length flamingo T-shirt to find him standing at the sink munching on a bagel—a bagel we didn't have in the house last night. Which meant he must've gone out to a nearby coffee shop, but he'd come back. Yep, there were my purse and keys on the table, and he'd probably memorized the elevator code when I punched it in Friday evening.

Well, what do you know? He *had* waited for me to wake up.

He gave me a long, slow once-over from my bedhead to my bare feet. A look that scorched a trail of awareness on my skin.

That darned light musky scent flared, but I brazened out getting what I needed in the kitchen: Starbloods.

I strolled to the mini-fridge as if I were fully dressed, took out a bottle (my behind facing away from him, of course) and turned back to my suite. I felt his eyes on me all the way, and I felt... power. Feminine power. Whoa, this was just like it looked in the movies—a real rush.

Except I let the rush go to my head and didn't watch where I was going. I nearly smacked into the doorframe.

"Uh, I'll be ready in ten minutes," I said, not daring to make eye contact.

"Great. Fine. I'll wait."

What, no snickering? No make-it-five-minutes comeback? Was his voice a little hoarse? Like Neil's got with Maggie?

I didn't need to go there. If his voice was hoarse, it was probably from lack of sleep. Maybe allergies. I threw on the dark blue jeans and gold knit top I'd laid out, then put my hair in a ponytail with a heavy-duty scrunchie, and slid on a pair of gold sandals. I didn't realize until I skidded back to the kitchen that Saber was in blue jeans, a yellow polo shirt, and the black jacket to cover his holster. Except for his jacket, we looked like we'd coordinated our clothes, for heaven's sake.

He gave me another long, appraising look that made goose

bumps prickle on my arms. Then one corner of that sensuous mouth lifted in a half grin. That's all it took to forget my fledgling feminine power and bolt for the door.

Millie Hayward lived on the island in an older but gorgeous condo building on the beach. Built in a U shape so every condo appeared to have an ocean view, her unit was front and center of the U on the first floor. It wasn't gated, so she had no warning we were coming. She opened the door wearing pink slacks, a sweater set, and an expression of surprise.

"Francesca?"

"Hi, Millie," I said, good manners coming to the fore to cover my nervousness. "Do you remember meeting Deke Saber on my tour Thursday night?"

She nodded. "I remember."

"Mrs. Hayward," Saber said, "we need to speak with you."

"About that awful man who threatened Cesca?"

"Do you mind if we come in?" Saber countered.

She eyed me for a long minute, reluctantly, I thought. It took a quick mental scrolling of vampire lore to figure out why she might be hesitating. So much for trusting me.

"It's safe to let me in, Millie. This isn't an open invitation for me to invade your home."

Relief—subtle but there—swept her features, and she stepped back to allow us by.

"Thank you," I said as she closed the door.

She motioned us to a cozy living room seating area of four overstuffed armchairs in sea foam green and a wood and glass coffee table. Original seascapes in oils and acrylics dotted the walls, and potted palms stood at the sides of the room-wide ocean-view windows.

"Sit, please," Millie said. "Would you like anything to—" She broke off, looking unsure what Miss Manners would offer a vampire guest.

She hugged me on the street but froze up with me in her home? I sighed. "We're fine, Millie, thank you."

With another flash of relief, she lowered herself into one chair, and we took the two opposite her.

"I don't know what I can tell you about that awful man that I haven't already said."

Saber leaned forward, his forearms braced on his knees. "You can tell us about James Peters, ma'am."

Millie's lips thinned until they were pinched white. "So you know."

"We know your nephew was married to Yolette before his death two years ago," Saber said.

"It was eighteen months," she said raggedly. "That woman killed him, you know."

Saber and I exchanged a quick glance but didn't speak.

"She was older and, I guess he thought, more worldly. She got him involved in unnatural sexual practices, spent his money like water, and ultimately killed him."

"Did she inherit his estate?" I asked softly. Saber shot me a warning look, but I didn't heed it, and Millie didn't see.

"Not the whole of it, thank God. James wasn't thirty yet and didn't have full control of his trust fund, but she didn't know that."

Millie growled so low in her throat, I glanced around for a dog.

"The bitch called James's mother, my sister Sarah. Not when James died, you understand. No, some French inspector told Sarah that James was dead. That woman," she spat, "was too *grieved* to bother speaking with her mother-in-law until six months later. Then she had the nerve to call Sarah to complain about being out of money and ask for more."

"Was Sarah already sick by then?" I asked.

"No." Millie blinked back tears. "She didn't even get to claim James's body."

"Why not?" Saber asked sharply.

"Because the little gold digger had him cremated. She said he wanted his ashes scattered in their garden or some such nonsense. Sarah had a memorial service in Tulsa, but—"

I spotted a box of tissues on a Swedish modern credenza and quietly retrieved them. When I'd set the box on the coffee table near Millie, Saber spoke gently.

"Mrs. Hayward, how did you know about James's personal life with Yolette?"

Millie dabbed at her nose. "When James called Sarah to announce he'd gotten married, Sarah was crushed. There was no wedding celebration, and James didn't invite Sarah to France for a visit. He didn't even offer to bring his wife home so Sarah could meet her daughter-in-law. It just wasn't like him—none of it. Sarah was heartbroken, but she carried on with a smile. I couldn't let it go."

"So you hired someone to kill her?"

I glared at Saber, and Millie snapped her spine ramrod straight.

"I hired a private investigator with contacts in Paris to find out what kind of trouble James had gotten himself into. I did not hire anyone to kill her." She narrowed her eyes. "If I had, James would be alive, and so would Sarah. She was perfectly healthy before James died. No cancer, no problems at all."

"Who did you hire, Millie?" I asked.

She held my gaze. "You haven't figured that out?"

"The Gomer-looking guy on the tours?"

She smiled. "I told him not to go over the top, but yes. His name is Eugene Cassidy."

"Where is he now, Mrs. Hayward?"

She blinked at Saber's intensity. "I don't know. I don't have him on a full-time retainer. Why? Is he in trouble?"

"We want to question him about the murder," Saber said, "and about a beating that took place early this morning."

Bewildered, Millie looked at me.

"The troublemaker from the tour is Victor Gorman, Millie," I said. "He's in the hospital and hurt pretty bad."

Millie shook her head. "Eugene wouldn't kill or beat up anyone. He had no reason to unless—"

"Unless what?" Saber asked.

"Unless that madman went after Francesca." She blushed. "Eugene told me you saw his gun Tuesday night and that you escaped as fast as you could. I haven't heard from him since."

"Have you tried to reach him?" Saber asked.

"Well, once. After I heard about that woman's death, I called to find out what I owed him...in case I needed to transfer funds." She waved it off. "He'll bill me, I'm sure."

I nodded, thinking about something that was bothering me. "Millie, I don't mean to be insensitive, but did Yolette really run through all of James's money? Did Eugene ever say?"

She snorted. "He reported she had plenty. She thought she

could play the poor bereaved widow and bleed Sarah dry, but I'll hand it to my sister. She didn't send that woman a red cent."

"This PI, Eugene Cassidy," Saber said. "Did he mention anyone else he was working for?"

"Of course not. He's an ethical PI," Millie huffed.

"But he might've said something in passing," Saber suggested.

"He didn't." Then she cocked her head as if considering. "I can tell you he's been in Daytona a good deal, but then he has an office there."

Saber and I traded another glance.

"Is Daytona important?" Millie asked.

Saber reached into his jeans pocket and handed her Rachelle's picture. "Do you know this woman?"

Millie inhaled a harsh breath. "It's the vampire from France. The one who was blamed for killing James."

"Are you sure?" Saber pressed.

She rose and went to the same credenza where the tissue box had been, opened a cabinet door, and pulled out a photo album. With one flip, it opened, and she handed it to Saber. "Eugene's Paris contact took these at some party or other about a month before James died."

I leaned in to peer at the pictures, some just of Yolette, two of a young, laughing man I presumed to be James, and two of Rachelle with Yolette. Oddly, none of James with Rachelle.

"Did you blame the vampire for James's death, Mrs. Hayward?"

Millie took the album back, traced one of the photos with her finger. "I blamed his bitch of a wife. I didn't know what to think about the vampire. Maybe she actually killed James, and maybe she didn't."

"Did you know she was in the States?" Saber asked. "In Daytona Beach?"

Millie looked up slowly. "When?"

"For over a year." Saber paused. "She was found dead last Saturday."

"Yolette was there," Millie said softly, almost to herself.

I tensed. "Yolette and Etienne were in Daytona?"

She nodded slowly. "They were there from Monday until last Saturday. In fact," she added, "they flew into Miami a month ago and drove to the Keys, then up the coast. According to Eugene they stopped in Key West, South Beach, Lauderdale, the Cape, and Daytona on their way here."

"Did the PI tell you what they did? Report on their movements or who they met?"

Millie shook her head. "Not in detail. He said they did typical tourist things and went to a vampire club here and there. I told him to warn me when they hit St. Augustine."

"How did you know they would come to St. Augustine?" Saber asked, his tone milder than his expression.

"Eugene deduced it. They were to fly out of Jacksonville this coming Wednesday."

"So you also knew where they were staying?"

"I knew," she sighed. "I thought about confronting them—or her. I thought about a lot of things, including," she said, looking Saber square in the eyes, "killing her."

"Is that why you went on Ms. Marinelli's ghost tours? To confront Yolette?"

Millie gave me a small smile. "I read about you in the paper. You seemed like a nice young woman, not a monster. We even have an acquaintance in common. Maybelle Banks."

"From my bridge club," I said to Saber and gave him credit for not rolling his eyes.

Millie sighed. "I knew Yolette would look you up sooner or later, just because you're a vampire. Was it a sickness with her?"

I spread my hands. "I don't know."

"Eugene found out they bought ghost tour tickets and that they specifically asked for your tour. He was going alone, but I decided to go myself, to see her firsthand. It didn't take much to get my friends together, and—"

Millie shrugged and twisted a tissue in her hands. "I wanted revenge. I wanted her to suffer. Now she's dead, and all I feel is cheated."

Millie gave us one of Eugene Cassidy's business cards. As we left, she also said she and her friends really had meant to guard me from "that nasty man," but they couldn't make it tonight. I told her not to worry, that Gorman was off the streets for at least another day and that Saber was guarding me now. She smiled, patted my arm, and promised to see me another time. I didn't count on it.

Saber called the number on the PI's card from the car while we were still parked at Millie's. He barked a message at voice mail, flipped his cell phone shut, and put it in a holder on his dashboard.

It rang not five seconds later.

"Saber." He listened, cut his gaze to me, and said, "She's right here. I'll put you on speaker."

"Ms. Marinelli, Detective March. We've gone over your truck but didn't find anything useful. It's ready to be released."

"Thanks. I'll call Tom and ask him to pick it up. At the impound yard, right?"

"Right. It'll be open until five."

"Got it."

"The second reason I'm calling is to tell you Gorman woke up. He wants to see you."

"See who?" Saber asked.

"Both of you. He won't talk to us without you. Officer Michaels from City—the same guy from last night—is already at the hospital, and I'll meet you there."

Saber flipped his phone shut, his expression as puzzled as I felt.

"Gorman wants to see me? That head injury must be worse than we thought."

Saber cracked a smile. "If he can identify his attackers, we're a big step closer to solving this before anything else happens."

Since he laid rubber turning out of the condo lot in front of a speeding jeep full of teens, I hoped the anything else wasn't a car wreck.

I reached Tom at the body and paint shop, and he promised to pick up my truck and call me with an estimate. Something else to think about when I had time.

At five thirty, traffic flowing off the island wasn't as packed as that coming on. Flagler Hospital was just on the other side of the 312 bridge on the left, and the way Saber drove, we were there in twenty minutes.

We met Officer Michaels and Detective March in the hall and entered Gorman's room. Michaels and March stood at the bedside, Saber and I took positions at the foot of the bed. I guess I expected Gorman to look frail in a hospital gown. Wrong. Oh, he looked worse for wear, but the bruising around his strange light blue eyes made them look colder than ever.

Detective March took the lead. "You see who did this to you, Gorman?"

"Son of a bitch hit me from behind, and I never did get a good look. But she," he pointed at me with a perfectly steady hand, "had to have somethin' to do with it. She searched my house and set me up for murder. Shit, I'd just had a little talk with her at Wal-Mart, so it ain't no coincidence I got beat up not three hours later."

Detective March shifted his weight. "Special Investigator Saber is supervising Ms. Marinelli. She's never out of his sight."

Gorman eyed us both. "That true?" he asked, his voice sounding harsher than ever. "You gettin' it on with Mr. Special Investigator?"

Saber and I looked at each other.

"And he wonders why he got beaten," Saber said mockingly.

"Poor people skills," I answered, then looked at Gorman. "I had nothing to do with the beating or any of your other troubles, Mr. Gorman. What's more, I think you know it."

"Well, somebody searched my house while I was fishin', and somebody planted things," Gorman blustered. "If it wasn't you, who the hell was it?"

I shrugged and spread my hands. "The murderer?"

"You didn't kill that Frenchie?"

"I just said I didn't set you up. I was sure *you* killed Yolette until I went to get my mail and found you bleeding."

"You found me?" His jaw went slack, his eyes bulged. "You didn't lick on me, or bite me, or anything, right?"

Lick on him? Gads, what a revolting image. "Mr. Gorman, I wouldn't bite you if you were the last meal on earth."

Michaels coughed into his hand. March harrumphed.

"Mr. Gorman," March said, "the Fourniers complained that you were stalking them."

Gorman's eyes shifted away. "I wasn't stalking 'em."

"But you were following them," March said.

"I live here. I have a right to keep track of what goes on in my city."

"You were also following them in Daytona last Friday," Saber said.

I looked at Saber, wanting to drop my jaw at this new piece of information. Instead, I clamped my teeth together and eyed Gorman anew. Maybe he *had* killed Yolette. Or Rachelle. Or both of them.

"So what if I was," Gorman said picking at the edge of the blanket draped over his belly and casting an uneasy glance at March. "I got a right to go where I want."

"Those surveillance photos you took of the Fourniers sure make it look like you were stalking them," March said. "We have your computer and your digital camera. The photos are dated. It could look to a jury like you were planning to kill the woman all along."

Gorman balled the blanket in his fist. "But I didn't. Hell, I got beat up last night, and I don't know who did it or why."

"Did you see the Fourniers with the Daytona vampires, Gorman?" Saber asked.

"Yeah," Gorman admitted cautiously.

"Any particular vampires?" Saber pressed.

"You got the pictures. You tell me."

Saber gave Gorman a long look. "You know their names?"

"No, and I'm gettin' tired," Gorman complained, a whine in his voice as he looked to March again. March stared back.

"We're almost finished." Saber leaned both hands on the metal foot of the bed. "How long have you been following Ms. Marinelli?"

"Three months, off 'n' on."

That bit of news made me want to shower for a solid week, but I managed not to gag.

"Who told you the Fourniers would be in St. Augustine?" March asked.

"I got friends," Gorman said defensively.

"The Covenant?"

"Yeah, the ones down in South Beach. They were on recon at the clubs and overheard the Frenchies invite a bunch of vampires to have sex with 'em. Then the sickos bragged that they were havin' sex with vampires all the way up the coast. They had a lure or somethin' vampires liked. That's when I knew I had to watch this 'un—" Gorman pointed at me again. "—extra close."

"Gorman," March said, "do you remember anything about the attack that can help us? How many there were? Voices, smells, anything?"

"Blood."

"Yeah, you bled a good deal from what I heard," March said.

"No, I mean what I remember. I was standin' at the bank entrance—"

"The entrance to Ms. Marinelli's building," Saber said.

"Yeah, yeah, but I'm trying to tell you I smelled blood."

"Describe it."

Gorman shot Saber a petulant look and smoothed his blanket over his belly. "You know, blood. A kinda sweet, metallic smell only a thousand times stronger. Like a whole bath of blood."

I felt myself sway and groped for the end of the bed.

Gorman saw my weakness and smirked. "Thinkin' about all that blood make you hungry, vampire?"

"It makes me queasy." *You nitwit,* I wanted to add but didn't. I was too busy taking cleansing breaths of chemically treated hospital air.

When I trusted myself not to lose it all over Gorman's hospital blanket, I said, "Are you sure that's what you smelled?"

"Yeah, I'm sure. What are you, some kinda wimp? Swoon at the sight of blood."

"Not the sight, the smell."

FIFTEEN

"What the hell happened in there?" Saber demanded as soon as we were in the hospital parking lot.

"You heard me," I said, pacing beside him. "I got queasy."

"Thinking about blood?"

"Smelling it." I shuddered and rubbed my arms. "For just a second, I was picking up what Gorman smelled before the attack."

"You mean a psychic thing?"

"Yes, and I never want to be in that guy's head again. But it triggered something."

"What?" he probed, beeping the car unlocked.

I sighed to throw off the memory of Gorman's evil thoughts and climbed in. "That same scent of blood was on my truck the night it was trashed, and a fainter version was on Yolette at Scarlett's last Monday. Fainter than it was when we found Gorman, but there." I rubbed my forehead. "I think I smelled blood on Etienne, too, but I can't remember when."

He slammed his car door. "What does that mean?"

"I don't know." I reached for my seat belt and suppressed another shudder. "But I have the gut feeling it's important."

"There wasn't any blood on your truck. Just paint."

"I know, and that's what's confusing."

"Yolette could've cut herself," Saber mused.

"I remember thinking the same thing and that I didn't want to be blamed for it."

He started the car but stared out the windshield as it idled. After a full half minute, he turned to me. "The smell of blood really makes you sick?"

"Yes," I admitted.

"How the hell do you feed?"

Darn, I knew this would come out sooner or later. Wouldn't it figure, Saber would be the first to know?

I grimaced and blurted the truth. "I hold my nose, okay?"

"You hold your—" He broke off and stared at me. Disbelief and amusement crossed his features. "But you drink flavored blood."

"You snooped in my mini-fridge."

"Why drink flavored blood if you hold your nose?"

"I like the caramel aftertaste."

He gaped, then simply shook his head. "You're the weirdest damned vampire I've ever met."

I gave him a tired smile. "Get me home, will you?"

We took U.S. 1 back downtown. I didn't feel like talking, and Saber didn't push me. True, he was probably trying not to laugh, but his silence gave me the space to think.

Whatever was tickling my memory or my psychic sense, it was driving me crazy by the time we arrived at the penthouse at six fifteen. I had more than an hour before I had to get ready for work. Maybe the notes we'd made last night would help crystallize what I was reaching for.

"Saber, where's the suspect list we made?"

"In my duffel. Why?"

"Just get it. Please."

He gave me an I'm-humoring-you look but wheeled down the hall. While he retrieved the papers, I checked phone messages and found one from Maggie I'd return before I went to work. In the kitchen, I set the timer and got a pen from the junk drawer. The alarm would remind me when to stop sleuthing and get ready for tonight's tour.

Saber met me at the kitchen table with the legal pad and notes but minus his jacket and holster. I shuffled through the papers twice, with Saber looking on but not interrupting. The third time I started through them, he slapped a hand over the sheets.

"What are you looking for?"

"I'm not sure, but work with me, will you?"

He gestured toward a chair and took one himself. I sat and spread the papers in an arc between us.

"Let's look at this again from the beginning," I said, pen poised. "We have Rachelle murdered last Friday night, right?"

"Early Saturday morning somewhere between midnight and three," he supplied.

I sketched out a time and crime grid and filled in Rachelle. "Then Yolette is killed, what, the following Thursday morning?"

He hesitated, then shrugged. "You're not a suspect now, so yeah. The ME figures she was killed between two and five."

I scribbled the time by Yolette's name. "Next we have my

truck vandalized on Thursday night between eight and eleve-
nish. It could've been a bomb or my brakes could've been tam-
pered with, but that didn't happen."

"So?"

"It's a less violent crime."

"If you consider extensive damage and DIE spray-painted on
your tailgate less violent."

"Who has reason to trash my truck? Only Gorman. He
threatened me, and he hates vampires, but, oops, he was gone."

"Everyone else in town *likes* vampires? Is that what you're
saying?"

"Are you going to carp or help?"

"Carry on, Sherlock."

I crossed my eyes at him but recorded the vandalism. "Now
last in this string of events, Gorman is beaten. I didn't do it, so
who did?"

"Too many people to count?"

I couldn't stop the quick grin at his deadpan expression. "He
is repulsive, isn't he?"

"He's worse, but I'll grant you, the beating probably wasn't
random."

"Okay, then," I said with a final notation, "we have two
murders—"

"And the victims knew each other."

"Yes, but the vandalism and the beating don't look connected. So, let's do a process of elimination." I folded my hands
on the legal pad. "Is it possible Ike or one of his nestmates killed
Rachelle?"

"If they had, there wouldn't have been a body to find."

I made a face. He was right. "Are the Daytona Beach police pursuing the case?"

"For all intents, no. They called me according to procedure and dumped it in my lap."

"Did you interview Ike?"

He threw me a dark look. "Where are you going with this?"

"We have two dead women connected by their past."

"Not to mention their broken necks and the .22 silver slugs in their brains."

"Which is odd, too. For a vampire, sure, the bullet has to be silver. For Yolette?"

"Maybe the killer forgot to change ammo."

"Or just didn't bother, but silver isn't dirt cheap, and breaking a neck isn't easy. It'd have to be someone with military training."

"That's not a given, but it's a good premise."

"Saber, what about the autopsy? Weren't there any handy finger or hand bruises on the victims?"

"To indicate how large the hands that snapped the necks were?" he said with a grin. "No. Both women's faces and bodies in general had some pre- and postmortem bruising, but nothing to give us a lead. The toxicology tests won't be back for at least another week."

"Damn. All right then," I pressed on, picking up my pen. "Who gains what by killing these women, and who'd know how to break a neck? Let's start with Gorman. There were guns at his house, correct?"

"Which he insists were planted."

"Is there a ballistics match, or do you know yet?"

"The results will be in by Monday, but even if there's a match, I don't think he did it."

"I agree. Also, there's no way he'd get close enough to Yolette or Rachelle to break their necks."

"Rachelle was shot first."

"Fine," I said scribbling another note, "but Gorman wouldn't use a little pistol to shoot her. He'd use something bigger, like an elephant gun."

"Or a rocket launcher."

"And he'd take pictures and brag about it."

"But his alibi holds, so who's next?"

I put a big *X* over Gorman and skimmed down. "There's Millie and Mick, but they're both off the list, too."

"Millie, yes. Why eliminate Mick?"

"Don't start on Mick."

"He has ties to the Daytona Beach vampires, and he's ex-military."

I raised a brow. "Really?"

"Navy," Saber said.

"But he doesn't really have ties, Saber. He has a history with them that would keep him far, far away from the nest. He wouldn't work for Ike in a billion years."

Saber didn't look sold but said, "Go on."

"Gomer aka Holland aka Eugene the PI."

"He knew exactly where the Fourniers were staying."

"But Millie's no fool. She hired a reputable PI, not an assassin. Although," I added, tapping a nail on the table, "Ike could've hired him to investigate Rachelle's death."

"Not likely. Vampires might enslave or enthrall, but they don't look in the freaking phone book for a PI."

I look in the phone book for all sorts of things, but I let it go. "Maybe Ike saw Eugene following Yolette and glommed on to him that way."

"That's possible."

"But it still doesn't make sense that Eugene would kill Yolette. Not for Millie *or* for Ike."

"You're right. Ike would want the killer brought to him for some old-fashioned vampire justice."

I knew from the past what that could mean, and Ike's reputation wasn't any kinder or gentler than King Normand's.

"So why don't you call Ike and ask him about Eugene?"

He pointedly cut his gaze to the living room windows. "It's still light out. Ike won't be up for at least an hour, and—" He stopped and gave me an odd look. "What time's the tour tonight?"

"Nine to about ten thirty. Why?"

"We could go see Ike after that."

"We who? I'm not going anywhere near him."

"Oh, come on, you've never met your closest vampire neighbors."

"And I never want to. I told you that." I tapped the pen on the pad. "Let's get back to our suspects. Etienne. What have you found out about him? Does he have an alibi? Is he really grieving? Has he demanded Yolette's remains yet?"

"Whoa," he said, leaning back in the chair. "Slow down before you hang the guy. First, he does have an alibi."

"What, pray tell?"

"He was fishing."

I blinked. "With a nor'easter coming in? I don't think so."

"He went inland, over around Gainesville. Lake fishing."

I wondered how far inland the lake wind warnings went.

Since I watch more HGTV than the Weather Channel, I had no clue.

"He has witnesses, I suppose?"

"Yep. He arranged in advance to rent a boat, and the guy working the marina signed it out to him at six fifteen. The only wrinkle in his story is that he was supposed to have been at the marina by five in the morning. He was over an hour late."

"Time enough to kill Yolette?"

"Technically, but he says he took a wrong turn, and that is possible. He showed us on a map where he went the wrong way."

I stared at him. "Doesn't that strike you as odd?"

"What? That he knew where he made the wrong turn?"

"That he consulted a map at all. Maggie says men are notorious for not following maps or asking for directions."

His lips quirked. "In a foreign country, even men use maps."

"What about the body? Is he having her cremated?"

"To destroy some other evidence, you mean?" He shook his head. "He's been patient, but that may not last long. He says he wants to take her home, and so far there's no other physical evidence in the house or car—or on her body—other than what there should be."

"No handy blood-soaked clothing or fibers under her fingernails, huh?" I said, disappointed.

"Nada. As for background, we don't know as much about Etienne as we'd like to. He's thirty-five, born in Paris, married Yolette a little over a month ago."

"Is he well off?"

"He's comfortable enough." He cocked his head. "You think he killed Yolette for her money?"

I chewed the tip of my thumbnail. "I don't know. Etienne could've killed Yolette for her money, but I don't know why he'd kill Rachelle."

Saber frowned and ran a hand through his hair. "Maybe she was a threat of some kind. Maybe she'd been blackmailing Yolette because Yolette really did kill James Peters."

"So Yolette and Etienne kill Rachelle to get rid of the loose end. It could've been planned, or they could've run into her in Daytona and jumped at the opportunity to kill her."

"That only works if they could get Rachelle alone and get the drop on her."

"Do the Daytona vampires travel in packs?"

"Not necessarily."

"Then it wouldn't be that hard to get her alone. Maybe they promised her a big payoff to lure her somewhere. Where *was* her body found?"

"On the beach about two hours before dawn. Some spring breakers stumbled over her."

"Had she been in the water? I mean Yolette washed up, but she didn't look like she'd been in the water long."

"More mystery novel trivia?"

"Will you just answer me?"

"Rachelle wasn't in the water at all, except for the waves washing over her."

"So we're down to Etienne, but there's no evidence."

"That's the size of it."

"It stinks."

"Yeah, but we can't charge him without evidence."

I looked at the notes spread on the table. "There has to be a piece we're missing." I tapped my pen on one name and circled it. "We need to talk to Eugene. He's been reporting to Millie since before James died. He has to know more than we do."

Three things happened at once. The timer dinged, the house phone rang, and Saber's cell vibrated across the table. I grabbed the cordless, eyed the caller ID, and greeted Maggie as I dashed to the kitchen to turn off the noisy timer.

"You sound out of breath," Maggie said as Saber disappeared down the hall, the cell to his ear.

"Just a little. How's Tallahassee?"

"Fun, actually. I found the most marvelous salvage yard and junk store. How about you? Is Saber still there? What happened with Stony?"

"His name is Victor Gorman, and it turned out he had an alibi, so Saber's still here."

"And you're good with that?" Maggie sounded half suspicious, half incredulous. "I mean, do you feel safe?"

I thought back to this afternoon when he'd seen me in my sleepwear. There was safe, then there was safe from myself.

"Cesca, you're not answering me."

"Oh, sorry, I just realized I didn't get the mail yet. Yes, it's fine. I'm safe and sound."

"Really?"

"Maggie, I promise. How was Neil's seminar?"

"He's in hog heaven. We have another meet and greet at the university at eight. Oh, and he's been asked to check a dig site a little west of here tomorrow morning, so we may be back later Sunday than I thought."

"No problem. I don't have a tour, so I'll probably stay in and study or—" I broke off when I heard Neil in the background. "What did he say?"

"He asked if you went shopping for a new surfboard yet."

"Haven't had time. Why?"

"Something about good waves next week. He's finally coming out of the bathroom. Gotta go. Take care, and I'll see you tomorrow night."

I put the unit back on the charger and headed down the hall to see if Saber was still on the cell. He was, judging by the one-way conversation I heard through the closed door. I might've eavesdropped, but I had hair to tame with a flatiron that wasn't hot yet. Keeping one ear peeled for Saber's voice or footsteps, I refreshed my makeup, took my Minorcan costume out of the closet, and went back to the bathroom to brush out tangles.

I leaned over from the waist to get to some snarls at my nape—they're the worst—when Saber said, "Guess who that was?"

I jerked up and whirled toward his voice. The hairbrush flew into the wall, and I fell back against the countertop.

"Geez, Saber, you startled me."

"Maybe you should have your vampire hearing checked."

"Or my head examined," I muttered and swept my brush off the tiled floor.

"Are you guessing who called?"

"Eugene Cassidy, PI."

"Yes, but the cell connection was bad. We're meeting him after your tour tonight."

"Okay," I said, suddenly nervous.

Sexy Saber was standing in my bathroom doorway, which is in my bedroom suite, which is where my bed is. My bed with my huge stuffed dolphin and my other personal touches. I felt an intimacy creep around us. Darkened rooms, hushed voices, my light musk scent and his stronger one entwined.

He must've felt the charge, too. He cleared his throat and stepped back. "I'll go eat something while you get ready."

"Right, good. I'll, uh, be ready to leave here at eight thirty."

He nodded and took off, as Maggie would say, like a scalded cat.

So why was I the one who felt burned?

SIXTEEN

It was a perfect, balmy night in paradise as Saber and I walked up St. George Street to meet my tour group. The stars shone bright in the unpolluted skies, the moon was waxing, and soon my psychic senses would be as normal as they get.

But not soon enough to prepare me for what waited at the waterwheel.

Vampires.

Damn. No wonder the street was eerily empty. My bad that I didn't notice sooner.

I stumbled to a stop a quarter block away. Saber halted, too, and swore under his breath.

Four vampires and the blood bunnies Cici and Claire, all of them dressed in assorted tight, black leather outfits, waited at the tour substation. At the center of the group stood the vampire who had to be Ike. He looked part Asian, part African American, his hair military buzz short and his face clean-shaven.

Compared to the strong line of his jaw, his lips were almost feminine, but his snake eyes were the color of deepest hell.

Janie and Mick in their usual tour guide costumes also stood sentinel at the station. I heard Janie's heartbeat flutter like the wings of a trapped bird, and Mick was darn near hyperventilating with agitation. A second later, he spotted us, grabbed Janie's hand, and hurried toward Saber and me.

I had a bad feeling that got worse as I looked past my friends at Ike.

The weight of his gaze settled on me like black ooze, and my skin prickled and crawled until I wanted to claw at my arms. As I stared, Ike languidly lifted a beringed hand and curled his fingers. Janie's steps faltered. Her tight expression slackened, and the fear in her eyes drained to nothing. In seconds my friend's vitality bled away. She pivoted and appeared to float back toward Ike before I could think to move.

Mick was faster. He wheeled after her yelling, "Janie, no!"

Ike said one word, "Tower," and an impossibly tall black male vamp held out his hand like a traffic cop to freeze Mick in his tracks.

Saber's breath hitched, and mine stopped, as Janie's shell snuggled her back against Ike's chest and exposed her neck. Ike flashed fangs and ran a finger across Janie's collarbone, but his gaze stayed locked on mine.

"God *damn* it, he's grandstanding." Saber whispered viciously. "I hate it when they do this."

Fists clenched in impotent rage, I turned my back on Ike to stand in front of Saber. "What now?" I asked, low and tight.

"We stop it before it gets out of hand."

"Can't you just shoot them?"

I heard the underlying wistfulness in my whisper, and Saber must've, too. He bent closer. "You have to face this, Cesca."

"Why? Because they're my people?"

"No." He tucked a tendril of hair behind my ear. "Because they're everything you work not to be."

My breath left my lungs in a whoosh as I stared into his eyes for an endless moment. He was right. Hard as I'd tried to hide from the horror of my past, from the ugly part of myself, I had to face this. We had to save Janie and Mick.

"I only hope," I said, jabbing my finger in his chest, "you brought an arsenal of silver bullets."

He slid his gun from the holster under his jacket. "Locked and loaded."

"Do we go in blazing?" I asked, straightening my spine.

"We play it by ear, but keep this in mind. Like it or not, you're a vampire, too, and this is your turf. If things go south, grab Janie and Mick, and stay out of my line of fire."

I nodded. "Let's go."

We turned as one to stride side by side toward the vampires. I envisioned an insane version of the shoot-out at the OK Corral, especially with Saber on my right hiding his gun at his thigh. Eight feet from the living and undead, Saber and I stopped.

"Ike," Saber said.

"Saber." Ike's fully dilated eyes showed only black as they flicked from Saber to me. "Francesca, Princess Vampire."

His rich voice slid over me like raw silk, an infinitely more dangerous sensation than the skin prickles. Even my defunct title sounded like a caress instead of merely a name, and my throat ached to answer him. I might have, if Saber hadn't shifted at my side.

In that second, I realized that Ike was pulling energy from my aura. That's what caused the tugging tightness in my chest and throat.

I threw up my shield with a force that made Ike's reptilian eyes widen. Surprised me, too, but life and death are powerful motivators.

"Public enthrallment is illegal, Ike," Saber said steadily.

"He's pulling aura, too," I said. "That's a staking offense, isn't it?"

"It is," Saber said, raising his gun hand in a slow, even motion. "Let the woman go."

"Or you will what?" Ike sniffed. "Shoot me?"

"In a heartbeat."

"A heartbeat? How appropriate when it would be your last," Ike sneered, his fangs flashing white in the streetlights. "You would not kill one of us before we ripped you all to shreds."

"You forget, Ike," Saber said. "I have a vampire on my side. That evens the odds some."

"Is this so?" Ike's slashing eyebrows rose mockingly. "Princess Vampire sides with mortals over her own species?"

"Don't put me in the middle of your pissing contest," I snapped. "I put up with this crap from King Normand, but I'm not taking it from you."

"We're not bluffing, Ike," Saber warned.

Ike ignored him, his beady eyes boring into mine. "Answer the question, Princess." He dipped his open mouth toward Janie's neck. "Do you choose mortals or vampires?"

Ike's fangs hovered inches from Janie's jugular. Saber was a deep breath from firing. Something in me snapped, and I acted on instinct.

I swung my gaze to the mocha-skinned female vamp in his entourage, and pulled her aura like a supersuction vacuum on full power. The vampire hissed as the first shock hit her, and she tried to fight me, but I'd siphoned energy to survive. I was a master at this, and I was ticked.

The vampire's will broke, and she staggered forward to sag at my feet on one knee. Her black hair was an art piece of long cornrows with what looked like bits of polished bone beads. Human bone. Yuck.

I looked at Ike. His expression was more thoughtful than angry, but he vibrated with tension.

"Now who is committing the staking offense?" he asked sardonically.

"Self-defense, Ike. Right, Saber?"

He looked a smidge pale, but his eyes twinkled. "That's how I see it." Saber raised a brow at Ike. "So, Ike, what'll it be? Play games, or talk about Rachelle's murder?"

That got Ike's attention.

He straightened and let go of Janie. She swayed but stayed upright, and I breathed a little easier.

Ike's eyes narrowed on Saber. "You have something to report?"

"A second murder with the same MO as Rachelle's," Saber said easily.

"Gee, Ike," I said, widening my eyes, "it's been all over the news. Didn't you know?"

"I do not watch mortal newscasts," he said repressively,

pupils bleeding back to as normal as they would get. "Saber, put your paltry gun away and explain."

"Let these people go first," Saber said. "Walk them to the street and break the thrall nice and slow so they don't panic."

"When Princess releases Laurel, I shall."

I startled, because I'd forgotten the woman kneeling in front of me. That I'd pulled Laurel's aura was one thing. That I'd effortlessly held it scared the hell out of me, but now was not the time to show it.

"Tell you what, Ike. Have Cici and Claire move the mortals, and send—" I motioned at the tall, white female vamp who'd stood like a statue through our face-off.

"Zena," Ike supplied.

"Send Zena over here to get Laurel. We'll each release on three."

Ike snapped his fingers at Zena. She rushed to help Laurel stand and positioned her near Ike. Cici and Claire carefully led Mick and Janie to the street. When Saber counted us off, Ike and his male minion broke the thrall on both Janie and Mick. I freed Laurel so abruptly the air crackled with energy.

As Saber holstered his gun, Mick and Janie blinked into awareness of the here and now. Mick shot Saber and me a surprised look, then grasped Janie's hand, and hurried off. They'd be missing time, but better that than missing blood.

Or an entire throat.

Which is what I might be missing if I'd let Laurel come back to herself at my feet.

"She insults you, my lord Ike," Laurel growled, black eyes shooting hatred. "She insults our entire nest. Let me kill her now and be done with it."

"Silence." Ike's voice cracked like a barbed whip. "Saber, tell me of your investigation."

"Saber is not investigating," Laurel pushed. "He is sniffing around this one. I smell them, each on the other."

"You're probably right, Laurel," I said, sugary sweet. "Saber's been living in my space for a few days. Protecting me."

Ike's posture stiffened. "From whom? Rachelle's killer?"

Laurel's jaw muscles tightened, and it hit me that she had something to hide from Ike. I filed that tidbit away.

"We don't know yet who killed Rachelle," Saber said, all business, "but a Frenchwoman named Yolette Fournier was killed here on Thursday. She knew Rachelle and probably visited your club in the last week or ten days."

"Many people visit my club," Ike sniffed. "How was this mortal acquainted with my Rachelle?"

I waited for Saber to drop the bomb.

"Rachelle was accused of killing Yolette's first husband," he said.

"In France." It was a statement not a question.

"That's right," Saber said mildly. "Did you know about the incident, Ike?"

"I knew. However, if this Yolette is herself now dead by the same killer—" He spread his hands as if looking for answers. "Surely you do not think I had anything to do with this."

"No," Saber said, "but you might be able to give us a new lead if you answer a few questions."

Ike tapped his chin, then shifted his gaze from Saber to me. "Are you assisting Saber in this matter, Princess?"

I glanced at Saber, who nodded. "Unofficially, yes. I'm helping narrow the suspect list."

"And are you privy to what Saber would ask me?"

I shrugged. "More or less."

"Then you must ask this of me."

"Why, so I'll owe you one? No dice." I'd exposed my only real vampire skill for Ike to see, might as well speak my mind. "It's *your* vampire who died, Ike. You can be a good citizen and answer questions here, or I'm betting Saber can talk to you in a more official capacity."

He paused so long, I thought we were headed for a standoff. "Very well. What do you and Saber want to know?"

I glanced at Saber. "Gorman first?"

"Start with Cassidy."

"Fine." I met Ike's black eyes again. "Did you hire a man named Eugene Cassidy to investigate Rachelle's death?"

"Rachelle's murder, and I did not hire him. Tower—" Ike waved at the tall vamp who'd frozen Mick. "—caught Mr. Cassidy lurking in our parking lot. I merely suggested it would benefit his health and the health of his loved ones should he look into the matter for me."

"Did Cassidy," Saber said, "say he'd been tracking anyone?"

"A Covenant man," Ike admitted.

"Have you had trouble with the Covenant in Daytona?" I asked, partly out of curiosity.

"They never seem to bother us for long."

I'll bet. Could I be as ruthless as Ike? Naw. In spite of pulling Laurel's aura, I couldn't pull off ruthless.

"Ike," Saber said, "Yolette probably visited your club, but she would've been with her new husband. Do you remember a French couple being there last week?"

"I am not in the club, only the office. Laurel?"

She jerked ever so slightly, but I noticed it, and so did Ike and Saber.

Laurel tossed her head. "They seemed to be groupies, Lord Ike. Only interested in sex with us."

Watching Cici and Claire from the corner of my eye, I expected them to flinch. They didn't, poor trapped souls.

"Yes, they were into sex with vampires," Saber said to Laurel. "We need to know what they did at the club. Did Rachelle leave with them?"

Laurel shrugged. "If she did, I did not see her go."

Liar, I thought, and knew I was right. Laurel had been jealous of Rachelle. That was plain in her eyes, never mind reading her thoughts.

"What about security cameras?" I asked. "Do you have those tapes?"

Laurel smirked but wiped her expression clean when Ike stepped to her side, mirroring Saber's stance beside me. He took her hand and tucked it in the crook of his arm.

"I am afraid," he said silkily, "that the cameras record digitally. They erase themselves after twenty-four hours."

"Bummer," I said.

"Any further questions, Princess?"

"Just one. Why did you show up tonight?"

"To take this famous ghost tour."

I blinked. "Are you serious?"

He waved a languid hand. "It seems a quaint way to spend an evening, and I paid for the privilege in buying every ticket."

"You bought thirty tickets?" Saber asked, sounding as astonished as I felt.

"Fine. Let's do this."

I spun to grab the lantern from the substation cabinet. When I straightened, I turned smack into Ike with Laurel still on his arm. He didn't budge an inch, just stood staring at me.

"What?" I snapped, only partly in irritation. The other part was nerves because, well, the guy *was* scary.

"Are you setting up your own little kingdom in St. Augustine, Princess Vampire? If so, be warned I will not tolerate competition."

"One vampire does not a kingdom make, Ike. I'm just doing my job and living a normal afterlife."

"One hears you do not need to work."

"One might also hear I'd be bored stiff if I didn't—no pun intended." I leaned forward, not into his face, but nearer. "Now, are we doing this or not?"

"Tut-tut," he said. "Your tour manners leave much to be desired. Perhaps I will turn in a complaint. I have ways of applying pressure to have you fired."

The tut-tut almost had me grinning, but when he attacked my manners—my excellent manners—that was it.

My free hand planted on my hip, I glared.

"I'm not in a power struggle with you, Ike. If you want to do the tour, fine. If you want anything else, you can go whistle Dixie, because you're not getting it from me."

Laurel and the tall twins hissed like snakes, but I didn't back off. "I'm free and way over twenty-one, and I'll do as I please. Got it?"

"We'll see," he said evenly, but he stepped back. "Please proceed."

I rolled my eyes at the whole lot of them and began the ghost tour, doing my best to ignore the jealous rage emanating from Laurel.

The spirits were out in force, but from the first stop, they scrambled to hide from the vampires. It might've been funny if I hadn't felt so bad for them.

While Saber watched my back, Ike's vampires did nothing but complain. They avoided the cemeteries and churches as sacred ground, and the fort and old Spanish hospital were snubbed as hallowed ground. The vampires bitched about walking instead of flying, and they flat-out heckled one of our most disturbing ghosts, Fay. The crabby ghost had gone berserk rattling windows. I'd need to mend fences with her before I took another tour by her house.

I would've loved for the biting ghost at the oldest drugstore to take a hunk out of someone—preferably Ike or Laurel—but it wasn't to be. When the building was moved back in 1887, it had been plopped down on part of the Tolomato Cemetery. If I really thought the vampires would fry on holy ground, I'd have cheerfully mustered all my vampire strength and speed to give 'em a shove and watch 'em burn.

Tacky, but true, and it would've saved me from having to see any of them again.

I suppose you can guess that the abbreviated tour didn't take long. In forty-five minutes we were back at the waterwheel, where music poured into the night from the Mill Top Tavern. I wrapped up my spiel with Saber at my side again.

"That was not as amusing as I had been led to believe," Ike said, eyeing his blood bunnies, Claire and Cici, as if contemplating punishment. "But the night is young. Perhaps you will both have a drink with us?"

"No, thank you," I said as I put my lantern away.

"Excuse me?" Laurel snarled, elbowing Saber aside to crowd behind me.

I was *really* getting sick of people invading my space, but I faced her and forced myself to smile pleasantly. "I said no thank you."

"Lord Ike allowed you to live this night," Laurel said, the beads on her cornrows quivering with her intensity. "You will not refuse him."

I stood my ground. "I believe I just did. No offense, of course," I said, glancing at Ike, "but I have other plans."

"What could possibly be more important than pleasing Lord Ike?" Laurel demanded.

Almost anything, I nearly said but figured that might get my head slapped off my shoulders. Laurel was itching for a fight to avenge herself.

"I'm waiting for an answer," she snapped. "Why do you refuse Lord Ike's gracious invitation?"

Wild horses wouldn't make me tell her Saber and I were meeting Eugene, so I shrugged and told her something shocking enough to shut her up.

"I'm going shopping at Wal-Mart."

"Wal-Mart?" she echoed faintly and actually fell back a step while the tall twins exchanged a glance of pure horror.

"Yes. They've rolled back prices this week on small appliances."

"Oooh, I need a fanthy blender," Cici lisped. "Do they have Cuithinargh—" Cici broke off when Claire elbowed her in the ribs.

Poor Cici. I felt sorry enough for her to take her to Wal-Mart myself—and talk her into doing something safer than hanging out with vampires.

Ike gave me a steely look, then surveyed his crew and growled so low in his throat the ground vibrated beneath my thin-soled slippers.

"Another time," he said with a mocking bow. "Perhaps by then you will decide, eh, Princess?"

"Decide what?" I asked.

"Whether to exist with the mortals or truly live as a vampire. You cannot straddle the worlds much longer."

He clapped his hands once and swept his entourage in a glance.

"Children, drive yourselves back immediately," he said to Claire and Cici. At the vampires he barked, "Come."

The vamps took five steps up the street and *poof*! They were airborne, flying. Not with arms out like wings, not facedown like birds. It was as if they'd hopped on a moving sidewalk powered by a wind current heading south.

"You have to admit," Saber said, leaning in to whisper in my ear, "that's damned impressive."

"Yeah, it is," I breathed. "Just think what they save in gas."

SEVENTEEN

When the vampires disappeared into the starry sky, I expected Saber to blow his stack.

I didn't expect him to glance at his watch and say, "You want a drink?"

"A drink?" I echoed stupidly.

"Sure. There's not enough time for you to drag me all the way to Wal-Mart before we meet Eugene."

I peered closer into the cobalt depths of his eyes and saw them twinkle. Then he smiled and took my arm. "Lighten up, Cesca."

I couldn't help but smile back as I fell into step with him, but I shook my head. "Aren't you, um—"

"Pissed as hell?" Saber supplied.

I gulped. "We can go with that."

He flashed a full-on grin. "I'm not angry. I'm surprised. When you told me you survived being buried by feeding off energy, I didn't picture you sucking it like water through a damn straw."

"I didn't feed that way," I said defensively. "I only had a sip here and there."

Saber leaned to peer at my face. "You didn't know you could pull aura like that, did you?"

"No, and it shocked me," I admitted. I'd be coming to grips with that knowledge for days.

"Shocked Ike, too," he said with an edge to his smile.

"He was threatening my friends, Saber. I couldn't just stand there."

He stopped and turned me, laid his warm hands on my shoulders.

"Cesca, you used your powers, your skills, to protect your friends and defuse the standoff. My skills come with a gun, yours come with being a vampire. You don't have to be like Ike to be what you are."

Maybe he had a point, but I'd still scared myself silly.

Saber tucked my hand in his arm, and we resumed strolling. "The only thing that worries me is that you showed your hand to Ike. He's sure not going to leave you alone now. You're a challenge."

"And you sound happy about that why?" I snipped.

"Because," he said, steering me the final steps to Scarlett's, "I'll just have to hang around and protect you."

A wave of pleasant shivers showered me, then my cell phone chirped. I fumbled it out of my pocket and checked caller ID.

"It's Mick," I told Saber.

He nodded. "Take it while I look for a table."

I flipped the phone open. "Mick, are you and Janie okay?"

"Yeah. We're exhausted but alive." He sighed. "Thanks for whatever you did to get us out of there."

"Sure." If they didn't remember what a close call it had been, they'd have fewer nightmares. "Can I do anything for you?"

"No. I brought Janie to my place. I have—" He hesitated. "—certain safeguards here. Janie's already sleeping, and I'm headed for bed."

"Good. And, Mick, I'm sorry."

"I don't blame you, Cesca. I just wish I'd asked more questions when the office told me your tour was a sellout." He sighed again. "Next time, huh?"

"Right," I said. "I'll call tomorrow."

I disconnected, then whirled at a touch on my back.

"Easy," Saber said, handing me a glass of sweet tea, heavy on the ice. His drink smelled like bourbon, neat, and Eugene Cassidy stood behind him holding a cola.

"I ran into Cassidy inside, but we can't find a table."

I glanced across the street at the courtyard of a closed coffee shop. Four people at one of the small metal tables were leaving.

"There?" I asked.

Saber nodded, and we trooped into the shadows of huge oaks.

"Miss Cesca," Eugene said as he pulled a chair out for me.

He still spoke in that deep North Carolina drawl, but it was no longer Gomer-ish. His black slacks and dark gray cotton shirt weren't tailored, but they fit him correctly.

"Miz Hayward said I can share any information with you, so where do you want to start?"

"With Etienne Fournier," I said as I settled in the seat. "What do you have on him?"

"You suspect him of killin' Yolette?"

"And maybe Rachelle, too," I said.

Eugene's gaze cut to Saber. "You were called in on Rachelle's case, right?"

Saber nodded. "And we know Ike drafted you to investigate the murder."

Eugene frowned. "How did you know?"

"Ike showed up for my tour tonight."

Eugene gave me a slow blink. "He left his lair?"

"Yes, so the sooner we figure this out, the sooner Ike will be off our backs. Did you see the Fourniers with Rachelle in Daytona Beach?"

"Briefly, in the parkin' lot at Ike's club. A client can't pay me enough to go into one of those places, so I ran surveillance from outside."

"Did Rachelle and the Fourniers leave together?" Saber asked.

"No. Rachelle went back inside, Yolette followed her, and Etienne went to their car. He sat a while, messin' with somethin' that looked like a flask."

"A flask? Like for liquor?" I asked.

"Yes, but I couldn't see what he did with it. After 'bout fifteen minutes, he went back inside."

"When you saw them outside the club," Saber pressed, "were they agitated? Seem to be arguing?"

"Tense. It seemed like a tense encounter," Eugene said slowly, his gaze going over Saber's shoulder as if picturing the scene. "Rachelle was holdin' herself stiffly. I didn't have my eavesdroppin' equipment set up, though now I wish I had."

"What about later?" I asked. "Did you see them again?"

He frowned. "Come to think on it, that was odd."

I waited with the proverbial baited breath, thinking I'd have to crawl down his throat to pull the words out.

"Rachelle and a whole group of 'em came out the second time. Most of 'em were actin' drunk or high. One of the females—not Rachelle—had herself draped all over Etienne. Kissin' on him, lickin' his ears. Hell, I thought she was gonna either bite him or sexually attack him right there in the parking lot."

I glanced at Saber. "Can vampires get drunk or high?"

"You don't know, Miss Cesca?" Eugene said, startled.

"I haven't hung around vampires for a long time, Eugene."

"Oh, a'course."

I raised a questioning brow at Saber. "Well?"

"On enough blood, yeah, vampires can get high. On booze and street drugs? I've never seen those affect them." Saber paused, then asked Eugene, "What was Rachelle doing in the parking lot the second time?"

"Talkin' to another of the female vamps, and that was definitely an argument. The one kept pushin' Rachelle—like she didn't want Rachelle back in the club."

"Do you know which vampire it was?" Saber asked.

"Not by name, but she was black, hair in cornrows. I'd recognize her."

I glanced at Saber, and we read each other loud and clear. Laurel.

"My wife called 'bout then," Eugene continued. "The hot water heater broke, and I had to get home."

"But the Fourniers were still at the club when you left?" Saber asked.

"They were. Even looked like they were headed back inside. Their car was empty when I passed it on the way out of the lot."

I sat back, picturing one vampire shoving another one as if to keep her outside. Laurel had been little miss bossy, zealous where Ike was concerned, and jealous, too. Could she have had a hand in bumping Rachelle off? Why would Etienne drink booze from a flask when Ike sold liquor? I couldn't see Etienne traveling with French brandy.

"...an engineer," Eugene was saying when I focused on the conversation again. "Etienne had never been married before Yolette, but he'd known her for a while. They both were deep into the vampire club scene for several years."

"You mean Yolette knew Etienne before she met James Peters?" Saber asked.

"Yep, and after." Eugene rubbed the back of his neck. "They were rumored to be lovers, but that lifestyle lends itself to sleepin' around."

"Wait, you think Yolette and Etienne were lovers during her marriage to James?" I asked. "Like a threesome?"

Eugene shook his head. "That I don't know. My Paris contact never got a consistent story about their activities." He turned his hands up in a go-figure gesture.

"Was there *any* consistent information?" Saber asked.

Eugene made a rueful face and pulled at his ear. "Only that Etienne hung around Yolette and James during the time they were a couple. Etienne might have a date, or he might be alone, but they socialized."

"Millie told us Yolette inherited some of James's estate," I said. "What about Etienne? Does he inherit from Yolette?"

Eugene shrugged. "My Paris contact might be able to find out about a prenup, but it won't be until Monday."

Eugene pulled out a small spiral, the kind Detective March used, and wrote *Inheritance* in neat script. We sat quietly for a minute, me trying to draw lines between the murders—all three of them, if I included James.

"Let's say," I mused aloud, "that Etienne is involved in the murders. The two humans wouldn't be difficult to kill—"

"But a vampire would be nigh on impossible," Eugene added.

"Right. Yolette and Etienne *seemed* obsessed with vampire sex, but were they really?"

Saber leaned forward, his elbows on the small table. "What are you cooking up now?"

"I can see Yolette into sex. She came off as bisexual."

Eugene nodded. "That fits what I saw."

"But," I went on, "Etienne seemed more—I don't know—remote? Like he didn't care one way or another but was mildly amused by Yolette's antics. That's how he acted when she propositioned me."

"Actually," Eugene drawled, "now that you mention it, he wasn't kissin' or cuddlin' the vampire who was all over him. He just sorta stood there. Yolette would be the one holdin' hands with a vampire or havin' her arm around one."

"Did Etienne look embarrassed? Tolerant? What?" Saber asked.

Eugene closed his eyes a minute. "Like Miss Cesca said, amused. Indulgent, maybe."

"Were you taking photos?" Saber asked.

"And video. I can e-mail the stills to one of you."

"Can't hurt," I said and rattled off my e-mail address. "So if Etienne wasn't in the vampire scene for sex, what drew him there?" I turned to Eugene. "What else do you have on him? Work, family, anything?"

He spread his hands as if at a loss. "He's the only child of parents livin' outside Paris. Works for a chemical company where he has a poor performance record. He's been demoted once and is on probation now."

"Why?" I asked.

"Comin' in late, sloppy work habits, that kind of thing." Eugene paused. "He had a good company reputation until he started carousin' at vampire clubs."

"What exactly does he do at the chemical company?" I asked over a buzzing noise.

Eugene shifted in the hard chair, pulled out his cell phone, and read the screen before he answered. "I guess he does whatever chemical engineers do. Develop chemicals, test 'em."

"Do you know what he was working on?"

"I'll check that with my contact Monday," he said, adding my questions to his list. "Anythin' else?"

"Just one other question," I said. "Why did you tell me you were Holland Peters?"

"Instead of stickin' with Gomer?" Eugene smiled and patted my hand where it lay on the table. "Truth is, I wanted to see if Yolette or Etienne would react to it. When Stony caused the scene and I had to give my name, I stuck with Holland."

"Did the Fourniers connect you with Yolette's first husband?" Saber asked.

"Didn't so much as blink when I said I was Peters," he admitted. "Cold fish, those two. I need to go, but if you get proof

Etienne killed Rachelle, I'd sure 'preciate bein' filled in. Ike is not a patient, uh, man."

Eugene had to stake out a hotel in Ormond Beach, but he left us his business cards, complete with his cell and fax numbers and his e-mail address. I tucked mine in the bodice of my Minorcan costume as he and Saber shook hands.

Bad move.

With Saber strolling beside me back up Hypolita toward the bay front, I was aware of the card in my bra and my musky aura. Each time Saber brushed my arm oh-so-casually, my body tightened, and my breasts distinctly tingled. I wasn't horny enough to chew nails yet, but my heart thu-thudded with every stray touch.

Distraction. I needed one, and fast, because getting it on with Saber was *not* on my agenda.

At Hypolita and St. George, we veered around a group of bikers reeking of beer and wearing almost as much leather as the vampire set.

"Can you take any legal action against Ike?" I asked when we passed the bikers.

Saber peered at me. "You mean to call him off Eugene?"

"Gee, no, I meant getting him to wear more cotton blends, less leather."

"Smart-ass," he said with a quirk of his mouth. "I could make noises about revoking his protected status, but he'll probably drop Eugene once the case is solved."

"What if it's not solved? I mean, we *are* down to Etienne as the killer, right?"

"He feels right for it, but we can't prove it."

"Then we're missing something. I know we've looked at this six ways from Sunday, but there has to be something we haven't stumbled on."

"Maybe, but this isn't one of your mysteries where the case is neatly resolved. Killers do get off, and Etienne isn't a U.S. citizen. We can't compel him to stick around without cause."

"Then we have to find cause," I muttered.

By unspoken agreement, we crossed Avenida Menendez and climbed the cement steps to the walkway running along the bay. I plopped down on the ledge of the seawall to think, leaned back where I thought one of the bollards was, and almost tumbled backward into the bay.

"Watch it!" Saber leapt to catch one of my flailing hands and jerk me off the ledge.

And into his arms.

We stood frozen, chest to breasts, pelvis to pelvis. His arms clamped around my waist, my arms encircled his neck. Breath caught and stuck in my throat as he looked into my eyes.

"You nearly went for a swim," he said, his softly exhaled words caressing my face.

"I wouldn't have been hurt."

"No, but the water's cold." His sensuous lips lifted in a seductive smile. "This is much warmer."

Warmer? If my body temperature careened any higher, I'd be a puddle at his feet. His hips rocked minutely against mine, and my breath came in hitches.

Then his cobalt gaze settled on my mouth.

"S-Saber," I whispered.

"Hmmm?"

"Are you planning to kiss me?"

His scent spiked—assertive, erotic, urgent. "Yeah, I am."

I waited a beat. "S-soon?"

He lowered his head with such excruciating slowness it felt like years before his lips brushed mine.

Once. Pause. Twice. Pause.

"Cesca," he said so low, my vampire hearing kicked in.

"Hmmm?"

"Close your eyes."

His mouth neared, his hand cupped the back of my head, and I let my eyes drift shut.

His lips nibbled mine, coaxed me to open to his tongue. I inhaled, drawing his scent into my lungs, his breath into my body. Fireworks exploded behind my eyelids.

Then it was over.

He broke off the kiss, slowly, and eased space between us.

I blinked against the glow of streetlights. In another second, I adjusted to standing without the brace of his body and slid my hands from his shoulders.

"Ready to go home?" he asked.

Home. With Saber. The idea didn't scare the bejeebers out of me anymore.

As we strolled southward, I listened to the muted sounds of sailing ships rocking at anchor in the bay. A rowboat glided toward one of the ships anchored nearest the seawall, but the rower didn't seem to be having an easy time of it.

A woman at the rail astern called down, "What's wrong, Cappy?"

"Damn boat's leaking again. It was supposed to be fixed."

"Honey, it was only a patch job."

Saber caught my gaze and grinned. We walked another dozen steps before it hit me. Yolette. A boat.

I stopped, spun, and stared at the rowboat. "That's it, Saber. That's what we've been missing."

He turned sharply. "What?"

"The boat. Yolette," I said fast, gut instinct telling me I was on the right track. "She was killed on land, but we found her in the ocean. How did she get there?"

Saber gave me a long look. "You think she was dumped on a sinking rowboat?"

I waved a hand and rushed on. "Not a rowboat necessarily, but I thought I saw a small boat just past the breakers before we all hit the surf Thursday morning. I reported it to March but didn't push it, because I figured it could have been a pelican riding a swell."

"With vampire vision you can't tell the difference between a boat and a pelican?"

"I didn't bother with vamp vision, not with the wind, spray, and blowing sand that morning. Besides, I was there to surf, not scan the horizon for whatever might be out there."

"Why do you think Yolette was in a boat?"

"One, because when Shelly Jergason mentioned the loud renters that night at bridge club, she also said they'd borrowed a rowboat from a neighbor without asking. That gives Etienne access. Two, if Yolette was dumped straight into the water, her body would've sunk. She wouldn't have been found for days."

"A body will float longer in salt water."

"How long?"

He shrugged. "Thirty minutes, maybe more. Water seeps into body cavities eventually."

"But you said she was killed between two and five in the morning. We were on the beach at six. And Etienne was getting his fishing boat somewhere in Gainesville—which is a good hour and a half away, even if you're speeding—at six fifteen."

"I'm following," Saber said slowly. "Etienne couldn't dump the body much after four thirty and still get to the lake."

"And with the nor'easter coming, isn't it more likely the body would either wash back up on shore or be pulled out to sea by the riptides?"

He frowned. "Could've been a fluke of the storm and incoming tides that she washed up when she did."

"But she hadn't been nibbled on by fish or crabs or whatever. She couldn't have been in the water that long."

Saber looked back at the rowboat, now tied off and riding low in the water. "If she were in a boat, it would tend to suck her body under as it sank."

"Not if it sank slow enough."

"Waves would've swamped it."

"Maybe, but it won't hurt to see if there's a boat missing from the neighborhood. See if there were splinters in Yolette's body."

"All right, I'm convinced it's possible," Saber said with a small smile. He took my hand and tugged to get me moving.

I worked at not hyperventilating when he kept his hand snug around mine. "So we'll call March right now?"

He sighed. "First thing in the morning."

"But Etienne's had days now to cover his tracks," I protested as we neared the Bridge of Lions.

"Yes, but since the murder, the neighbors have been watching him every second he's outside the house or on the beach." Saber waggled his brows.

I pictured Shelly, then a neighbor like Mrs. Kravitz on *Bewitched*, and grinned. "I take it these are nosy neighbors?"

He gave my fingers a squeeze. "Civic-minded. March said dispatch is sending deputies out there at least once a day."

I chuckled and matched his steps as we crossed the street. The bank parking lot, shrouded in shadows on my right, reminded me that Etienne was our vandal as well as our murderer.

"Etienne trashed my truck, too."

"Like you said, it was a diversionary tactic, and so was planting evidence at Gorman's house."

We passed a Greek restaurant and small shops closed for the night, and I fished in my skirt pocket for my keys. Only steps from home, I wrinkled my nose at the still-lingering coppery odor. Saber gave me a sideways glance.

"What's wrong?" he asked, holding his hand out for my keys.

"The blood smell is still here, but there's not a drop of blood on the sidewalk, the stoop, or the walls."

"Could be some of Gorman's blood soaked into the soil." Saber pointed to a planter box nestled against the sidewalk wall.

As he unlocked the door, I leaned over the neatly cut shrubs and native lantana and sniffed. "It could be in the dirt," I conceded, straightening, "but the scent is awfully strong. Like if an artery or vein were opened. You can't smell it at all?"

He ran a hand through his hair. "No. Don't take this the wrong way, but is there a chance you're imagining the smell?"

"As in the power of suggestion?" I challenged him, fists on my hips. "No. It's too similar to the blood smell on Yolette and on my truck."

"Then there has to be an explanation," he said, pocketing my keys and stepping over the threshold.

"Wait, are you saying you believe me?"

"Come here." Saber came back to the stoop, caught my hand, and gave me a gentle tug up the single step. In another second he'd kiss me right there in the doorway. I saw it in his eyes as cobalt darkened to midnight blue.

A sound between a crack and *pufft* came from the plaza, and Saber's eyes widened as I lurched into his arms, a blaze of burning pain in my right shoulder.

As he pulled me through the door to safety and laid me in the hall, cursing all the way, I had only two fears: that the shooter was coming for Saber and that the bullet in my shoulder was silver.

EIGHTEEN

~⚊~

I'd never been shot, so I didn't know what physical symptoms to expect from silver in my body any more than I knew exactly what to expect from sex.

Except I didn't figure sex would hurt as much.

Turned out the bullet wasn't silver. It was plain lead, shot from a .22 rifle, according to Saber, who saw it come out of my shoulder and *pling* into a surgical steel bowl. From there, an officer from the St. Augustine Police Department took custody of the slug as evidence.

Saber insisted on staying with me in the treatment room. The same doctor who'd changed out my GPS tracker was on duty, and, because my vampire body was already healing the wound, the doc decided to remove the bullet on the spot in the ER.

Facedown on the exam table, I cringed when the doc cut away the blouse of my Minorcan costume and my bra, squirmed when the nurse cleaned the wound. The scent of my own blood might've made me woozy, but the doc smelled of lime cologne, antiseptic, and pine cleaner. A freaky combination, but an effective distraction.

Of course, Saber stroking the back of my legs from knee to ankle during the impromptu surgery was darned distracting, too.

We left the ER just over an hour after we'd arrived. I wore a blue cotton hospital gown over a bulky bandage and my costume skirt. Saber wore a scowl so fierce it sent a young ER clerk scuttling back to his desk.

The crime scene still crawled with activity when we returned to the condo building. Saber's hand at the small of my back, subtly guiding me through the onlookers and some press, was reassuringly warm.

So many city and county cop cars and uniformed personnel milled around, I wondered why they were all needed. Yellow tape cordoned off most of the block and plaza, breaking only at the street where police stopped anyone attempting to get in or out. The cop we checked in with was the same woman who'd shown up when my truck was vandalized Thursday night. Only two days and a lifetime ago.

Detective March and another man in plain clothes met us in the street in front of the bank and condo entrance.

"You find the weapon?" Saber asked immediately.

"Negative," March said. "This is Detective Balch, St. Augustine Police Department."

"Balch," Saber acknowledged, shaking hands with the thin, blond man.

I murmured a greeting but kept my arms pinned at my sides so my flimsy gown didn't flap in the off-bay breeze and expose more than I wanted seen.

"Ms. Marinelli," March said, "I imagine you want to get

upstairs, and Balch and I need to get statements from both of you, if you're up to it."

Saber's hand flexed on my back, and from the corner of my eye I saw his look of surprise. "You've finished processing the front stoop and hallway?"

Balch answered. "I made it a priority when March explained the victim's, uh, special needs."

I didn't like the way Balch's eyes slid away from mine, but putting him on the spot wouldn't be mannerly. Besides I was tired, so I aimed a grateful smile at both Balch and March.

"You're right, I need to be in my own space. Thank you."

Balch ducked his head and turned to lead the way to the tenant entrance as he filled us in.

"Looks like the shot was fired from a .22 rifle somewhere between the gazebo and the old market," he said, gesturing across the street to the plaza. "If the guy didn't keep the rifle with him, he could've tossed it anywhere."

"Including the bay," Saber agreed, running his hand through his dark hair.

I stopped on the sidewalk and shuddered.

Saber eyed me a second. "You still smell the blood?"

I glanced at Balch and March, who'd walked ahead of us. "Not as strongly now, but yeah, I do."

Saber nodded and turned to the detectives. "Do me a favor," he said. "Take a sample of the soil in this planter by the entry. Test it for blood—fresh and old blood."

"Why?" March asked, his frown puzzled. "Ms. Marinelli wasn't on the stoop long enough to bleed into the planter."

"I know, but Cesca keeps sensing an odor we're trying to track down."

"You're smelling blood?" Balch asked, his voice heavy with distrust. "Is this a vampire thing?"

"Yes, Detective Balch." I met his guarded gaze matter-of-factly. "I don't know if it *is* blood, or if I'm just sensing it that way, but it could be important."

"And you'd like us to check it out." Balch held eye contact a moment, then shrugged and called a female tech over. Once he'd given her instructions, he said, "Ready to go up?"

I glanced at Saber. Judging from his impatient expression, we were more than ready.

In the condo, I excused myself to change into blue nylon elastic-waist pants and a dark green cotton shirt. I'd bought the shirt large and loose to wear as a light jacket over sweaters. Tonight it helped hide the fact that I was braless. My shoulder hurt more by the time I'd finished, but I managed not to grit my teeth when I returned to the living room.

Saber handed me a glass of ice as I settled at one end of Maggie's blue couch. He held a Coors bottle and sat on the middle cushion. March and Balch took the armchairs and held little spiral notebooks.

"We got the basic facts from Saber while you were changing," March said. "What do you remember, Ms. Marinelli?"

"We got near the tenant entrance," I started. "I don't remember what we were talking about, but I smelled blood and mentioned it to Saber."

"Who's blood did you think it was?" Balch asked.

"I didn't think it was anyone's in particular, but Saber said it could've been Gorman's." I stopped and looked at March. "Gorman is still in the hospital, right?"

"Right," March said, "but I sent a deputy to talk to him anyway."

"On the chance," Saber added, "one of his Covenant buddies did it."

"And?" I prompted looking from Saber to March to Balch.

"According to the nurses and hospital call records," March said, "Gorman hasn't had a single call or civilian visitor— other than when you saw him this afternoon." March paused and smiled. "But then, he's not your main suspect, is he, Ms. Marinelli?"

"My what?" I asked, looking to Saber for help.

Saber shrugged. "I told them we've been eliminating suspects."

"Then you know we think Etienne is the killer. What's bothering me is the plain lead bullet." I gestured with my glass of ice. "I mean, Etienne used silver ammunition on Rachelle and Yolette. Why change if he wanted me dead?"

"Maybe he only wanted to scare you," Balch said.

"Or," Saber piped in, "he ran out of silver ammo."

"Or maybe," March added, "Saber was the target, and you got in the way."

The fine hair on my arms stiffened as I turned to Saber. "Why would Etienne want you dead?"

He shrugged. "I have no idea."

"Did you hear or see—or smell—anything else before the shot?" Balch asked. "Anything at all?"

"Sorry, no. Like I said, Saber and I were talking. I was focused on that."

"What happened after the shot?" he pressed.

"My shoulder burned, and I pitched forward. Saber pulled

me in the door and about halfway down the hall. I think he drew his gun, and I heard him call 911."

"And that's all you remember?" Balch asked.

"That's it."

"Ms. Marinelli," Balch said, shifting in the chair, "could Etienne Fournier want to kidnap you? Extort money from you in exchange for, say, letting Saber live?"

"Depends on how crazy he is. Vampires aren't exactly easy marks. Even if he'd wounded Saber, Etienne had to know I'd fight back if he came after us in the building." I blew out a frustrated breath. "That's why it doesn't make sense."

"We can speculate all we want, but it won't catch the bad guy." March tucked his little spiral notebook in his pocket as he rose from the chair. "I need to get back downstairs. Balch, you have more questions?"

"Not at this time." Balch and Saber stood, too, and Balch shook Saber's hand. He didn't offer his hand to me, but he did smile. "Hope you heal up fast, Ms. Marinelli. We'll call to have you come sign your statement."

Since Saber had my keys and knew the elevator code, he played host and showed the detectives out. I slumped into the fluffy couch cushions and tried to dig up some enthusiasm for yet another trip to a cop shop. Sleuthing was sure taking up my formerly spare and uncomplicated time.

I don't know how long I drifted, thinking of nothing much but catching up with my online classes and getting my life back on a schedule, when the door lock snicked and Saber's footsteps crossed to the kitchen. The fridge door opened. Bottles clinked. Liquid sloshed as if in a bottle being shaken.

He was shaking beer?

I heard my mini-fridge motor kick on. The door had been opened. Damn!

I jackknifed up to glare over the couch back as Saber saundered toward me with a bottle of Starbloods in each hand.

"You opened both fridge doors at the same time, didn't you?" I accused as I jumped off the couch.

"Yep, and you can complain about my snooping after you drink up." He held both bottles out to me expectantly.

I crossed my arms, wincing when my right shoulder protested the stretch. "I only drink one at a time."

"No, you have two sometimes," he argued with a smile.

"How would you know?"

"Old-fashioned detective work," he said. "I counted the bottles in the bin. Your recycling day is Monday, so you should have six used bottles. You have nine. Ergo, you've had extra shots—I suspect when you had the tracker changed out."

"Fine," I said, plucking first one, then the other bottle from his hold with my good arm. "I'll be back in a minute."

"Hold it," he said, moving fast to block my escape. "You don't have a microwave in your room."

"So?"

"Aren't you going to warm up the Starbloods?"

"I drink it cold."

I veered around Saber, but he caught me around the waist and spun, not hurting my shoulder but backing me into the kitchen island. He braced his hands on the countertop, and his arms brushed my sides.

"What," I snapped, "are you doing? I told you I'd be back."

"I want to be sure you drink it all. Now." He stared like a stern nurse. "Down the hatch, Cesca."

"Saber, I don't drink in public."

"You're not in public. You're in your own home."

"I don't let people watch me drink," I ground out.

"You do now. Come on, stop stalling," he cajoled. "You need to heal that shoulder, and I'm making sure you drink every drop."

I reached over his arm to set one bottle on the counter, and shook the other one gently. Not the best delaying tactic, but Saber didn't look ready to budge.

"The least you could do is turn around."

"No."

I ground my teeth. "Fine, then *I'll* turn around."

His lips twitched, but he didn't laugh when I wiggled in the circle of his arms until I faced the far kitchen wall. The protective plastic made crinkly noises as I ripped it off, and the cap came off with a *thwunk*. With a deep breath, I pinched my nose shut and chugged my Starbloods. No sooner did I put the first bottle down than Saber held the second one over my shoulder, already uncapped. As I downed that one, Saber stepped away from me and over to the dining table.

"See, that wasn't so bad."

It wasn't, but I didn't have to let on. I took both bottles and metal lids to the sink, rinsed them, and put them in the recycling bin before I had the nerve to look at Saber again.

"Happy now?" I asked.

"Ecstatic."

"Good. Now, if you'll excuse me," I said rounding the counter to head for my room, "I need to brush my teeth."

"Hurry back. I brought your mail in."

I stopped in my doorway. "I should say thanks, but I bet you snooped through that, too."

"Only a little."

From behind his back, he produced the set of *Monk* DVDs I'd ordered, flourishing them as if he were a magician. "Unless you're too tired, I thought we could curl up on the couch and watch a marathon."

"I thought we'd discuss the shooting," I said.

"What's to discuss? It wasn't Gorman, and much as Ike might want to off one or both of us, he wouldn't bother with a gun."

"But what good would it do Etienne to shoot either of us?" I asked, surprised that he seemed so, well, blasé about the incident now. "It just doesn't make sense."

"No, it doesn't," he agreed as he opened the DVD box. "But rehashing it won't solve anything either."

"Saber," I said, crossing to stand nearer and plead my case. "We can at least check the photos Eugene was supposed to e-mail. Maybe there's a clue in them. Something to really tie Etienne to the murders."

Saber tossed the box on the couch and lightly laid his hands on my shoulders. "We've done all we can, Cesca. We gave March solid information. It's his jurisdiction, his job to finish."

I fought to ignore the thrill of Saber's touch. "March will call us after he talks to Etienne?"

"Tomorrow. Maybe he'll have made an arrest by then. And," he added, sliding his fingertips down my good arm and capturing my hand, "if you don't feel like watching *Monk*, we'll do something else."

The way his voice deepened, I knew what that something else might be. Kissing I could handle. Sex? My heart thumped double its usual time. Nope, I wasn't ready for that. Was I?

Besides, maybe watching Monk solve cases would inspire us with some brilliant way of catching Etienne. Couldn't hurt.

After sharing so much action with Saber, it was weird to do something mundane like watch TV together. The intimacy made me twitchy, or maybe it was just my shoulder aching, but I couldn't seem to settle in one spot.

We were half an hour into the first episode when Saber hit the Pause button.

"Are you hurting?" he asked, peering in my eyes.

"Why?"

"You keep squirming over there," he said, "over there" being my end of the couch.

"I'm a little uncomfortable," I admitted, "but I'll find a good position in a minute."

"No, you won't. Come here."

He took my hand, braced his back against the sofa arm, and tugged me into the V of his spread legs until my hip brushed his crotch. I started to scramble away, but he slung his arm around my waist and snuggled my left side to his chest.

"Does that take the pressure off your shoulder?" he asked.

"Um, yes." It put pressure other places, like low in my belly, but I didn't say that.

"Good, now relax."

Surprisingly, after my hormones stopped spiking, I did.

Three episodes into our marathon, Saber decided he was hungry. We found Maggie's stash of microwave popcorn and, while it popped, Saber inched my shirt off my right shoulder to check the bandage. His touch should've been clinical, but to me it was erotic. So was his warm breath on my neck. Our kiss at the bay front leapt to mind in vivid detail, and my pheromones fired. In the nick of time, the microwave beeped. Instead of chewing nails to take the edge off my horniness, I munched on a few handfuls of the extra buttery popcorn, then washed the salt taste away with water, heavy on the ice.

When we'd finished snacking, Saber pulled me against his chest again, but he didn't use the remote right away. He used his lips, kissing my temple through a curtain of hair, then lifting it from my neck to plant a kiss on my shoulder. My body reacted, but my brain did, too.

"Uh, Saber," I said, as he turned me in his arms. His cobalt blue eyes had darkened to midnight. "What are you doing?"

"Making a pass," he whispered. "Why, am I doing it wrong?"

"Oh, no, you're doing it, ahhh, fine," I breathed as he swirled his tongue around my ear. "But," I gulped, "but you're a vampire hunter and, uh-oh, executioner, and I'm—"

"The weirdest vampire I've ever met?"

"Uh-huh."

"I'm forgetting all that right now."

"Why?"

"Because you're also," he said, kissing my jaw as if to punctuate the words, "a delectable, desirable woman."

"I-I am?"

"You are." He cupped my jaw. "Now, are you going to analyze or enjoy?"

"Just remember," I murmured as his lips neared, "you started this."

His mouth settled on mine like it was there for the long haul. And it was. Hurt shoulder? What shoulder? Saber's legs and arms encircled me, his sensuous lips and teeth nipped and teased me into a hot, panting puddle of need. It would probably kill me, but I could hardly wait for more.

That's when the kissing stopped and Saber rested his forehead against mine.

"God, you're responsive," he said hoarsely.

I fought to get my brain back in working order. "That's a good thing, right?"

He raised his head enough to look in my eyes. "Hell, yes. It's great."

"So why are we stopping?"

"Because," he said, grabbing the remote and shifting me back to rest on his chest, "I won't stop at all if we go any further."

"And that's a bad thing?"

"Cesca, watch the show."

I was still cooling off when Saber proposed a contest to see which of us could solve the mystery before Monk did. Maybe Saber was still coming down, too. The rod in his jeans sure hadn't softened during the postkiss *Monk* episode. I found some satisfaction in that. Not as much as I wanted, but, hey, since Saber showed no signs of making another pass, and since I wasn't blinded by flashes of insight into our own case, I took him up on the contest.

Four episodes later, we were tied at two solutions each.

During the last episode, near dawn, I felt Saber's breathing go slow and rhythmic, and I let my eyes drift shut.

I awoke on my bed, the rose-colored chenille throw from Maggie's room covering me, Saber whistling from the kitchen. I sat up to read the clock on the other side of the bed. It was three thirty, but I noticed more than the time of day.

The second pillow on my bed held the impression of a head. The head that made the dent wasn't mine.

Oh, my.

Had Saber really slept with me? And I missed it?

Did I snore? Oh, please, let me not have snored.

Before I worked myself into a tizzy, Saber knocked on the bedroom door, and I whipped around to face him.

"Hey, how's your shoulder?" he asked as he came to stand by the bed.

Dressed in blue jeans and a lighter blue cotton shirt, no shoes, he smelled of soap, shampoo, and vital, virile man.

I gulped. What had he asked me?

"Here, let me take a look at it," he said, reaching for me.

I hurriedly held the shirt against my chest. "It's fine. Really. I bet it's all healed."

"Then I'll get the bandage off for you." He pulled the neck of my shirt back slowly enough for me to keep my breasts covered, then peeled off the tape and gauze as he casually added, "It healed. Good. Oh, by the way, March called."

"When? Did he arrest Etienne?"

"He called at three. No arrest."

"Why not?"

Saber shrugged. "No evidence."

"None at all? What about a boat? Did the divers find one?"

Saber sat on the bed and took my hand. "No, and Etienne is

hinting at harassment. Said he wants Yolette's body tomorrow so he can leave. If we try to detain him, he'll be on the phone to his consulate and the press."

"But, Saber, we know he did it."

"Technically, we don't know. We need hard evidence to make murder charges stick." He shook his head. "We could still get lucky, but I'm not optimistic."

"We could trick him into admitting to the crimes."

"Not without stomping on his rights."

"But he's not a U.S. citizen."

"All the more reason we can't entrap him," Saber said.

"So there's nothing we can do?"

He waggled his brows. "Well, I can think of a thing or two, but you need to return a call from your tour company, and Maggie phoned to tell you she'll be home by seven."

"Oh." I bit my lip but had to ask. "Are you going back to Daytona?"

"Not tonight," he said, rising from the bed. "You're down to one bottle of Starbloods, and I thought you might need a ride to the health food store tomorrow."

It was a lame excuse, and I knew he knew I knew it. But what the heck. Saber was staying a little longer.

"Sure, that would be great." I smiled as I rose from the bed and stood within a foot of him.

"Fine, then. I'll let you return your call and get dressed." But he didn't move toward the door. "I'm going out for a sandwich. You want anything?"

"No thanks."

I stood rooted to the floor. So did Saber.

"I'll lock you in, just in case."

"Okay."

Pheromones spiked—his and mine. His eyes darkened and, when he stepped closer, I swayed toward him.

He lifted a tangled lock of my hair and tucked it behind my ear. "Princesca."

I blinked at the nickname. "What?"

"I watched you sleep this afternoon."

I nodded. "I saw the indention in the pillow."

"You don't sleep like you're dead."

"I don't?"

"No," he said, cupping my jaw. "You make little sighing noises in your sleep."

"Oh." *I didn't snore? Yes!*

"I'm going to do now what I wanted to do then."

"Wh-what?"

He framed my face with his hands, his fingers sliding into my hair. "Kiss you again."

My body went liquid. "Will this be soon?"

He smiled. "Oh, yeah."

His thumb teased the crease of my mouth for the barest second before his lips closed on mine. Next thing I knew, we were locked pelvis to pelvis, tongues tasting each other in a kiss so hot I felt fevered. He rubbed his jean-clad erection across my lower belly, and my ears rang with the force of my own blood pumping hard through my veins. When he gripped my butt to lift me higher, fit me into him, my knees buckled. He kept us upright, but only until he angled me onto the bed and followed me down. Breath harsh, he nuzzled my neck as he settled between my legs.

"Princesca," he whispered hoarsely, his voice as deep as I wanted him to be inside me.

"Saber, my ears are ringing," I breathed as he flicked my shirt buttons free. "Is that supposed to happen?"

"It's the phone," he murmured as he kissed the slopes of my partly bared breasts.

"What phone?" My nipples tightened as Saber slowly slid the soft shirt fabric over them.

"Do you care?" He closed his mouth on one aching nipple.

"Nooo, ohhhh."

The tug of his suckling shot straight to the spot his erection teased, and I gasped and arched into him. He thrust back, and laved my other breast, flicking the nipple with his tongue. Waves of pleasure rolled through me, and yet there was more, just out of reach.

Skin. I needed to touch his skin.

"Saber," I said, hardly hearing my own voice as I pulled at his shirt.

He groaned when the material rent and fell away. I smoothed my hands over his back, learning his shape and texture from broad shoulders to spine to narrow waist.

He rolled off me, and I felt my nylon pants and panties peel off with a few sweeps of his hand. When the air hit that much bare skin, reality hit, too. The pros and cons of sex with Saber raced through my brain, but the biggest pro was that we were here now, hot and ready.

I opened my eyes to find his smoldering gaze steady on my face.

"Do you want to stop?"

"Do you want me to raid Home Depot?"

He blinked. "Home Depot?"

"Yeah," I said, my voice husky. "Maggie says when you're horny enough to chew nails, it's time for sex."

His sensuous lips lifted in a killer smile. "I'm gonna give you a lot more than sex, love."

I knew he didn't mean *love*, and, as he ran his hand lightly down the center of my body from neck to belly, it didn't matter. Saber would initiate me, and, however odd a couple we might be—even for this one time—I was safe in his arms. When his fingers inched lower still, he kissed me, and I lost all reason. He stroked me with his torturing fingers, sliding over my folds, into me and out again. The pressure built, and he urged me to let go, but I didn't know how.

"Saber, I need more," I gasped. "I need you."

Through a haze of lust, I saw him chuck his jeans and black boxers, and, when he braced his body over mine, I spread my legs to welcome him. He probed, and I stretched to enfold him. My legs locked around his waist, and with a long quick thrust, he filled me. After a moment to adjust to him so deep inside, he stroked, nipping at my mouth, my neck. I rode a swell that crested but wouldn't break.

"Princesca," he cried out, and sank his teeth into my neck.

Suddenly, the crest peaked and crashed, and I tumbled in waves of pulsing pleasure.

When the tremors eased, and our breathing slowed, Saber gave my neck a lingering kiss, then pushed up on his elbows to smile into my eyes.

"Good thing you heal fast," he said, pushing a strand of hair off my forehead. "I just gave you the mother of all hickeys."

Memory flooded back. "That's right, you bit me," I said, awed. "I'm pretty sure I'm supposed to do that."

"Nope," he said, teasing me with another thrust. "You. Don't. Bite. People."

"True." I squirmed under him. His eyes went lusty again. "And I guess that's fair, since I tore your shirt."

"Ummm. My last clean one." He slid out of me just a little, then slowly back in, deep, hard, hot.

My legs locked low on his, I caressed his butt. "Saber?"

"Yeah?" he croaked.

"Kiss me again."

"Soon?" he asked, flexing inside me.

"Now."

NINETEEN

Cosmil sat on the shanty porch in the willow wood rocker. The dappled late afternoon light danced in the clearing, but it did not soothe him.

"Francesca was shot last night," he said, rustling the newspaper as he refolded it. "The animal attack is reported as well." He sighed and glanced at Pandora. "I should not have recalled you so soon, my friend. I put you both in danger."

Cosmil watched Pandora for a reaction, but the big cat sat on its haunches beside the rocker and calmly licked a massive paw. Too calmly, perhaps, yet Cosmil would not scold Pandora for defending herself against the drunkard who had cornered her as she'd made her way home. It had only been a small bite, after all, not a kill.

Pandora ceased licking and raised her amber gaze to Cosmil.

You foresaw only the vampires as a threat last night. Magick is not infallible.

"True." Cosmil paused. "She handled herself well, did she not? Used her power without abusing it."

You no longer see her as a monster, Old Wizard.

Cosmil sighed. "Not for a long while now, though I see more tests for her before the week's end."

Then Triton comes at last?

"Yes, and we must protect Francesca until he arrives."

You wish me to watch her again?

Cosmil buried a hand in Pandora's ruff. "Please, Pandora. I must concentrate on cloaking Triton while he travels."

Shall I kill this man who smells of blood?

"Not out of hand," Cosmil said. "Human justice must be served, if possible."

Pandora snorted but leapt off the porch to head for the city. Cosmil drew a circle in the air, and the concealing spell he'd conjured for Pandora's extra protection snapped into place.

Showering with Saber was my erotic dream come true, only better. Unsure and shy at first, I was soon hotter than the water cascading over us. Saber showed me a creative use for the built-in tiled bench and the term *pulsating showerhead* took on a whole new meaning.

We toweled each other off and might have drifted back into bed, but the phone rang incessantly. Finally I dashed to answer the cordless extension unit that had fallen on the floor—don't ask me when—while Saber went to dress in Maggie's room.

It was the ghost tour company asking me to fill in for a guide who had a family emergency. I wanted the evening free to spend with Saber, but they'd tried everyone else on the backup list, so I agreed to take the gig. I'd be safe with Saber, and though I didn't know where he'd be sleeping tonight, I hoped to grab more alone time with him.

Let's face it, I hoped to grab more of him, period.

Ten minutes later, I was wearing terry cloth shorts and a T-shirt and blowing my hair with my hurricane-force dryer when Saber padded up behind me, barefoot and bare-chested but wearing his dress slacks.

"Heard anything more from Maggie?" Saber yelled over the noise of the blow dryer.

"Nope, but she's due home in a little over an hour," I called back, smiling as our gazes met in the mirror.

He caressed my hip and held up a black turtleneck pullover. "You think Neil would mind if I borrow this?"

"He'll never notice."

"He will if you rip it off me," he said and pulled the thin sweater on. His muscles rippled under the fabric, and my hair dryer suddenly seemed too hot.

I switched it off and turned to Saber. "Need I mention the biting incident again?"

"That little bitty hickey isn't healed yet?" He hooked one arm around my waist and lifted my hair for a peek.

"Not quite." I laid my hands on his forearms to brace myself when Saber nuzzled the fast-fading bruise. "I'll wear a shawl for the tour tonight."

He froze and pulled back. "I thought you had the night off."

"The guide on the schedule had an emergency, and no one else was available. We can go together and, um, do something later."

"I can't go, Cesca." He let go of me and raked a hand through his hair. "I have to go to Hastings to investigate a suspected werebite, damn it."

"A werebite?" I echoed. "I thought werecreatures were extinct."

"They are, far as I know, but it's my job to check out this kind of report. Problem is, Gorman's out of the hospital."

I tensed, then shook it off. "Saber, it'll be fine. Hastings is only twenty or thirty minutes away, and Gorman isn't likely to take a run at me so soon—not after the beating he took."

Saber gathered me in his arms and hugged me tight. "You're overestimating his intelligence."

"I'm gauging his self-preservation," I replied, hugging him back, enjoying his scent and how natural it felt to be in his arms.

He dropped a kiss on my head and stepped back. "Still, an ounce of prevention won't hurt." He flipped his cell phone open. "You have the late tour?"

"No, the eight o'clock."

"Let's see if March can suggest an off-duty deputy to hang out with the tour."

"Saber, a bodyguard isn't necessary. Really. By Murphy's Law alone, I should have an easy tour tonight."

"I trust firepower, Cesca, not fate," he said, wheeling out of my room when March came on the line.

I admit his protectiveness was endearing. I eavesdropped on his end of the conversation while I wielded the flatiron—until he went into Maggie's room. I lost the words then, but made pretty darn good inroads on my hair by the time Saber came back carrying his duffel bag and looking grim.

I set the iron on a towel and gave Saber my full attention. "What's wrong?"

He dropped his bag on my bed. "March gave me an update. Ballistics positively matched one of the .22s we found in Gorman's house as the murder weapon, but the serial numbers were filed off. We can't trace it."

"And Gorman swears up and down that it was planted, right?"

"You got it. There's no sign of a .22 rifle, and if Yolette was set adrift in a leaking boat, it hasn't shown up yet."

"What about the soil samples from the planter box?"

"No word yet. Hell, that could take a week. And," he added darkly, "Etienne made good on his threat to call the French consulate. A small jet is on standby to fly him out of here Monday with Yolette's body."

"A small jet to go all the way to France?"

"We think he may go to Miami. There's no flight plan filed yet."

"Saber, how soon do you have to leave for Hastings?"

He glanced at his watch. "The sooner the better. March doesn't seem to have a deputy available tonight. If I can wrap up the bite business quick, I can be back before nine and catch up with your tour."

"Before you go," I said, heading for my desk and laptop, "let's see if Eugene sent those photos he took in Daytona."

"What do you expect to find?"

"I don't know, but it can't hurt to look."

I slipped into my chair and retrieved my e-mail. Saber leaned over my shoulder, his hand braced on the desk. A few minutes, and there they were in an attachment, Eugene's surveillance photos ranging from wide angles to telephoto shots. They weren't all as clear on my system as they might be firsthand, but he'd captured several good shots of Yolette and a frightened-looking Rachelle.

"What did Yolette do or threaten to do that would spook a vampire as much as Rachelle looks spooked?" I asked aloud.

"And, if she was under Ike's protection, why didn't she ask him to help her?" Saber said.

"I don't know, but get a load of Laurel in this one." I enlarged a picture of Laurel shoving Rachelle away from the club's doorway.

"Pull up the shot of Etienne in the car again," Saber directed.

I did and enlarged it several times until we could make out the flask in his hand. A flask that seemed to wink silver in the parking lot light.

"Why carry a flask when the club sells booze?" I asked.

"Maybe he had something else in it. Is there a shot of him drinking from the flask?"

I scrolled through the photos again, enlarging here and there, but only one showed the flask.

"Damn, another dead end," I said, closing the file.

"At least these put the Fourniers with Rachelle on the night before she was found dead," Saber said. "And did you notice Gorman's not in these shots? Not even in the wide-angle crowd shots."

"Which means," I said as I stood, "he wasn't close enough to pose a threat, even if he was armed."

Saber cupped the back of my head and stepped close to me. "I need to hit the road, but promise me you'll be careful." He moved his mouth over mine and murmured, "I have plans for us."

Saber left at six fifteen with his gear, but his declaration of having plans for us lingered. I replayed it as I finished my hair,

drank my last Starbloods, and cleaned Maggie's suite. Not that
Saber had left a mess. He'd even stripped the sheets and cleaned
the bathroom.

I made the mistake of inhaling his scent from the sheets as I
carried them to the laundry room, and fantasies exploded. Us in
a hotel room making each other pant and sweat and climaxing
at the same time the way it happened in romance novels. Too
bad I'd taken *The Kama Sutra* back to the library. I got so hot
thinking about getting wild with Saber, I had to stick my head
in the freezer.

Which is where Maggie found me when she blew in the door
at seven.

"Is the ice maker on the fritz again?" she asked as she
propped her little wheeled suitcase by the table.

"Uh, no," I stuttered and slammed the freezer door. "It's
fine. I'm just, um, making sure it's on."

She gave me a raised-brow look. "Did Saber do something to
upset you?"

"Oh, no. Not a thing. We're fine."

"Where is he any—" Maggie broke off and stared. "Cesca,
why on earth are you blushing?"

"Come talk to me while I get ready for the tour," I said,
rounding the island and heading for my room.

"What tour? I thought you had tonight off."

"I'm filling in," I told her as I broke out my makeup supplies.
"Saber had to go to Hastings to investigate something, but he's
coming back later."

Maggie leaned against the bathroom counter and frowned.
"Is what's-his-face, Stony, on the streets again? Because I don't
feel good about you working with that nut running loose."

"They can't lock Gorman up, Maggie, but it's fine," I assured her while I swiped on eye color. "He took a good beating, you know, and I doubt he's up to following me around tonight."

I didn't remember if I'd told her Etienne was our real culprit, but I didn't mention it now. She'd only freak.

"I can go with you," Maggie offered.

"No," I said, wielding the mascara wand. "You just got home. Saber cleaned your suite, and I put fresh sheets on the bed. I'm sure you have things to do before work tomorrow."

"What are you doing after the tour?"

"You might want to make that *who* am I doing." I opened the face powder and waited for my wording to sink in.

Maggie's eyes went saucer round. "Oh. My. God. That's why you were blushing. You've had sex. With Saber. Oh. My. God. How did it happen?"

"Well, first, it happened with him on top."

"Too much information, smart-ass," Maggie said and lightly slapped my arm. "Come on, you know what I mean. Thursday you didn't want anything to do with him, and now you're an item? What changed?"

"I'm not sure exactly," I said, sweeping the powder brush over my face. "He kissed me on our way back from the tour last night, and then when I was—"

I caught myself before I said "shot," put the powder brush down, and locked gazes with Maggie.

"The good news is I'm fine. Well, you can see that, right?"

"Spit it out, Cesca."

"I was shot last night, but," I said, holding up a hand to keep her from interrupting, "it wasn't Gorman, because he was in the hospital. The cops don't know who did it."

"You were shot?" Maggie's eyes slitted.

"In the back of my right shoulder in front of the building," I confirmed. "The paramedics took me to Flagler, but I was already healing by the time the doc saw me."

I rounded out the event by telling her that the sheriff's office and the city police were investigating.

"You were shot last night, but you're traipsing off to do another tour tonight when Saber's not going to be there to protect you?"

"He couldn't protect me last night, Maggie. Neither of us saw it coming, but I wasn't in a crowd then," I said as I packed away my makeup. "Tonight I will be, and Saber's going to catch up to the tour by nine."

Maggie took a deep breath and unballed her clenched fists. "Let's skip over this and get to the good stuff. What happened with Saber? Not the intimate details," she said, giving me a wicked grin, "just the overview."

I laughed. "You know, I'm not sure." I grabbed my Regency outfit from the closet and filled her in as she helped me into the gown. "After the detectives left, we were watching the *Monk* DVDs I ordered, and he kissed me again. Then, this afternoon, he took the dressing off my shoulder and things just happened."

"Good things, I take it?"

"I thought so," I said, trying not to sound dreamy.

"That's all that counts. And Saber's coming back tonight?"

"Well, maybe not here to the condo."

"Ah, so you may not be home until the wee hours? If then?"

I waggled my brows. "I can only hope."

Maggie was quiet a minute, then said, "Do you think this is a good idea? You'll have challenges most couples don't have."

"In the first place," I said as I put my slippers on, "we're not exactly a couple."

"But you trusted him enough to sleep with him."

"I did, didn't I?"

I gazed at the bed, smiling what was probably a goofy smile, but Maggie was right. I had trusted Saber. I *did* trust him.

"Are you both ignoring the vampire issue?"

I shrugged. "He is, and I finally feel desirable. Right now, I'm letting that be enough."

I strolled north on St. George headed for the tour substation, cell phone and key in my reticule, a spring in my step.

Okay, so I lied to Maggie, but only a little. I did wonder where Saber and I were going, if anywhere. I was in like with the guy, and most definitely in lust. I might be a romantic, but I'm a practical one. Love takes time. More than the four days I'd known Saber—except maybe in old wartime movies where the guy and girl meet and marry days before he ships out.

For all I knew, Saber would hightail it back to Daytona and never visit. Never invite me to visit him. Or he could be off investigating all over the state and see me once in a blue moon. And never call in between times.

Shoot. Now I was depressing myself.

A man on a red Vespa zipped by on Treasury Street, and I stopped in my tracks. Note to self: Knock it off.

A week ago I had a new job and the itch for a man. Four tours from hell and a dead body later, I still had a job and a very hot guy who was hot for me. Saber made my teeth sweat, sure, but just because he was my first didn't mean he'd be my last. One step at a time.

Some Sunday nights are hopping on St. George, but tonight it was quiet at the north end of town. Even the music from the Mill Top Tavern seemed muted. Maybe I'd have my first normal tour, and nothing would crop up to interfere with a long night of passion with Saber.

My hopes for that elusive normal tour ended when I saw the ten college students waiting for me. Spring breakers. They had the worst earmarks of the breed. Sunburned from hitting the beach, drunk from hitting the bars. A lot of bars, judging from the way they behaved. Loud, rowdy, stumbling, weaving. And that was just the girls. Two of them wore shorts so short and halters so brief, they were a deep breath away from public indecency.

No telling how active the ghosts would be tonight or how they'd react to this bunch. The weather was too calm to stir up the ghosts, and after they'd dodged vampires last night, they could be hiding from me or ticked off and ready to get even. Ghosts could be every bit as touchy or cranky or playful as they had been when they were alive.

It would be nice if none of the spring breakers barfed on me. Since my Minorcan costume blouse was shot—literally—the Regency gown was all I had for work.

My phone rang just as I was about to start my opening spiel, and I fumbled in the reticule for it.

"Hey, Cesca," Saber said when I answered. The connection wasn't great but adequate. "Have you started the tour yet?"

"Nope, what's up?"

"I'll be late catching up with you. I'm in Palatka chasing down this werebite report."

Palatka was forty-five minutes southwest of St. Augustine. Not a bad drive, but he wouldn't make it back by nine.

"It'll be closer to nine thirty before I get there. Should I find you in town or meet you at the condo?"

"I'll call you when I finish, and we'll take it from there."

"Great. No vampires on the tour, right?"

"Nope, just spring breakers."

"Drunk?"

"Pretty snockered."

"Give 'em the full show. That ought to sober them up."

I laughed. "Oooh, evil, Saber."

"Be careful, Princesca. I'll see you later."

I couldn't help the grin I felt spread over my face. Saber had sounded like he missed me. What a high. Now I could deal with anything. I set the cell phone to vibrate, dropped it in my reticule, and turned to my group to implement Saber's advice.

"Good evening and welcome to Old Coast Ghost Tours. I'm Cesca, and we have an exciting night ahead of us." I waded through their beer and tequila fumes to snag the lantern. "If you'll give me your tickets, we'll get started."

Nine pairs of eyes blinked stupidly. One set still held some awareness.

"Are you the designated driver?" I asked the not-drunk-stupid young man with shaggy brown hair.

"Yes, ma'am."

Ah, manners. "Are you also the designated ticket holder?"

"Oh, yeah, here," he said, thrusting a handful at me.

"Thank you."

I stashed the tickets in the substation and prepared to find out how functional this group was. I'd stick to the most brightly lit and well-traveled streets first for safety. If one of them fell off a curb, I could get help fast.

"St. Augustine was founded in 1565 and is one of the most haunted cities in America. Tonight we'll even go into a few of the buildings where ghosts have been reported, but we'll start with the Huguenot Cemetery."

I told the Judge Stickney story, and before I could go on, two of the girls screeched that someone was pulling on their clothes and hair. The ghost culprit was either Erastus Nye or John Hull playing pranks. Both were thought to have contracted yellow fever, I explained. The encounter began the sobering process for the whole group.

Sobering to me were the occasional whiffs of blood in the air and the periodic *rrryyyow* of the magick cat. Or I thought it was the magick cat's howl. Perhaps it was just a cat in heat. I never saw the animal or sensed the source of the blood smell as I traipsed the college kids all over haunted downtown for the full hour and a half.

We skipped Fay's House, but we had chills and thrills from the other ghosts with no stumbles, falls, or upchucking. The ghosts didn't seem to hold a grudge against me for the vampire tour, and I got through the night without threats or injuries from or to humans. The way my tours had gone? This was a major victory.

I parted ways with my group back at the waterwheel at nine thirty-five and pulled out my phone to call Saber.

I found three messages waiting. Figuring one was from Saber, I called voice mail.

The first message was from PI Eugene Cassidy who'd rushed his contact in Paris for answers. My mouth fell open as I listened. The chemical company that employed Etienne, he said, had done some investigating while Etienne and Yolette were gone. They proved Etienne had been using their facilities for a private project. From the company's own chemical analysis and Etienne's project notes, they concluded Etienne had created a blood scent designed to lure vampires.

Damn, no wonder I smelled blood every time Etienne was around. I thought of the photo Eugene had taken of Etienne with a vampire hanging all over him. He'd put the scent on himself. Maybe from the flask.

Eugene's message ended with the tidbit that he suspected Etienne and Yolette's honeymoon trip was a cover for Etienne to peddle the formula to the U.S. Covenant organization.

Double damn, that fit. The Covenant could lure and kill almost any vampire with Etienne's invention.

I saved Eugene's message, then listened to one from Saber. He'd talked to Eugene, too, but also to March. Etienne and Yolette's rental house was empty, and the sheriff's office had issued a BOLO—be on the lookout—for Etienne.

The last message was from Maggie, and her voice froze the blood in my veins.

"Cesca," she said, her tone tense and too controlled. "Come to Fay's House right after the tour. Don't call the police. What?" she snapped at someone in the background.

Someone whose voice I recognized.

"All right. Cesca, the French guy says to come alone or he'll kill me."

The message ended. Reality sank in. Etienne had Maggie.

TWENTY

Instinct urged me to streak to Maggie's rescue, tear out Etienne's beating heart, and hand it to him. Reason prevailed.

Don't call the cops? Screw that. They could catch Etienne red-handed if they got rolling fast enough.

I saved Maggie's message as evidence and found Saber's number on my incoming list.

"Saber," I said when he answered. "Call 911. Etienne has kidnapped Maggie."

"I'm ten minutes out. Where is she?"

"At Fay's House," I said, pacing. "On Cuna and Spanish, I think, but I could be off by a block."

"You grew up here and you don't know the damned address?"

"Nag me later," I snapped.

"Cesca, he'll want you in exchange for Maggie."

"I don't know why the hell he would, but I'll do what it takes to protect her."

"Can I talk you into waiting for the cavalry?"

"Can pigs friggin' fly?"

"Then be careful."

"Just get here in time to catch him in the act, Saber."

I disconnected and, with only a smidge of conscious thought, I was there in vampire-speed seconds—just five feet from Fay's front porch.

Maggie, pale and gagged, sat on the wooden steps, her hands and feet bound to the stair rail with large red plastic cable ties.

Etienne, reeking of blood scent, stood over her with the barrel of a big, black pistol trained at the top of her head. He aimed a second, sleeker black gun at me.

Fay's furious ghostly face floated at the window, and she rattled the panes until I was sure the glass would break and rain shards on Maggie.

I took in the scene in a matter of seconds and moved slowly closer. No point in spooking Etienne.

"Did he hurt you?" I asked, kneeling at Maggie's feet.

Maggie shook her head, a tumble of emotions in her eyes.

"Ah, Francesca. You arrive at last, and with touching concern for your friend."

I looked up. "Etienne."

I wanted to full-out energy-drain the bastard on the spot, but he'd been around a lot of vampires. At the first tug on his aura, he might shoot Maggie. I couldn't risk that.

"What do you want to let Maggie go?"

"You, *ma petite*."

I stood, fists clenched. "Fine. You've got me. Now what?"

Etienne laughed. "Do you not care to know why I want you?"

"Knock yourself out," I said through gritted teeth. "Tell me."

He gave me a slow, chilling smile. "You are a vampire and a virgin and have power *magnifique* waiting to be—how do you say it? Tapped. I, Etienne, will initiate you to lovemaking and *vos pouvoirs fleuriront*. Your power, it will blossom. Ah, what sexual delights await you with me as your lover."

I let the virgin thing pass as he descended two steps.

"What I do not understand is why you have not come to me sooner. The *formule*, it has worked *fabuleusement bien* on all the other vampires."

"The blood scent formula?"

"*Oui*. It worked so well, it rid Yolette of her rich husband."

Suddenly I was in Etienne's mind, reading his twisted thoughts. Pictures whirled, vile pictures of shredded flesh and spattered blood. Of death-stare eyes and a soul locked in the memory of terror. Of a woman with a pointed chin in the throes of passion on a beach, then broken in the sand and washed by waves. I saw more, saw everything Yolette and Etienne had done, and words tumbled out.

"Yolette used too much of your scent on purpose, and Rachelle killed James in a bloodlust, didn't she? You helped Yolette cover the crime, but you knew the truth, because you were there watching from a safe room. It was you I heard on Monday night. You said James's death was an accident, but you thought the word *Murder*."

His eyes widened, then narrowed as he came down another step.

"Very good, *ma petite*. Your powers, they may be even more formidable than I thought. What else do you know?"

"You lured Rachelle to the beach, but Yolette killed her. Then you used the same method to kill Yolette."

"You are correct. Fitting, *n'est-ce pas?*"

"But you didn't kill Yolette for her money—or rather James's money. You killed her because she threatened to frame you for James's and Rachelle's murders and take your formula."

Etienne shrugged. "*Oui,* it is true. Yolette, she is *jaloux* of you and your powers that will be. She does not wish me to have you. Pah, she has no vision. *Mais moi,* I have the grand plans."

"How did you rig it so we'd find Yolette's body?"

"Ah, *ironique,* was it not?" He chuckled. "Yolette, she was meant to sink with the boat. I report her missing. Days go by, and she is found eaten by the fishes or not found at all. I am the grieving husband. *Très tragique,* but now I have you, *mon cher.*"

Etienne came down the last two steps, the pistol now aimed at me, the sleeker gun at Maggie.

A low, menacing *rrryyyow* sounded close, and I heard soft footfalls from the back of Fay's house. Cat was here? Were the cops? Had Etienne heard? His gaze flicked toward another, louder *rrryyyow.* Full diversion time.

"Too bad you've done all this for nothing, Etienne," I said. "I'm not a virgin, and your formula doesn't work on me. The smell of blood makes me sick."

His eyebrows rose to his hairline. "Then you will become accustomed to the scent, and you will crave it as you crave me. I will control your desire, your powers and the *formule.*"

"Wrong," I said, fists on my hips. "I'd rather stake myself than have sex with you, and no one—no one—will control me again. Ever."

He pressed the smaller gun to Maggie's temple, and my heart tripped.

"You want your friend to die?"

"No, damn it."

"Then we will walk. My auto is in the next block."

Walking was good. I'd get him away from Maggie and then use one of these powers everyone kept yammering about.

I gave Maggie a reassuring smile as Etienne stuck the smaller gun in his waistband. He hooked an arm around my neck, and we turned from the main part of town.

We hadn't taken five steps when Gorman stepped from behind a huge hibiscus bush, a honking huge gun pointed at us.

"You ain't leavin' yet, Frenchie. I got a score to settle for that beatin' you gave me."

In one smooth motion, Etienne raised his pistol and shot Gorman dead center. It was so fast, I thought I'd imagined it until Gorman folded in half and hit the pavement.

As he did, I caught a flash of movement from between two buildings on the other side of the street.

Time slowed, but events didn't.

Etienne aimed, Saber aimed, and I leapt into the air, half pulling Etienne with me. From the astonished look on Saber's face, I might have honest-to-goodness flown toward him until one bullet tore through my thigh, another through my back. Saber tried to break my fall, but I fell short of his arms and bounced on the pavement.

Two more shots, and a vicious *rrryyyow* echoed in the street, then silence except for the wail of sirens.

Maggie. Saber. Had Etienne shot them both like he had Gorman? Raw fear like I hadn't known in centuries drove me to my feet.

Yowling, screaming, and pain-racked French curses erupted behind me as I looked for Maggie. She was still tethered to the rail, her eyes the size of saucers, but she was alive and not bleeding.

Saber lived, too. He stood with his gun wavering between Etienne and Cat in her full panther form. Cat held Etienne's throat in her jaws and had drawn blood but hadn't torn his throat out. She rolled her amber eyes at me as if to ask what I wanted her to do.

"No, Saber," I shouted and staggered to him. "Don't shoot Cat. Please."

"Cesca, get back. This cat is a fucking werepanther."

"Trust me, she's not." I gently sank my hand into the stiff ruff of fur at Cat's neck. "Release the man and hide."

She obeyed but met my gaze before she spun, loped between the two buildings across the street, and disappeared.

From the corner of my eye I saw Saber shove the gun in his holster as officers poured into the street from both ends. He dealt with the officials, and I lurched to Maggie's side to carefully remove the gag.

"Are you all right?" I asked, awkwardly hugging her. "Oh, Maggie, I'm so sorry. I should've warned you about Etienne."

"Wouldn't have made a difference," she croaked, her throat obviously dry. "He surprised me. Acted like you'd told me all about him."

"Why did you leave the condo?" I asked, cautiously tugging on the plastic ties I saw were biting into her skin. I might've been able to snap them with vampire strength, but couldn't risk hurting her more. "Damn, I need scissors to get these off."

I called Saber over as Maggie said, "I was coming on the tour. To protect you." She gripped my hand. "Guess my little girl's grown up this weekend."

"Your little girl," Saber said from the foot of the stairs, "is in a shitload of trouble. Here, let's get you free."

He flipped what looked like mini–wire cutters from a Swiss Army knife and, in under a minute, Maggie was on her feet, supported between two paramedics. She insisted I needed medical attention, too, maybe to save me from the wrath blazing in Saber's eyes.

But Saber moved fast. He grabbed my shoulders and backed me up the steps almost to Fay's front door.

"Why the hell did you jump into my line of fire?"

"I was jumping in Etienne's way, not yours."

"He didn't get the first shot off."

"And I should know that *how*? He shot Gorman before I could move. I thought I was saving your butt."

"If you wanted to save butts, why didn't you drain that SOB's energy the minute you got here?"

"Besides protecting Maggie, I wanted to get the truth. He confessed, Saber. And even if what he told us isn't admissible in court, you have him for kidnapping and killing Gorman and attempted murder."

"You're almost right, Ms. Marinelli." March's voice rumbled from the steps.

Saber swung to face him, and I caught Fay in the window looking smug. Smug instead of angry? That had to be a first.

"We've got Fournier," March continued, "on a whole list of charges including multiple counts of attempted murder."

"Attempted? Gorman's alive?"

"He is for now, and I'd appreciate it, Saber, if you'd finish your chewing out somewhere else. Ms. Marinelli is bleeding, and my evidence techs need the space."

"Of course, Detective March," I said, head high.

Too bad I missed a step on the way off the porch and fell flat. I ruined a perfectly regal exit.

I could've sworn Fay laughed.

Flagler Hospital's ER was hopping. My implant chip doc wasn't on duty, but a guy who really did look a little like George Clooney was. I imagined comparing notes on him with Maggie. It kept me from brooding about Saber's dark glances and thunderous silence.

Gorman was taken to a hospital near the interstate, and Etienne Fournier arrived by ambulance and under guard. Saber's second shot had caught Etienne's arm—a through and through. No bullet to dig out, but he needed stitches to close the tears and punctures on his neck. He babbled constantly in mixed French and English about the wild panther that had attacked him.

Maggie and I were also transported by the EMTs, and Saber followed. Maggie was diagnosed with mild shock and given an IV for dehydration. She didn't call Neil, but Saber did. I don't know what Saber said to Neil—or what Maggie said to him for that matter—but Neil bopped into my treatment room at one point. He joked and told me he'd take me surfboard shopping when Maggie and I were well. I nearly fell off the examination table.

Saber's shot had hit my thigh, but it, too, had gone through the muscle and out again. Since the healing had begun, the doctor left it alone. My back was another story. The bullet had sheared across a rib and lodged in my side. Since it was evidence, it had to come out. I tried to take off my precious one-piece Regency gown myself, but the attending nurse slit it with scissors, avoiding the bullet holes, and handed it to a deputy as more evidence.

Saber stayed with me but didn't stroke my legs through the procedure. He kept up the silent treatment until the doctor mentioned giving me a transfusion to speed the healing.

Saber insisted I ingest the pint of blood.

I told them both to shove it.

Well, what could Saber do? Stick a straw in the bag and pry my mouth open? Hardly.

Neil took Maggie home at four in the morning and spent the night in her bed. Saber took me home at six and camped on the couch. We didn't say two words worth repeating from the time March broke up Saber's rant at me until the following afternoon.

I came to awareness sluggishly until the mattress shifted and my eyelids flew open. Propped on his elbow, Saber's cobalt gaze solemnly assessed me.

"How's Maggie? Where is she?" I asked rapid fire and started to rise.

Saber pulled me back to bed. "Maggie's fine. She had a call about some breakthrough on the house. Permits and a dedicated crew or something like that. Neil's with her." He paused a long second. "How are you?"

"I need a shower," I said, then realized that last shower I'd taken was with Saber. "I mean, I'm good."

"You need this before anything else," he said, reaching behind him to the bedside table. He hooked two bottles of Starbloods in his tanned fingers.

"I wish you'd stop shoving blood at me," I said, snagging both bottles and setting them on my side table.

"I wish you'd stop taking chances with your life," he said sternly.

"Afterlife," I corrected.

"Whatever. You scared about ten years off me last night."

"It wasn't that chancy," I said quietly. "I am a vampire."

"You're also someone I'd like to keep around for a while."

"You would?"

He raised a brow. "You think I sleep with vampires all the time?"

"I didn't say that." I picked at the sheet edge, then met his eyes again. "I don't know what to think, Saber."

"Neither do I," he admitted, taking my hand, "but I'm willing to take the ride to see where this goes." He paused a beat. "Are you?"

"I don't know how much time we'll have together. I have to make new costumes. I have to study."

"I have investigations to conduct. Like into the werepanther."

"It's not a were. It's a shape-shifter. A bewitched cat that turns into a panther. Or maybe the other way around," I said, wishing I could think of a better description. "But it's not a were."

"A bewitched animal?" he asked, eyes narrowing in thought. "How do you know for sure?"

"Weres, real lycanthropes, have a certain smell. Cat smells completely different, and I sense magick on her."

"Is this a psychic thing?" he pressed.

I debated a nanosecond, but I trusted him. "I've seen something similar. My friend Triton. The one from the old days."

"The one you were in love with?"

"Yes. He shape-shifted into a dolphin, but I always felt the same sense of magick from him. Triton wasn't a were, and Cat isn't, either."

He looked at the oversized stuffed dolphin that rested on my desk, quiet for so long I thought he'd up and leave.

Instead he gave a single nod. "Okay, then."

"That's all? Just okay?"

"Yeah, that's all." He reached to tuck a sprig of hair behind my ear. "I trust that you know the difference, and I trust you to tell me the truth."

"Oh. Well, good." Feeling awkward, I cleared my throat. "What's happening with Etienne?"

He grinned. "He's booked into St. Johns County jail. In the infirmary for now."

"Will he go to trial?"

"Oh, yeah. He can't seem to confess fast enough."

"Even to Yolette's murder?" I asked, surprised. "I didn't think there was solid evidence on him."

"There wasn't, but he's wearing Detective March thin unburdening himself of his crimes."

His too-innocent expression made me ask, "Did you talk to Etienne?"

"I had a word or ten with him."

"And you said what?"

Saber waggled his brows. "I may have mentioned prison as a viable alternative to another cat attack."

"Have I mentioned you're evil?"

Saber shrugged. "He shot you twice."

"I can add. That nutcase owes me two costumes and a paint job for my truck."

"Princesca," Saber said, shaking his head and shifting closer, "are you going to shut up long enough to let me kiss you?"

"Are we finished fighting?"

"Yep."

"Is kissing all you have in mind?" I asked as I snuggled against him and wrapped my arms around his neck.

"Hell, no," he said with a grin. "I need a shower, too."

I didn't drink my Starbloods until a long time later.

My first real date with Saber wasn't a normal one, but nothing in my afterlife had been normal since he swept into it.

He wanted to see me surf, so Friday about two hours before sunset we met at Crescent Beach. I brought my new surfboard—the one Neil helped me select—and an Igloo ice chest stocked with wine for Saber and store-bought sweet tea for me. Saber showed up in his sexy swim trunks—the man did have well-muscled legs and a butt I could squeeze forever. He also brought crispy fried chicken with all the fixin's.

We rubbed our wet bodies together in the waves a while. I wanted to reenact the beach scene I'd seen in an old movie, but Saber insisted I surf before darkness fell.

Now, as I paddled out to catch the last wave of the day, Saber sat on the shore watching from our beach blanket. The sunset burst in pinks and purples and indigo blues. Maybe the scene wasn't everyone's picture of a romantic setting, but with Saber there, it was mine.

A big wave surged under my board, and I sprang to my feet to ride it in. I waved at Saber; he waved back. The moment was perfection.

Then my gaze was drawn to the dunes and to a man who stood with one hip cocked. Just the way Triton used to stand.

I squinted at the lone figure, vampire vision kicking in.

It was him. Triton. From the distance, our gazes locked. Then he looked down at Saber.

I don't know if I made so much as a peep out loud, but in my head I cried Triton's name and all but flew out of the surf. I was still attached to my board by the leg leash as I hit the sand, and I stumbled a step before ripping the Velcro free of my ankle. Saber shouted and pounded after me as I scrambled up the dune, but it was empty.

I scanned the boardwalks to the beach houses, the patio of the nearby restaurant, even the rolling dunes of native scrub plants. No one was there.

Triton had vanished, but a golden dolphin charm just like the one he used to wear twinkled in the sand.

Saber stood quietly at my side for a moment while questions I couldn't ask swirled. Why did Triton leave? Would he find me again? Where did he live now, when did he get to town, how long was he staying? I waited for the wrenching ache of longing for Triton to rip into my heart, but it didn't come.

Oh, I still yearned to see him—to touch him and talk to him—but only as a long-treasured friend. The soul-deep pain was gone. Somehow, somewhere, I'd let it go.

Saber shifted around me and scooped up the charm. He cradled my hand, dropped the charm in it, and closed my fingers over the precious metal warm from the sand. Then Saber threaded his fingers through my hair and tilted my face to his.

"Did that belong to Triton?"

"I think so."

"The way you streaked out of the water, you just think so?"

"It was his. I saw him."

Saber's thumbs made little circles on my temples. "I can't compete with your past, Cesca."

The charm in my fist, I slid my arms around Saber's waist and smiled.

"There is no competition, Saber."

"You sure?"

"Mmm-hmm." I fit my body into his and felt him stir. "I'm through brooding over my past."

"You are?" His voice went just a little hoarse. "Why?"

"Because my present with you is such a kick."